Professor Bernard Knight, CBE, became a Home
Office pathologist in 1965 and was appointed Professor
of Forensic Pathology, University of Wales College of
Medicine, in 1980. He is the author of twelve novels,
a biography and numerous popular and academic
non-fiction books. **The Sanctuary Seeker** is the first
novel in the Crowner John series.

Also by Bernard Knight in the
Crowner John Series

The Sanctuary Seeker
The Poisoned Chalice
Crowner's Quest
The Awful Secret
The Tinner's Corpse
The Grim Reaper
Fear in the Forest
The Witch Hunter

visit the author's website at
http://mysite.freeserve.com/bernard_knight

THE SANCTUARY SEEKER

A Crowner John Mystery

Bernard Knight

POCKET
BOOKS

LONDON · SYDNEY · NEW YORK · TORONTO

First published in Great Britain by Pocket Books, 1998
This edition first published by Pocket Books, 2004
A imprint of Simon & Schuster UK Ltd
A CBS COMPANY

3 5 7 9 10 8 6 4 2

Simon & Schuster UK Ltd
1st Floor
222 Gray's Inn Road
London WC1X 8HB

www.simonandschuster.co.uk

Simon & Schuster Australia
Sydney

A CIP catalogue record for this book is available
from the British Library.

ISBN 978-1-84739-997-7

Typeset by Palimpsest Book Production Limited,
Polmont, Stirlingshire
Printed and bound in Great Britain by
CPI Group (UK) Ltd, Croydon, CR0 4YY

Author's Note

Any attempt to give modern English dialogue an 'olde worlde' flavour in historical novels is as inaccurate as it is futile. In the time and place of this story, late twelfth-century Devon, most people would have spoken early Middle English, unintelligible to us at the present time. Many others would speak western Welsh, later called Cornish, and the ruling classes would have spoken Norman French. The language of the Church and virtually all official writing was Latin.

Exeter Cathedral, as described in these pages, is not the same building as can be seen today, with the exception of the two massive towers, which were there in Crowner John's time.

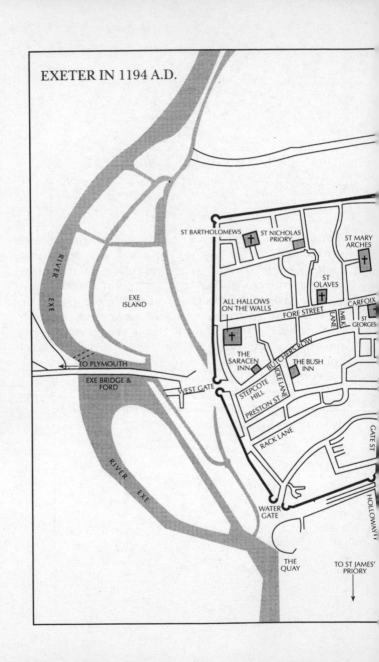

EXETER IN 1194 A.D.

RIVER EXE

EXE ISLAND

ST BARTHOLOMEWS

ST NICHOLAS PRIORY

ST MARY ARCHES

ST OLAVES

ALL HALLOWS ON THE WALLS

FORE STREET

MILK LANE

CARFOIX

ST GEORGES

TO PLYMOUTH

THE SARACEN INN

BUTCHERS ROW

THE BUSH INN

EXE BRIDGE & FORD

WEST GATE

STEPCOTE HILL

IDLE LANE

PRESTON ST

RACK LANE

GATE ST

RIVER EXE

HOLLOWAY

WATER GATE

THE QUAY

TO ST JAMES' PRIORY

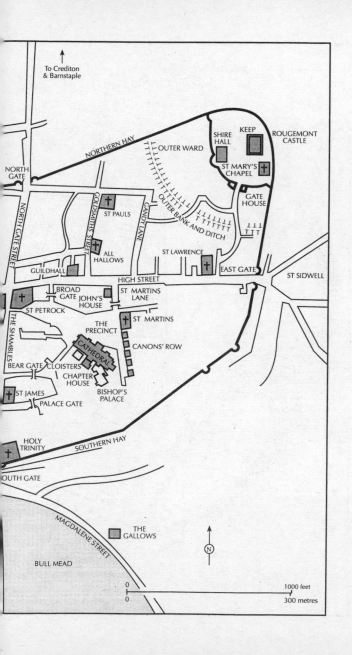

To Crediton
& Barnstaple

NORTHERN HAY

SHIRE HALL

KEEP

ROUGEMONT CASTLE

OUTER WARD

NORTH GATE

NORTH GATE STREET

GOLDSMITHS STREET

CANDLE LANE

OUTER BANK AND DITCH

ST MARY'S CHAPEL

GATE HOUSE

ST PAULS

ALL HALLOWS

ST LAWRENCE

GUILDHALL

EAST GATE

ST SIDWELL

HIGH STREET

BROAD GATE

ST MARTINS LANE

JOHN'S HOUSE

ST PETROCK

THE SHAMBLES

ST MARTINS

THE PRECINCT

CANONS' ROW

CATHEDRAL

BEAR GATE

CLOISTERS

CHAPTER HOUSE

ST JAMES

BISHOP'S PALACE

PALACE GATE

HOLY TRINITY

SOUTHERN HAY

SOUTH GATE

MAGDALENE STREET

THE GALLOWS

N

BULL MEAD

0   1000 feet

0   300 metres

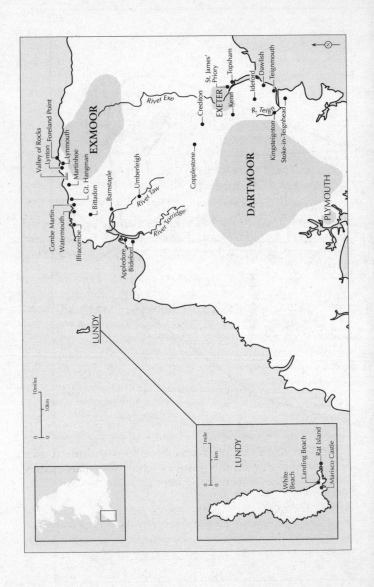

Glossary

ABJURER
A criminal who sought sanctuary in a church and elected to 'abjure' by confessing his sin to the coroner and leaving the realm of England for ever, to avoid being hanged.

ACRE
City on the north coast of Palestine, where Richard the Lionheart landed in June 1191 during the Third Crusade. A two-year siege by other crusaders had failed to dislodge the Saracens, but Richard succeeded within a month, much to the chagrin of his French and German allies.

AMERCE
To impose a financial penalty (fine) on a person or village. The coroner (*q.v.*) would not collect it straight away, but record the amercement on his parchment rolls to present to the King's justices when they came; they would confirm or cancel the fine.

ARCHDEACON
A senior clergyman, responsible for the administration of areas within a diocese. Bishops in Norman times were rarely resident and their archdeacons ran affairs

for them. In the diocese of Devon and Cornwall, there were three Archdeacons, one responsible for Exeter.

ASSART
A new piece of arable land cut from the forest, to enlarge the holdings of a village.

BAILIFF
Overseer of a manor or estate, directing the farming and other outside work. A steward or seneschal (*q.v.*) might be above him in a large establishment; he would have reeves working under him.

BALDRIC
A diagonal strap over the right shoulder of a Norman warrior to suspend his sword scabbard on the left hip.

CANON
A member of the cathedral chapter (*see* Prebendary).

BURGAGE
A town property, usually a house on a plot, occupied by a burgess.

BURGESS
A freeman of substance in a town, usually a merchant or craftsman. A group of burgesses ran the town administration and elected the portreeves or later a mayor.

CAPUCIN
Medieval headgear, consisting of a long length of cloth wound round the head rather like a turban, the free end hanging down to one shoulder.

CHAPTER
The administrative body of a cathedral, composed of the canons (or prebendaries) and the senior clergy. They met in the chapter house, usually attached to

the cathedral. The name derived from the reading of a chapter of the gospels before each meeting.

CONSISTORY COURTS
The ecclesiastical courts, which had the right to try clerics, rather than the secular courts. Anyone who could read and write could claim to be tried by this court, as literacy was virtually confined to the clergy.

CONSTABLE
Has many meanings, but in the twelfth-century context, a senior military commander, often the custodian of a castle, alternatively called a castellan.

CORONER
Senior law officer in a county, after the sheriff, first officially appointed in September 1194, though there is a mention of a coroner in Saxon times. The name derives from the Latin *custos placitorum coronae*, meaning Keeper of the Pleas of the Crown, as he recorded all crimes and legal events for the King's justices.

CROFT
A small area of land around a village house (toft), for vegetables and a few livestock, used by the occupier (cottar), who was either a freeman or a bondsman (villein or serf).

CUIRASS
A breastplate or short tunic, originally of thick leather but later of metal, to protect the chest in combat.

DEODAND
Literally 'a gift from God', it was the forfeiture of anything that had caused a death, such a sword, a cart or even a mill-wheel. It was confiscated by the coroner for the King, or sometimes given as compensation to the victim's family.

EYRE
A meeting of the King's judges to decide legal cases; the General Eyre was introduced by Henry II to bring justice to the people by the judges moving from county to county to try cases. Later these became the Assizes ('sittings') and in modern times, the Crown Courts.

HAUBERK (OR BYRNIE)
A chain-mail tunic to armour the wearer from neck to knees; often had a hood extension (aventail) to reach under the helmet and sleeves to the elbow.

HONOUR
A holding of land from the King, Baron or Church. It might be a large estate or a single manor. A manor might be one village or several, under the same lord. Some large villages were split between manors. The administration of a manor was run by a steward and one or more bailiffs, under whom were the manor reeves (*q.v.*)

JURY
Unlike modern juries, the medieval jury were witnesses, local people who were obliged to gather to tell what they knew of a crime or dispute. The coroner's jury was supposed to be all men over twelve years of age from the four nearest villages, though this was often a practical impossibility.

JUSTICIAR
The chief minister in Norman times, a great noble or churchman appointed by the king. In the reign of Richard I, there were several justiciars, the most effective being Hubert Walter, who was Richard's military second-in-command in Palestine before returning home during the king's imprisonment in Austria to help raise his ransom. Richard made him Archbishop of Canterbury

and Chief Justiciar, and he virtually ruled the country after Richard's permanent departure from England only two months after returning from captivity.

MANOR REEVE
A foreman appointed in each village by the lord of a manor to oversee the daily routine. He would allot the farming work to the freemen and serfs and, though illiterate, by means of memory and tally-sticks (marks cut on sticks to check numbers), he would keep a record of crop rotation, harvest yields and tithes, etc.

MURDRUM FINE
A fine or amercement (*q.v.*) levied on a village by the coroner when a person is found slain and the locals cannot 'present Englishry', thus raising the presumption that they had murdered a Norman.

ORDEAL
An ancient ritual, abolished by the Vatican in 1215, where suspects were subjected to painful or potentially fatal ordeals, such as walking across nine red-hot plough-shares, carrying a red-hot iron bar nine paces, picking a stone from a barrel of boiling water or molten lead, licking white-hot iron, etc. If they suffered no injury, they were judged innocent; another ordeal was to be thrown bound into deep water – if they floated they were guilty, if they sank, innocent!

OUTLAW
Literally, anyone outside the law, usually an escaped criminal or a fugitive. They often lurked in the forests and any person was entitled to kill them on sight to collect a bounty, as they were 'as the wolf's head'.

OUTREMER
The four Christian kingdoms in the Levant at the time of the Crusades, including the Kingdom of Jerusalem.

PHTHISIS
Tuberculosis.

PORTREEVE
One of the senior officials in a town, elected by the other burgesses. There were usually two portreeves, later superseded by a mayor. The first mayor in Exeter took office in 1208.

PREBENDARY
A canon of a cathedral. A priest who is granted a prebend, the income of a church in the diocese to support him. Many canons employed a vicar to look after their parish, while they stayed in the cathedral.

PRECENTOR
A senior cleric in a cathedral, responsible for organising the religious services, singing, etc.

PRESENTMENT OF ENGLISHRY
Following the 1066 Conquest, many Normans were killed by aggrieved locals, so the law decreed that anyone found dead was Norman and the locals punished by a murdrum fine (*q.v.*) unless they could prove the deceased was English (or Welsh). The presentment of Englishry by relatives of murdered people continued for several hundred years, as even though it became meaningless it was good source of revenue.

SANCTUARY
An ancient religious offer of mercy, where a fugitive from pursuit or a gaol-breaker could claim forty days immunity from the law if he reached a church or even the precincts of a church. This was not available for crimes of sacrilege.

SENESCHAL
The senior steward or head of the staff of a great household.

SHERIFF
A 'shire-reeve', the King's representative in a county, responsible for law and order and the collection of royal taxes.

TITHE
A tenth part of the harvest, demanded by the church.

UNDERCROFT
The ground floor of a fortified building. The entrance to the rest of the building was on the floor above, which had no communication with the undercroft. Removable wooden steps prevented attackers from being able to storm the main door.

Acknowledgements

The author would like to thank the following for historical advice, though reserving the blame for any misapprehensions about the complexities of life and law in twelfth century Devon; Mrs Angela Doughty, Exeter Cathedral Archivist; the staff of Devon Record Office and of Exeter Central Library; Mr Stuart Blaylock, Exeter Archaeology; Rev Canon Mawson, Exeter Cathedral; Mr Thomas Watkin, Cardiff Law School, University of Wales; Professor Nicholas Orme, University of Exeter; and to Clare Ledingham, Editorial Director at Simon & Schuster, for her unfailing interest and support.

CHAPTER ONE

In which Crowner John rides to Widecombe

The three riders plodded miserably along the rutted track. The hoofs of their animals splashed in the muddy water that trickled down to meet the Webburn river, a mile away. Leading the trio, Crowner John cursed as he felt the rain beginning to trickle from the edge of his leather hood into the neckband of his cloak. Even the hardships he had endured during the Crusades or the Irish campaigns had failed to immunise him against the purgatory of a wet autumn in the West Country.

Close behind his great grey stallion came a brown mare, carrying the gaunt shape of the coroner's bodyguard, his ginger hair wrapped turban-wise in an oat-sack that dripped water down his frayed leather cuirass. 'I thought November was for fog on these bloody moors, not this endless rain,' he grumbled. Though he knew Saxon English well enough, Gwyn of Polruan spoke in his native Cornish, mainly to annoy the third member of the party.

'Stop complaining, if that's what you were doing in that barbaric tongue!' whined the man bringing up the rear. He was half the size of the other two and sat his mule side-saddle, like a woman. An unfrocked priest, Thomas de Peyne was the coroner's clerk and, in Gwyn's eyes, as evil a little bastard as ever fouled the soil of Devon.

The weather had frayed their tempers more than usual, though they were ever a quarrelsome band. It was now more than three hours since they had left Exeter and the ceaseless downpour along the eastern edge of Dartmoor was enough to rot a man's soul.

At last, the coroner's horse breasted the ridge at the edge of Rippon Tor and Sir John de Wolfe could look down with relief on the wretched hamlet that was their destination. He brushed the rain off his eyebrows and wiped the drops from his hooked nose as he reined in his stallion. A tall, dark, sinewy man, John had a pair of deep-set, brooding eyes surmounting a long face with high cheekbones. It was a face that was not given to much humour – not that his previous soldiering life had offered much to laugh about.

The two other riders stopped alongside him and they sat in a row, gazing down without enthusiasm on the saturated countryside. To their right, a grey slope of bare moorland swept up to the granite crags of Chinkwell Tor and Hameldown Beacon, stark against the skyline. Below, the land canted away to the left, with clumps of trees thickening to forest as the moor gave way in the distance to the Dart valley. Strips of cultivated fields filled the middle foreground, with a dozen mean houses clustered around a wooden church. Further away they could see a band of dense woodland, beyond which drifting smoke indicated the next village, which the coroner thought to be Dunstone, though the few available maps of Dartmoor were a mixture of fact and speculation.

'Another God-forsaken place,' complained the hunch-backed clerk, in his irritating high-pitched voice. At frequent intervals he crossed himself nervously, where another man would pick his nose or belch.

John tapped his horse's belly with his heel. 'Come on, let's see what they've got for us.'

He led the trio down the slope, their mounts picking their way carefully over the slippery mud and stones of the path down to the village of Widecombe.

A hundred paces from the muddy mound that served as the village green, they were met by a man with a reeve's staff, who had ambled out of the nearest thatched hut. He was a rough-looking fellow, with unkempt hair plastered to his skull by the rain. Touching his brow in a grudging salute, he approached the grey horse. 'You this crowner man, then?' he demanded.

The rider glared down at him from under heavy black eyebrows that matched the dark stubble on his face, for against the fashion of the times he had no beard or moustache. With his black hood and dark riding cloak, he looked like a great raven perched on the horse.

'*Sir* John de Wolfe to you, fellow! The King's coroner in this county – so show some respect, will you?' Though not a vain man, John was conscious of his new royal appointment, foreign though it might be to most people in this westerly limb of Coeur de Lion's kingdom.

The manor reeve caught the snap in the coroner's voice and became vastly more deferential. 'Yessir, begging your pardon. Ralph the reeve, I am. Come indoors out of the rain, sirs.'

They squelched after him through the cattle-churned mud towards his long-house. Though the best in the village, it was a rickety low structure of frame and wattle, with a roof of tattered straw that sprouted grass and green moss. One end was a byre, from which came the lowing of cattle, most destined soon for the butcher's knife as few could be kept fed through the coming winter.

The other half of the building was a windowless dwelling, smoke filtering from under the low eaves of the thatch. A puny lad hurried out from somewhere to take the reins of the horses and lead them off to feed.

The three travellers followed the village headman, the tall figures of John and Gwyn having to stoop under the doorway to enter the house. In the dim light, they saw a bare room with an earthen floor. A smoky fire burned dully in a clay hearth-pit in the middle, over which a small cauldron hung on a trivet. One crude door led to the cowshed and another to the luxury of an inner room, where two runny nosed barefoot children gaped with round eyes at these visitors from the unknown outer world.

'Sit yourselves, sirs,' invited the reeve. He pulled forward a low bench and a milking stool to the fire, virtually the only furniture, then called brusquely to a woman lurking in the darker recesses of the room. 'Martha, bring ale, bread and some bowls for this broth you've got warming here.' His English was thick with the local accent.

The official party shrugged off their sodden outer clothes and the reeve hung them on wooden pegs fixed into the wall-frames. He wondered where Gwyn and the small man fitted into the system. The Cornishman, betrayed by his accent, was even taller and certainly more massive than the crowner, but with his ginger hair and moustache, was a complete contrast to the saturnine blackness of Sir John. Although the man had no beard, his moustache was so profuse that is bushy tails hung down on both sides of his mouth and chin almost to his chest. His unruly shock of hair ran down as sidewhiskers to join his moustache.

Gwyn had been born forty-two years earlier, to a tin-miner who had turned to fishing and moved to the coast at Polruan, on the opposite side of the river entrance to Fowey. Gwyn had followed the fishing trade until he was seventeen, then come to Exeter to be a slaughterman in the Shambles. His huge size brought him an invitation to become bodyguard-cum-squire to a local knight off to the wars. Fourteen years ago, in 1180, he had come to Sir John de Wolfe and they had remained together ever since, fighting and travelling in Ireland and to the Third Crusade.

The coroner's clerk, Ralph saw, was a furtive little man with a dropped shoulder from old spinal disease and a shifty pair of eyes that darted everywhere and missed nothing.

The visitors were served a simple meal by the silent woman, who was pale and toothless though probably no more than thirty. While they slurped meat broth over the edges of wooden bowls and champed at the hard bread, the coroner sat and listened to the story of Ralph the reeve.

'Found him before milking time, yesterday morning, we did,' the village overseer said, with a certain morbid relish. Little happened in Widecombe and the finding of a body made an intriguing change from sheep foot-rot and mouldy oats, the only local topics of conversation. 'Lying on the bank, he was – head in the water. In the little stream that runs into the Webburn, between here and Dunstone, a fair way beyond the old Saxon well.'

Gwyn's ruddy face followed the story carefully, while the button eyes of the sparrow-like clerk jumped restlessly about the room.

Crowner John held up a large hand, keeping his half-consumed bowl of broth in the other. 'Wait a minute, man! Whose side of the stream was it on – yours or the next village's?'

The reeve looked shiftily from John to Gwyn and then to the clerk.

'The truth, man!' snapped the coroner.

Ralph's acne-scarred cheeks twitched and the single yellow tooth in his upper jaw stuck out like a spike as he grinned feebly. ''T was on our side, sir . . . though I'll swear those damned Dunstone folk put him across in the night.'

The big Cornishman grunted. 'Why should they do that? And how could you know they did?'

The reeve scratched vigorously at the lice on his head as an aid to thought. 'To save themselves the trouble of all this new-fangled crowner's business – beggin' your pardon, sirs,' he added hastily. 'That body wasn't there the night before, for our pig boy was down in that there meadow till dusk.'

'He could have come there and died during the night, you fool!' whined Thomas.

Ralph shook his head. 'His belly was blown up. Been dead a while – a good few days at least, at this season.'

'Washed down the stream, then?' hazarded John.

The reeve rocked his head again. ''Tis but a trickle of a brook before it joins the other stream. Not enough to move a badger, let alone a man's corpse. No, them

Dunstone people dumped him on us, so as not to be first finders, that's for sure.'

The law laid an obligation on those who discovered a body, the so-called 'First Finders', to raise the hue-and-cry by immediately rousing the nearest four households and starting a chase for the culprit, as well as notifying the authorities. It was an obligation that carried penalties for errors, and most people made every effort to avoid being involved.

The coroner finished his soup, put the bowl on the floor and stood up, his head all but touching the rough beams above. He moved to stand right over the fire, letting the moisture steam off his worsted breeches and the grey knee-length surcoat, slit back and front for sitting a horse.

'Any idea who this corpse might be?' he snapped at the reeve. The battle-scarred veteran of a score of years spent campaigning in Ireland, France and Palestine, John had a demanding manner. A man of few words, he wasted none and, in turn, expected no fancy turns of phrase or beating about the bush.

Ralph shook his head again. 'No one from these parts, Crowner. Not a serf nor villein, neither. More a gentleman, by his garments.'

John's eyebrows rose a little, crinkling the forehead scar he had won from a Saracen sword outside Acre. 'A gentleman? We'll see about that. Where've you got him?'

The abruptness of his deep voice sent Ralph scurrying to get their cloaks, still dripping on the wall hooks. 'In the tithe barn, just inside the entrance. Starting to smell a bit, he is.'

They trooped outside to find that the rain had eased to a fine drizzle. The sodden village sat dejected in its valley and now a pall of white mist had settled on the moor above, heightening the feeling of isolation from the rest of the world. A few curious souls watched covertly from the doorways of their cottages as the procession left the reeve's dwelling.

'Over this way, sirs,' called Ralph, splashing ahead towards the small church and larger barn that sat slightly below the crest of the village green.

John saw that the hamlet, set in a valley, was all slopes and mounds, but fertile from the soil washed down from the moors over aeons of time.

'We called you right away, Crowner, just as we should,' said Ralph virtuously. His initial truculence had long vanished, now that he realised that under the new law Sir John de Wolfe was a force to be reckoned with.

It was only a month since his own lord, Hugh FitzRalph, had assembled his six manor reeves and told them of various new laws that had filtered down from the royal court, where the King's justiciar, Archbishop Hubert Walter, was ruling England now that Richard had returned to France.

One new regulation had come from the General Eyre, sitting in the county of Kent: in September, it had revived the ancient Saxon post of coroner.

To the ignorant reeves, including Ralph, Kent was as remote as the moon and coroners were equally incomprehensible. They had gathered that the new men would record illegal events and enquire into dead bodies, but their interest waned rapidly as FitzRalph's clerk, the only man in the manor who could read, droned on. All that Ralph remembered was that if a death occurred violently or unexpectedly, a runner had to be sent straight away to Exeter to notify the sheriff and this new official – otherwise the village would be amerced, which meant a heavy fine. As he heaved at the tall, rickety door of the barn, it occurred to Ralph that if he wanted to keep the perquisites of his job as village reeve, he had better find out a little more about coroners and stick to the rules: if this hawkish black beanpole was crossed, he might prove a handful of trouble. As he wrestled with the door Ralph looked covertly at Sir John de Wolfe and decided that the stern, sallow face, with the deep furrows running down to the corners of the mouth, was that of a hard man. His great height and slightly hunched shoulders gave him the appearance of a bird of prey, ready to swoop on any wrong-doer. De Wolfe's lips, though, made Ralph wonder if the new crowner made himself more agreeable to the ladies than he did to men: they had a full sensuality at odds with the man's otherwise flinty appearance.

He jerked his mind back to reality and pushed the door wider, aiming a kick at several small boys who had followed them across the green. Three other men came and stood a respectful distance from the group.

'Here we are, Crowner, I threw this sack over him for decency.' He flicked off the rough hessian from the still shape on the ground and stood at the head of the cadaver with an almost proprietorial air.

John de Wolfe and Gwyn stood each side of the corpse and bent to view it more closely, while the clerk crossed himself and stood further away, holding a grubby cloth over his nose.

'Smells a bit, don't he?' muttered Gwyn. It was merely an observation.

'Told you he was corrupt,' said the reeve, trium-
phantly. 'He never died in our stream night 'fore last,
that's for sure.'

John tilted his scabbard out of the way and squatted
at the side of the body.

The front of the tunic and undershirt were ripped
open and greenish-red veins could be seen across the
swollen belly, making it look like marble. The face was
slightly puffy and the open, sightless eyes were sunken
and clouded.

'His features are still fairly good, if we had someone
who knew him,' remained Gwyn.

'They won't be for long, though. Another few days
above ground and his own mother wouldn't recognise
him.' The coroner was an expert in corpses; he had
seen thousands in all states of decay in the Holy
Land and other campaigns. He prodded the flank
with a finger, feeling the bubbling tenseness of the
gas within.

'Good clothing, as you said, reeve. Worn and dirty,
but fair material. Looks French in style.'

'What did he die of?' grunted the ever-practical
Gwyn, crouching on his large haunches alongside
his master.

For answer, the reeve bent down and grabbed the
shoulders of the body, oblivious to the wave of stench
that came up as he heaved it over onto its face.

'There, on his back. We saw it when we carried him
in.' Bending closer, John saw a bloody stain diluted
with rain, on the green tunic. In the centre was a
small tear, narrow and just over an inch in length,
sitting obliquely between the man's shoulder-blades.

'Have you looked here under his clothing?' he
boomed at the reeve.

Ralph shook his head. 'Left it to you, sir, like we were told,' he said obsequiously.

The coroner grabbed the lower hem of the tunic with a bony but powerful hand and pulled it up. It would come no further than waist level. 'Gwyn, let's get this up.'

The ginger giant moved around to the other side to raise the limp arms, as they wrestled away the tunic and pulled the undershirt up to the armpits. At least the early putrefaction had got rid of rigor mortis, which would have made the process even more difficult.

As Gwyn let fall the left hand of the corpse, he grunted again, his favourite form of communication. 'His fingers . . . they're cut.' He picked up the hand and pulled back the curled fingers to expose the palm and finger pads. Between the thumb and first finger was a deep slash to the bone, and across the inside of the first joints of all the fingers, the flesh was cut to the tendons.

Even the squeamish Thomas de Peyne was intrigued. 'How did he come by that?' he squeaked.

'Caught hold of a blade, trying to defend himself. A knife or a sword,' answered John shortly.

'Perhaps the same blade that did this, then.' Gwyn pointed to the now exposed back of the corpse, reddened and blotchy where the blood had settled under the skin as it lay on its back after death. Under the rip in the tunic and shirt, the surface of the body showed a clean-cut deep wound, an inch long, sharp at the lower end and blunt at the top. As they watched blood and gas blew slow bubbles out of the injury.

Without hesitation, the coroner poked his forefinger into the wound and pushed down until his knuckles were level with the skin. 'A stab, deep inside

11

him. Slashed his heart and lights, no doubt.' There was a sucking sound as he withdrew his finger and wiped it clean on the hay that littered the floor of the barn. Thomas the clerk retched and John looked round at him with a scowl.

'If your stomach is to be turned by every little thing like this, a useless clerk you'll be to me. Pull yourself together, man, or I'll get rid of you, even if the Archdeacon is your uncle!'

Thomas gulped back his bile, crossed himself and nodded. Since his trouble with the girl novitiates in Winchester, he had had no employment and only the intercession of the Archdeacon of Exeter had persuaded Sir John to take him as his clerk.

The coroner rose to his feet and looked pensively down at the corpse.

'It's clear *how* he died. What we need to know is *where* and *when* he died . . . and who he is.'

Gwyn ran a hand through his tangled hair, which so often looked like a haystack after a gale. 'Murdered, no doubt. Stabbed in the back, a coward's act with dagger or short sword by the size of the wound.'

He never called his master anything, not 'Crowner', not 'Sir John'. Yet he was utterly loyal without being servile, a Cornishman deferring to a man with Saxon, Norman and Celtic blood in his veins.

The coroner stood scowling down at the body. 'Stabbed in the back, yes . . . But he had the chance to grab the blade with his left hand, maybe setting aside a second thrust.'

Gwyn nodded in agreement. He, too, had had ample experience of the ways of assault and sudden, violent death. 'That wound may not have struck him dead on the instant. Mortal though it was, he could have had time to turn and start fighting. I've seen men with three wounds worse than that carry on swinging a sword for five minutes before falling to the ground.'

John looked up at the reeve. 'No pouch or wallet, was there? Nothing about him to say who he was?'

Ralph shook his head dolefully. 'If they were robbers, they'd have taken anything of value. He has no ring, no brooch.'

The coroner shrugged and turned away. 'Clerk, earn your keep by writing all this in your roll. Make a note of all his clothing, exactly as to nature and colour. His age – would you say about twenty-five or somewhat older? His eyes look brown, though it's hard to tell when they've been clouded in death as long as this. Hair is very pale, though that's common enough around here.' He was still staring at the corpse, his lips pursed thoughtfully. 'How long would you reckon he's been dead, Gwyn?'

His henchman pursed his own lips and considered for a while. He was no man for rash judgements. 'November? This weather, wet but not cold. At least a week, probably a few days longer.'

The coroner nodded: that fitted with his own estimate. 'Yes – no maggots, but it's late in the season.'

Gwyn pointed down at the body. 'He's also got that.' It was a large brown mole, low down on the right side of the neck, from which a cluster of long hairs stuck out. 'Some one may know it – it's obvious enough.'

Crowner John nodded. 'He was born with that, so his family would know of it – if we ever find them. Add it to your roll, clerk.'

While Thomas pulled out his quill, ink-vial, a roll of sheep parchment and sought a flat-topped sack for a desk, Gwyn looked at the stout shoes still worn by the dead man. He bent down again and felt the heels with a finger. 'He had a horse, that's for sure. There are marks of prick-spurs rubbed into the leather.'

John pursed his lips. 'Good clothing and owned a horse. Not a common peasant. Should make him easier to trace, if he's a man of better birth. So long as he's from these parts.'

'And so long as he's not a Frenchman, as you suggested from his garments,' put in the clerk, now busy with his quill.

The inquest was to be held that afternoon, in the barn in which the body lay.

As putrefaction was worsening rapidly, Crowner John decided that there was no point in going back to Exeter only to return the next day. They would give themselves miles of weary riding and allow the corpse to get more foul by the hour. 'Summon a jury by noon – and your priest. We'll get the poor fellow buried before evening,' he commanded the reeve.

'Every man and boy over twelve years old, mind you, from the four nearest villages,' yapped his clerk, officiously latching himself on to the power of the coroner.

Ralph stared at them with a return of his former truculence. 'I can't do that! Many will be working the fields, cutting wood, tending sheep and cattle, some far from the villages up on the moor.'

Thomas de Peyne waved his arms at the village headman. 'Do as you're told, man. The law says every male in the Hundred has to come forward and see the corpse, then stand as juryman.'

The reeve stuck sullenly to his objections. ''Tisn't possible, sirs. I couldn't even get word by midday to

14

everyone from this village, let alone the Hundred. And who's to tend the animals, work the mill? The sheep will have roamed half-way to Exmoor while folk are here gawping at the corpse.'

As the little clerk was about to continue his ranting, John put out a large hand to push him aside. 'Do your best, reeve. Just get as many men as you can in the time. The pig boy, the first finders, anyone who knows anything about how the body was first seen. And get someone to dig a fresh grave in the churchyard. He'll have to go in unnamed, but at least you can get your priest to read a few words over him.'

Ralph ambled off, relieved that the big man was not going to apply every letter of the disruptive new law.

Gwyn pushed the barn door closed and they strode off through the mud, back to the reeve's house.

'We may as well dry off properly around his miserable fire while we wait,' muttered the coroner, squinting up at the low clouds draped over the moors above. It had stopped raining for the moment, but the threat hovered over them.

The silent wife produced more soup and bread, and they slowly steamed dry by the hearth, now brightened a little with a few new logs. Afterwards, like the old campaigner he was, Gwyn of Polruan wrapped himself in his cloak and stretched out his massive frame on the hard-packed floor. He never missed the chance to eat, rest or relieve himself, on the principle that he never knew when the next opportunity might come along.

The coroner gave more instructions to his new and not very cherished clerk. 'Get all this down on your rolls without fail. The reeve's name, names of the first finders and anyone else who has anything useful to say.

And a note that the village is to be amerced, whatever transpires at the inquest.'

'Why should that be, then?' grunted Gwyn from the floor, not yet asleep.

'Because the dead man's not been presented as English by the village. Nor can he be, as they don't know him from Adam – and he looks every inch a Norman gentleman.'

Even though it was almost a hundred and thirty years since the Norman invasion, the assumption was still made that anyone found dead of foul play was a Norman killed by Saxons.

'Will they have to pay for that, then?' demanded Gwyn.

'Depends on what the King's justices decide. If we find the real killer, then the villager's fault is transferred to him. If not, I dare say they'll be made to pay up.'

Gwyn sniffed loudly in disapproval. He thought this new coroner system merely another way to screw money out of the poor for the royal Treasury. Only his dogged loyalty to his knight made him keep his criticisms to himself, but the occasional grunt and sniff gave vent to his Cornish independence.

John de Wolfe was well aware of his henchman's feelings, but chose to ignore them. 'At least the village did the right thing in sending for me straight away – especially as I suspect they were right in thinking that the next village planted the body on them,' he said. 'Anyway, put it all down in that fair priest's hand of yours, Thomas. It will have to be presented to the justices in the Eyre when they next come to Devon.'

Gwyn sniffed again. 'Whenever that may be. They took five years to get to Bodmin last time.'

The bandy little clerk couldn't resist a quick jibe at his enemy. 'That's because Cornwall's so far from civilisation. A peninsula full of hairy Celtic savages.'

Gwyn threw a dead coal from the nearby hearth with unerring aim, hitting Peyne on the side of the head. The bird-faced ex-cleric let out a screech of anguish.

'Stop it, you two!' snapped John. 'You're like a pair of damned children, not grown men.' He slumped on his stool, hunching over the fire, steam rising faintly from his leather jerkin.

Tranquillity reigned for a time and when the coroner and his officer were sleepily silent, Thomas de Peyne sat with his back to the wall, huddled in his worn cloak. He thought again of the coroner's threat to sack him if he couldn't stomach the job, even though he had the Archdeacon's patronage. A fear of impending unhappiness seemed to be his lot: for almost two months now he had been almost content, with at least some purpose in life and a few pence from the coroner's purse to cover his minuscule needs. Common sense told him that Sir John's threat had been only half meant, but Thomas's insecurity dogged his every waking hour. As he crouched on the damp earth floor, his crooked back against the rough wall, he mulled over his own unhappy history. He was not a devout man, in spite of his former vocation, but he believed in God and trusted that, when he died, his next incarnation would be a damned sight better than the present one.

The fourth son of a minor Hampshire knight, there had been no land for him in their small honour near Eastleigh, so at the age of twelve he had been put into the cathedral school at Winchester. The entrance of such an unprepossessing lad, the runt of the litter, into such a prestigious college had been eased by his father's cousin John de Alecon, now Archdeacon of Exeter but who had then been one of the prebendaries of Winchester Cathedral. As he sat nursing his knees under his thin cloak, Thomas reflected on the years he had spent at school, never seeing his home for a full five years. As a small child, he had suffered a cold abscess of his upper spine, contracted from the phthisis that affected his mother and which had killed one of his older brothers. Though his had eventually healed, it had left him slightly stooped and twisted, the object of ridicule by his schoolfellows. Yet he had survived and had been strengthened in resolve by his persecution. He excelled at his letters, perhaps as compensation for his physical disadvantage. He could soon read and speak Latin and Norman French, as well as native English, which was looked on with scorn by his aristocratic Norman contemporaries – even King Richard had never bothered to learn a word of English. His penmanship earned even the grudging praise of his strict monkish tutors, but with these narrow talents, only one course was open to him – to go into the Church. Thomas de Peyne had no particular interest in theology, liturgy or pastoral care, but had a strong liking for books and manuscripts, and an insatiable curiosity about other people's business – probably because his own was so dull.

In due course and after years of study of logic, mathematics and more Latin, he became a junior deacon at Winchester. Gradually, over the next decade, he had become a workhorse in the administration of the cathedral and chapter. He was employed mainly in the treasury, his participation in religious life minimal, confined to obligatory attendance of the several daily services – but he had also become a teacher of reading and writing, which had helped towards his eventual downfall.

On his elevation to Archdeacon John de Alecon had moved to Exeter eight years ago, and was now one of the right-hand men of the Bishop. Before he left Winchester, his valedictory act for Thomas had been to get him ordained. Soon afterwards, he was made prebendary of one of the smallest parishes on the outskirts of the city, although he still laboured as a cathedral administrator and schoolmaster.

Thomas's reminiscences were halted briefly by a shattering snore from Gwyn, which disturbed the Cornishman sufficiently to make him mutter and grunt, then turn over and go back to sleep. Crowner John seemed to be dozing quietly on his stool, and the clerk's thoughts drifted back for the thousandth time to the events of his fall from grace.

Over the years, the malady that had affected his spine had grown worse: although the tuberculous abscess had subsided, the sinews and bone had contracted and shrunk so that his head was pulled slightly to one side and the lopsided lump on his back had become more obvious. His skin had seemed to coarsen and, though he was by no means grotesque, he was far from attractive. Although a prebendary was supposed to be celibate, many had mistresses or even illicit families – some had a whole clutch of bastards, often by different mothers – and although the cathedral precinct, where many canons lived, was forbidden to women, this rule was openly flouted.

Despite his physical shortcomings, Thomas de Peyne had a normal sex drive. He liked women, he desired women and, if he had been like his fellow prebendaries, his lust could easily have been satisfied. If only he had confined his activities to the stews that peppered Winchester – as they did every busy town – life could have carried on in its own humdrum, but comfortable way. But two years ago, one of his reading pupils in the cathedral day school, a fat fourteen-year old girl, had been his nemesis.

Hunched against the cottage wall, with the rough boards cutting into his bent back, Thomas wondered if her obesity and his crookedness had attracted each other – or whether she had been taunting him. For lead him on she certainly did, with requests for an extra hour of reading practice after the other scholars had left, coy looks, fluttering eyelashes and suggestive conversation. Either he misread the signs, from wishful thinking, or was deliberately trapped by her, but his eventual clumsy efforts at seduction in the dingy schoolroom off the cloisters were met with screams that could have drowned the cathedral bells. The proctors came running and he was imprisoned for the next week in a punishment cell under the chapter house. Thankfully, the whole abortive ravishment had taken place on episcopal premises so no sheriff's sergeants had been called. If they had, he would probably have been hanged within days for attempted rape.

As it was, he kept his life, but lost almost everything else. After interminable delays, he was hauled before the consistory court of the diocese, found guilty on what he considered perjured evidence by the girl and her family, and stripped of his holy orders by an irate bishop and ejected from the cathedral precincts.

The loss of his priesthood meant little to Thomas, but deprivation of the prebend, his living accommodation and the comfortable ecclesiastical life were a disaster. He was thrown out of the religious community and escaped having to beg for his survival only by scribing letters and bills for tradesmen and tutoring a few youths for rich families.

This went on for a year and half, until his commissions dwindled as he became more and more dishevelled and despairing. Cut off from his family by the disgrace, he even contemplated suicide, but eventually summoned the last of his courage to walk to Exeter to throw himself on the mercy of his kinsman. Grudgingly, the Archdeacon agreed to help him, if and when he could, and some months later, when the new coroner system was introduced, he had prevailed on John de Wolfe to take on Thomas as his clerk, recommending strongly his capabilities with pen and parchment.

So here he was, he reflected, a crook-backed ex-canon, with no money and few prospects other than tramping the countryside acting as a scribe and spy for King Richard's new law officer.

He sighed a great sigh and hunkered down into his hooded cloak, trying to submerge his chronic worries in the stupor of sleep.

CHAPTER TWO

In which Crowner John opens an inquest

Miraculously the rain held off until noon, when the inquest was held outside the great doors of the tithe barn. They now stood open to reveal the body of the murdered man lying inside on a rough bier. The only decent chair in the village had been brought from the church and placed a few yards in front of the entrance. It was a plain high-backed settle, kept in the small chancel in case the Bishop of Exeter ever visited – a penance he had so far managed to avoid.

Sir John de Wolfe sat augustly in the Bishop's seat. A motley collection of about thirty men and boys stood in a ragged half-circle before him. They ranged from skinny youths to arthritic grandfathers. The only thing they had in common was a sense of awe and bewilderment as to what this new-fangled 'Crowner's quest' was all about. They looked with interest, tinged with anxiety, at the predatory figure sitting there. To them he was dark and menacing, an almost demoniac messenger from the dimly perceived outer world.

For his part, John felt anything but messianic – he was cold, damp and would have killed for a good fire and a decent meal. He was the least intro-spective of men, practical and unimaginative. Unlike his brother-in-law, the sheriff, he had no sense of his own importance, other than a simple will to be an agent for the King's peace. In fact, he was a simple man, uncomplicated, lacking subtlety or romanticism. Devotion to his leader, King Richard, was enough for him; it was at the heart of a code of loyalty by which he had lived since he had become a fighting man, more than twenty years ago. Now forty and getting too old for battlefields, he had welcomed this chance to uphold the Lionheart's kingdom by doggedly and single-mindedly enforcing the royal laws as best he could. Whereas other more sophisticated minds might see that the King's feet were at least partly made of clay, John de Wolfe saw him in the same light as others held religion: to be revered and obeyed with blind faith. Now, though, none of this was going through his mind as he sat in the Bishop's seat and wished himself back in the warmth of the Bush tavern in Exeter with a jar of good ale in his hand, instead of in this miserable hamlet with its boggy soil and sodden inhabitants.

The burly Gwyn opened the proceedings by bawling in a voice that could have been heard far up on the moors 'All ye who have anything to do before the King's coroner for the county of Devon, draw near and give your attendance!'

There was some shuffling of feet as the gathering waited expectantly for something to happen. The women of the village, excluded from the menfolk's participation, loitered in the background, whispering behind their hands at this unexpected entertainment in their drab lives.

'The first finders – they who discovered the body – step forward,' commanded the coroner.

With a jostling of neighbours' elbows, a young man

with curly blond hair stepped out reluctantly and made a diffident nod of obeisance before the coroner. He had a bad cold and his nose was running like a tap. A rough hessian smock, with a knotted rope for a belt, left his arms bare, which like his face, had many bramble scratches, some still bleeding.

'Give your name and age to the clerk.'

Thomas was crouched on a milking stool at John's right hand, his parchments and inks spread on a small bench before him. His quill moved rapidly.

'Cerdic, of this village, sir,' he muttered, between sniffs. 'English, I am,' he added, superfluously as, with a name like his, he could be neither Norman nor Celt.

'Your age, boy?'

'Seventeen . . . I think,' he added uncertainly.

Crowner John ignored the muffled titter that came from the women at the back. 'And this body – tell us how you found it.'

The lad drew a brawny arm across his nose to wipe away a dribble. 'On my way to the bottom wood to cut withies, I was. Down the path by the brook, I saw this here body, lying face down in the water, his head on our side.'

The clerk scribbled away furiously, as the coroner sought more detail. 'What time was this, boy?'

'Just after dawn, sir. A bite to eat and I was out. First up in the village, I reckon.'

'What did you do then, boy?' rasped John.

Cerdic ran a forearm across his nose, then spat noisily onto the ground. 'I met Nebba when I was running back to the village. I told him, and he came back with me to look at the dead man. Then we both went to find Ralph.'

John pressed him for more facts of how the body lay and what wounds he had seen, but nothing new emerged. The young man was allowed to step back into the village ranks, which he did with obvious relief.

The next witness was a small boy, who had been tending the pigs the night before. He was marched forward by his mother, a formidable woman of extreme ugliness, who gripped her reluctant son by the shoulder to propel him before the Bishop's chair. Wide-eyed and overawed, all he could stammer out was a vow that there had been no body in the stream late the previous evening when he had scoured the area for a roaming pig.

After the child had been dragged away by his mother, John turned to the manor reeve. 'Who's this Nebba that the first witness mentioned?'

Ralph looked uneasy and shifted his feet about on the wet earth. 'He's a stranger in the village, Crowner. Been here a month or so.'

'Let's hear from him, then,' snapped John.

There was much gabbling and moving among the onlookers, many of whom turned round to look across the village green. A man, whom the coroner had noticed earlier at the back of the crowd, was walking quickly away.

Gwyn yelled at him to come back and, when the fellow took no notice, strode after him. Immediately, the man began to run, but he was no match for Gwyn's long legs. Although the cornishman was built like a bull, he could move fast over short distances and before the fugitive had gone fifty yards, he had him by the neck and was dragging him back to the inquest, his heels scraping along the ground.

Pushing his way through the ring of villagers, Gwyn shoved the man before the coroner.

John glared at him. 'What's going on? Why did you run away, knave?'

Nebba was thin, with tangled blond hair and moustache. He wore a dirty, torn tunic down to his knees, held by a worn leather belt that must once have been of good quality. His face was set in an expression of defiance rather than fear. 'I don't want to be mixed up with the law. All I did was go and look at some poxy corpse when that daft lad asked me to see it.'

Gwyn, who still held the man firmly by one shoulder, suddenly grabbed his right hand and pulled it up to show the coroner.

John leaned forward in his chair to see that the index and middle fingers were missing, old healed scars covering the stumps. 'Ah, Master Bowman, where did you lose those, then?' he grated. If a captured archer escaped hanging or having his throat cut, the two fingers that drew back the bowstring were chopped off, so that he could no longer practise his deadly profession.

Nebba scowled and remained silent, until Gwyn shook him until his yellow teeth rattled. 'Answer the coroner, damn you!'

'In Le Mans in 'eighty-eight,' he muttered sullenly.

The coroner's forehead scar crinkled as his brows rose in surprise. 'You fought with the old King?' He meant one of the last battles of Henry II, in which his rebellious sons Richard and John had combined with Philip of France both to defeat their father and break his heart.

Nebba nodded. 'That's why I didn't want to get mixed up with you. You're one of Richard's men.'

John gave one his rare laughs, a bellow of incredulity. 'Do you think I'd hold it against a man for being faithful to Henry, you fool?' he snapped. 'I'm not proud that Richard turned against his father, even though he was provoked by the old man's indulgence of John.'

The crowd was silent, mainly because they had no idea what Nebba and the coroner were talking about, but Thomas and Gwyn were well aware that Nebba was no ordinary villager. He was more likely a soldier on the run from justice.

'I know nothing of this dead one, sir. All I can say is that he lay in that bloody brook with his face in the water.'

'You had never seen him before?'

'Never. Neither do I know his name nor anything about him. I just want to be left in peace.'

John stared at him, suspicion competing with respect for a soldier who had been maimed for fighting for his king. 'This is not your village? You have a strange accent.'

Nebba shook his dirty locks. 'I have no village. I wandered here and work for my keep in the fields, sleep in the cow byre, until I move on.'

Like Gwyn, the coroner had suspected that Nebba was an outlaw who had tired of an almost animal life in the forest and who was trying to slip back into conventional life, even at risk of summary beheading.

Nebba was questioned further, but stubbornly maintained that he knew nothing about the corpse in the stream. The coroner persisted for a time, but could think of no reason why a former bowman should have been involved in the death of a young Norman, other than robbery. But if that were the case, reasoned John, why should he hang around the village?

He beckoned to Gwyn and muttered to him, 'What d'you think of the fellow? He's patently a runaway, beyond the law.'

Gwyn felt the same grudging sympathy for a former soldier down on his luck. 'No doubt he's a man of the forest, not bound to any lord or manor now. We could slice his head off his shoulders if we wished, but what good would that do? The woods of Devon hold a thousand more like him.'

John nodded. As usual, his man was thinking along similar lines to himself. 'I suspect he's working his way nearer a borough, probably Exeter, to try to get his twelve months within the walls.' Serfs and villeins could claim their freedom if they escaped their manor and resided in a borough for at least a year and a day, without being recaptured by their lord. Some outlaws impersonated villeins on the run and some even regained wealth and positions of importance. If Nebba could achieve this, the coroner had no desire to prevent him, so long as there was no proof that he had been involved in this killing.

John dismissed him, and the Saxon archer melted away into the crowd. The coroner shifted on the hard chair, aware that his investigation was getting nowhere.

Gwyn motioned for Ralph the reeve to step forward. As a gesture to the occasion, he had washed his face and tied his long hair back with a piece of twine. 'The lad Cerdic and that Nebba called me when they found the corpse. I took a couple of men and pulled him out of the stream on to the bank. We carried him up here to the barn, then I sent word to the manor bailiff at North Hall.'

Crowner John nodded, his long black hair bobbing about his neck. 'What about this Nebba? Where did he come from?'

The reeve looked furtive. 'Seems a good man, sir. Walked into the village at harvest time, wanted labour in return for food and shelter. We needed extra hands and our lord's steward said he could stay for the winter.'

It was unusual for a manor to shelter a stranger, other than the itinerant craftsmen that passed through. Probably some looted or stolen silver had changed hands as a bribe, but John felt that although he should drag the fellow to the sheriff for interrogation, he did not wish to interfere in a village matter.

He paused while his clerk caught up with the proceedings on the parchment roll.

'And you have no idea who the deceased might be, reeve?'

Ralph shook his pigtail. 'No, sir. But I reckon the corpse didn't die where we found him – too rotten he was. We'd have seen him long before if he'd been there the week it would have took to get that foul. Next village dumped him there, I'll swear.'

There was a commotion in the crowd as someone forced his way forward. 'That's a damn lie! We never laid eyes on him before.' A big, red-faced man in a faded blue tunic pushed Ralph aside and stood truculently before John. He had a hare-lip, which added to the malevolent look on his coarse features.

'I suppose you're from Dunstone?' asked the coroner.

The man grunted affirmatively. 'Simon, their manor reeve. You sent for me, Crowner. But we know nothing of this. Widecombe is just trying to avoid your amercement by putting the blame on us. Might have known this here Ralph would try a trick like that.'

John grinned inwardly. It was typical that villages – even belonging to the same manor – should be at odds with each other when it came to avoiding a fine.

Ralph loudly contested the denial of the neighbouring village's reeve. 'It wasn't there the night before, Simon, so how come a corpse corrupt more than a week suddenly appears in our stream, eh?'

'I don't know. That's your problem. Just don't go trying to put the blame on us in Dunstone, that's all.'

'Maybe you or one of your villagers killed him,' Ralph sneered.

Growling with anger, the stocky Simon stepped nearer to take a swing at Ralph, who hopped out of range.

John nodded at Gwyn, and the Cornishman ended the developing dispute by pushing Simon back into the throng with a hand the size of a small ham.

The coroner thoughtfully stroked the dark stubble on his long chin as he deliberated about what to do next. He had decided that neither of the manor reeves was to be trusted and he put them firmly into his pool of suspects, which also included Nebba.

'You both claim that neither Widecombe nor Dunstone know anything about this victim, yet even in this wet weather, his body could not have washed any distance down that tiny stream. And the killers would hardly return after ten days to shift the corpse. One of you is concealing the truth.'

An ominous silence followed.

'I will therefore amerce both villages in the sum of ten marks, unless in due course some other explanation appears.'

There was a murmur among the crowd. A mark was two-thirds of a pound, more than thirteen shillings. Ten marks was a great deal of money for such small hamlets to find – and FitzRalph, their lord, would be unlikely to contribute to the fine. The only consolation was that it would not be payable until the King's justices confirmed it, which might be a year or more in the future when the General Eyre next came to Exeter.

However, Simon was not one to leave the matter there. 'Crowner, this foul death is surely nothing to do with our folk, neither Dunstone nor Widecombe. The woods here abound with outlaws.' He scowled as he looked around for Nebba, who had vanished. 'They steal our sheep and fowls year in, year out. Around Spitchwick and Buckland the forest is thick with them – escaped felons, abjurers and runaway serfs. Why should we get the blame for the evil they do?'

There was a mumble of agreement from the jury, though no one wanted to be identified as challenger to the coroner.

Ralph was emboldened by his fellow-reeve's words and added, 'There are other evil men up on the moors. They live by theft – and murder, if needs be.'

'Men like that Nebba you've just heard from. Where did he come from, if it weren't outlawry? What about him for a suspect, eh?' Simon suggested.

At that another row broke out, Ralph defending Nebba, which Gwyn ended by pushing the two men apart and standing between them.

John de Wolfe jabbed a long finger at both reeves. 'I'm not amercing you for the killing, as there is no proof. The fine is for trying to deceive me and for obstructing my duties by not raising the hue-and-cry much earlier. One of you knew of this body before the lad found it in the stream. Even if outlaws were responsible, they wouldn't have kept a stinking body for near two weeks, then brought it to your village boundary. One of you is trying to shift the blame for a slain corpse to the other.'

There seemed no answer to that, and as no other witnesses had anything to say, the coroner thankfully eased his backside off the Bishop's hard chair and walked back through the doors of the barn.

The jury straggled behind him, still muttering under their breath about the amercement money, followed by the women and urchins. Thomas gathered up his writing materials and scurried after them.

When the throng had assembled in a wide circle around the bier, John approached the head, his hands clasped behind his back. His tall, stooped figure was like that of a learned pedagogue about to give a lecture on anatomical dissection.

He intoned his findings for the benefit of the clerk's quill. 'I, John de Wolfe, Knight, King Richard's coroner for the county of Devon, examined in the village of Widecombe on the third day of November in the year of our Lord eleven hundred and ninety-four, the corpse of an unknown man found yesterday in a brook between this village and Dunstone.' He bent a little nearer, oblivious of the burgeoning odour of putrefaction. 'The victim appears about five-and-twenty to thirty years of age, well built of medium height. Fair hair, not recently trimmed. Fair moustache, no beard. Eyes sunken, colour not discernible.' He motioned to Gwyn, who picked up the limp hands of the cadaver. 'Not the hands of a bondman or heavy craftsman, nor soft like a courtier,' he added, with a hint of sarcasm.

Gwyn, aided by Ralph, began to undress the body as the coroner continued his commentary.

'Wearing a good green tunic over an undershirt and linen shift. Black breeches, woollen hose, cross-gartered. No cloak present in spite of the season.' Probably stolen by his attackers, John thought. 'Leather belt, with embossed patterns, Levantine in style. Empty sword scabbard, curved shape – again from the East. Dagger in place in scabbard on back of belt.'

Here, Glyn drew out the dagger, a good but unremarkable weapon. 'No blood upon it,' he grunted, pushing it back into the leather sheath.

'Riding boots, again hammered leather pattern, coming from Jaffa or Acre in my estimation.' John could never resist airing his knowledge of the Levant. 'Bandages wound around feet, the sign of an experienced horseman used to long distances. Marks of spurs on boots, but none present now.' Also stolen, he thought.

Gwyn, well versed already in the coroner's routine, held up in succession the tunic, the shirt and the shift for inspection. In each was a clean slit about an inch long, under the left shoulder-blade. There were further cuts in the left forearm and in the upper part of the right sleeve.

The clothing, which smelt of the corpse's peeling skin and weeping body fluids, was bundled up and given into the care of the village, with instructions to wash and guard it safely until it was claimed by the victim's family.

The crowd shuffled nearer as the now naked body, belly swelling with gas, was displayed on the bier.

'The face and arms are deeply sun-browned, though fading. Corruption is present, of a degree that in this season and weather might token death at least a sennight, maybe almost a fortnight, since.'

Once more Gwyn held up the hands and arms, and John continued, 'A deep slash through skin and flesh on the left arm between wrist and elbow and a three-inch wound below the right shoulder. Sustained during a sword fight, the left arm raised in protection, the right struck to disable the sword arm.' Gwyn pointed a thick finger at the left hand to remind him. 'And defending cuts on the fingers, thumb and palm of the left hand, where the victim gripped a sharp blade.'

John waited for his clerk to catch up, then told Gwyn to roll the body over on to its face. When it rested with its limp arms dangling over the edge of the bier, they saw that the settled blood under the skin on the back now had a lacework of darker putrefying veins that contrasted with the greenish pallor of the upper skin.

The coroner proclaimed the significance of the slit in the clothing, pointing out the stab wound under the shoulder-blade, now dribbling fluid blood that had already collected in a large pool on the oak of the crude bier.

Gwyn leaned over to look again more closely at it, the ends of his moustache almost brushing the corpse.

A voice spoke from alongside him. 'A dagger, that was, not a sword. Double-edged, by the sharpness of the ends of the cut. Pulled downwards as it was withdrawn for there's a shallow cut tailing away from the lower end.'

It was Nebba. He had unobtrusively rejoined the throng, and Gwyn turned to scowl at him, annoyed at his challenge to the monopoly of knowledge of wounds that he and the coroner professed. A murmur went up from the onlookers near enough to hear him.

'Stabbed in the back. A wicked thing,' said Simon of Dunstone solemnly. Ralph looked at him suspiciously, but said nothing to provoke another squabble.

The coroner made his own close inspection. His lips thinned in distaste. 'Not killed in fair combat, for sure. He was fighting to the front and got two sword cuts for his efforts when someone else stabbed him between the shoulders. Then he turned and grasped the blade, getting his hand cut for his trouble.' There was nothing more to be seen, so after telling Thomas to note down the dead man's hairy mole, John walked back to his episcopal chair, the crowd shambling back to face him.

'The inquest can go no further than to declare the victim murdered and to state that his identity is unknown. It is obvious that no one can present Englishry to me, so the village of Widecombe is also amerced in the sum of ten marks as a murdrum fine.' There was another collective groan from the crowd at this additional burden for the future.

'Neither have I any way of telling where he died or whether you villagers are telling me the whole truth. I have the gravest suspicions of some of you, but further enquiry is necessary on my part.' He glared down accusingly at the two reeves. 'However, Widecombe guarded the cadaver and sent for the King's crowner without undue delay, as is the law now. That law requires me, if I can, to name the deceased, if he be a stranger and to tell where he spent the night before his death. Neither of these can I do, and so this inquest is laid aside for now.'

He turned to his clerk. 'Make sure everything is recorded on your rolls for the sheriff and the next visit of the justices.' He raised a hand to signal that the performance was over. 'If further information arises in the meanwhile, I will reconvene this inquest on this same spot.' Looking round the squalid village, he added, in an undertone, 'Which, God forbid.'

Rising from his chair, he gave instructions to Ralph, the bailiff and the parish priest to have the body buried in the churchyard with proper dignity and to erect a wooden cross at the head of the grave. 'Whatever else he was, he was a gentleman soldier and almost certainly a Crusader and thus deserves our respect.'

Striding away through the villagers, John de Wolfe's tall figure led Gwyn and Thomas back to where their horses were tethered. Within a few minutes, the trio were winding their way back up the track towards the county town of Exeter, some sixteen miles distant.

CHAPTER THREE

In which Crowner John falls out with his wife

The shortening days and the leaden sky made it almost
dark when John arrived home. The trio had spent an
hour in a tavern at Fulford on the road back from
Widecombe where they ate better food and drank
better beer than the reeve's wife had provided.

At the walls of Exeter they separated, the clerk
going off to his room in the cathedral precinct –
which he had obtained in spite of his expulsion from
holy orders. Gwyn went back to his wife and children
in their thatched hut outside the East Gate, while the
Coroner, with a noticeable lack of enthusiasm, went
slowly home to his burgage in St Martin's Lane, a
passage between the High Street and the cathedral.

He stabled his horse at a nearby farrier's and,
after seeing the stallion fed and watered, plodded
up the muddy cart-tracks to the timber town-house
that leaned over the tiny street. It was too large for
him – he had no children with whom to share it – but
his wife would hear nothing of moving to a smaller
dwelling. 'You are a knight, and the King's coroner
for the country, and I am the sister of the sheriff!'
she would declaim in her grating, high-pitched voice.
'How could we hold up our heads among our peers
if we moved to some miserable little tenement?'

At forty-six, Matilda was six years older than John. Though she had once been a handsome woman, now she looked every month of her age, in spite of the constant ministrations of her French maid, Lucille, who with powder and curling tongs attempted to keep back the ravages of time.

The coroner had been pushed into this lacklustre marriage sixteen years ago by the ambitions of his late father, Simon de Wolfe, who saw in a match with the de Revelle family the best road for the advancement of his eldest son. After less than eighteen months with his shrewish bride, John escaped from her with repeated absences at the Irish wars and then with King Richard in Palestine. In fact, his enthusiasm for warfare was founded less on patriotism and the removal of the Saracen from the Holy Land, than on his desire to stay away from Matilda.

The street door was ajar when he reached it and he pushed it open to find Brutus, his house dog, sitting in the vestibule beyond. The old hound's ears were held back and his feathery tail slowly swished the floor in a rhythmic welcome.

'At least someone's glad to see me home,' he murmured, as he bent to fondle the dog's head.

As he shrugged off his damp cloak and unbuckled his sword-belt, another figure appeared from a door at the rear, who also seemed pleased to see him. 'Master, you're back! Let's have those filthy boots off you.'

He sat on the inner step, watching strands of Mary's long blonde hair slip from beneath the linen kerchief that she wore on her head, as she tugged off his riding boots.

Mary was their serving maid, a handsome, if over-muscular, girl of twenty-five. Exuding good health, she had a briskness and determination that brushed aside all problems. She never failed to make John feel better when he was low – a frequent condition for the coroner.

Mary was the by-blow of a Norman squire and a Saxon woman from Exeter. In this divided household, she was firmly, if discreetly, John's ally against Matilda and Lucille. He had given her her job against his wife's wishes and, an eminently sensible girl, Mary valued it too highly to risk losing it over household politics – but short of open warfare with the mistress, she aided and abetted the coroner whenever she could in his campaign of survival against his strident wife. As she fetched him a pair of soft house shoes, she whispered to him conspiratorially, 'Her brother is here again, master. They're in the hall, complaining about you as usual.'

John groaned. His damned brother-in-law seemed to spend more time in this house than he did himself, and if Matilda were not such an obnoxious woman, he might have suspected Richard de Revelle of incestuous inclinations.

Reluctantly he rose from the chair and moved to the other door in the vestibule. This opened into the hall, which occupied the front half of the house from floor to roof. Behind it on the upper level was the solar, his and his wife's private chamber and sleeping place, reached by an outside stairway at the rear. Here Matilda did her needlework and Lucille primped her hair. In the small yard at the back of the house were outhouses where the two servants lived, and where the cooking, brewing and washing were done.

Mary picked up the boots, thickly coated with mire.

'I'll get these cleaned and polished – and good luck in there!' she added impishly.

John ruffled her fair hair affectionately. In the past they had had a few clandestine sessions in bed, but Mary had refused him in recent months, fearing that the mistress, through the hated Lucille, may have developed suspicions.

As she vanished outside to the domestic area, John lifted the wrought-iron latch on the hall door and, with a sigh, stepped into his own domain.

The room was high, gloomy and cold, in spite of a big log fire in the cavernous hearth at the further end. Much of the bare timber of the high walls was covered with tapestries and banners, but even these were sombre and depressing. A long oaken table stood in the centre of the room with a heavy chair at each end and benches down either side.

Flanking each side of the stone fireplace was a settle, a double wooden seat with a high back and side wings to keep out the draughts, and directly before the hearth, a pair of monk's chairs, each with a cowled back like a beehive, again to protect the occupant from the cold.

As John walked across the bare flagstones – Matilda would not suffer the usual scattered rushes on beaten earth as being 'common' – a mutter of voices echoed from the high walls. 'Matilda, I'm back,' he called.

A face appeared around the side of one of the cowled chairs. 'Indeed, so I see! A wonder you bother to come home at all. I've not laid eyes on you in daylight all this week.'

His wife's square face was set in a perpetual expression of disdain, as if a bad smell was ever under her nostrils. Though handsome once, a faint moustache and fleshy pouches under her blue eyes and along the jawline suggested both a lazy lifestyle and an over-enthusiastic appetite. Her elaborately curled hair was partly hidden under a brocade cap, which matched a heavy gown to keep out the November chill.

John crossed to the hearth and stood with his back to the fire, both to warm the seat of his breeches and to emphasise that he was master of the household.

Two pairs of eyes stared at him. 'And how did my new law officer fare today, in the dung-hole they call Widecombe?'

Sarcasm fell easily from the thin lips of his brother-in-law, lolling in the other chair. Though sibling to Matilda, his face was as long and lean as hers was broad, but he had the same cold blue eyes.

'Good day, Sir Sheriff, though I'm not *your* law officer. I answer directly to the King, who appointed me.'

Sir Richard de Revelle sighed, assuming a pitying smile as if indulging a naughty child. 'Of course, John, of course! Though faint chance you have of ever reporting to our good King – or even of seeing him. I hear reliable reports from France that he intends never again to set foot in England.'

Matilda snorted. 'And very good sense he shows, too. If I had my wishes, I'd not stay a day longer in this miserable rain-sodden country, full of Saxons and Cornishmen.'

In her youth she had once spent a few months in Normandy with relatives and had played ever since the martyred role of a reluctant Norman exile, though she had been born in Exeter and had spent nearly all her life in Devon.

John had heard it all a score of times, but familiarity

did not lessen his exasperation. 'The King may not be in Winchester or London, but he's still the sovereign of this land, Richard. And we remain his officers, wherever he is.'

The sheriff's face, with its thin dark moustache and small pointed beard, kept its patronising smile. 'Agreed, brother, and I'm sure you need no reminding that I am his representative in this country. What the Justiciar was thinking of when he meddled with this coroner business in September I still cannot fathom.'

John was not overburdened with patience and although the argument was familiar, the other's sneers were like a red rag to a bull. 'I'll tell you why, once again, brother-in-law. It was because the sheriffs were milking too much of the revenue due to the Exchequer into their own purses. Hubert Walter has had the good sense to set someone trustworthy in each county – the coroners – to keep a record of what's due.'

De Revelle waved this aside with a languid flip of his hand. 'Nonsense, John. You should know the truth better than any man, having been with Richard when he was taken in Austria. It was to raise the huge ransom that Henry of Germany demanded for him. Our wily Hubert dreamed up this scheme to screw even more cash out of the long-suffering populace.'

There was more than a grain of truth in what the sheriff said, and it touched John on a sore spot: his conscience still pricked him for not having saved his king from capture near Vienna, two years ago. As a knight in Richard's army, he had left the Holy Land with the King's retinue in October 1192, leaving Hubert Walter, now Chief Justiciar and Archbishop of Canterbury, in command of the remaining English force. During the voyage, which included shipwreck and attack by pirates, John proved such a staunch protector to his king that Richard took him into his personal bodyguard. The king had decided to return home by sailing up the Adriatic and travelling overland through Bohemia. Several times evading capture, he was eventually trapped in an inn at Erdberg, just outside Vienna. At the time John had been out with Gwyn, searching for fresh horses, and for ever after blamed himself for not having been on hand to fight for his royal master. Richard was imprisoned for a year and a half, first by Leopold of Austria, who sold him on to Henry VI of Germany. Eventually a ransom of a hundred and fifty thousand marks was agreed, a terrible burden for England, which had already been stripped by Richard to finance his army for the Third Crusade and later his campaign against Philip of France.

However, his loyalty to Richard the Lionheart forced John to deny his brother-in-law's argument and they bandied words for several minutes, neither willing to agree that the other was partly correct.

Matilda had tired of these political joustings in which she could take no part. 'You use your coronership as an excuse to be away at all hours, John!' she complained. 'You are never at home, seeing to our affairs and keeping me company.'

John's gaunt face reddened above the black stubble on his unshaven chin.

''Twas you pushed me into the damned job, woman. Didn't you plead with your brother and the Bishop to petition Hubert Walter on my behalf?'

The sheriff looked from one to the other, a smug

expression on his lean features. He enjoyed a good row between his relatives.

'Of course I wanted you to have the appointment, you clod of a man. Did you think I wanted you be a crude soldier all your life, lumbering about the country waving a sword?' She hauled herself out of the chair and stood threateningly in front of her husband, hands propped on her bulging hips. 'You needed decent employment – like a law officer high in the county, where you wouldn't shame me with your soldier's ways. Something appropriate to our position – a king's knight and a sheriff's sister!' She advanced another step towards him and even the redoubtable John moved back a little along the fireplace.

'By Mary Mother of God! John de Wolfe, be glad you have such a post. I don't want you skulking around, like some unemployed squire waiting for a new war – or, even worse, sinking to become some merchant or trader. Could I ever hold my head up then?'

The veins on his forehead bulged and the Coroner slapped his hand violently on the stone of the fireplace.

'It's always you, you, you!' he shouted. 'Damn what I might want as long as you can walk in a new gown in the portreeve's procession or in the judge's train, flaunting your airs and graces!'

He kicked at a log violently, sending a shower of sparks dancing up the wide chimney, and ignored her brother's smirks.

'You should make up your mind, wife!' John fumed. 'One moment you want me to be a county coroner, then you complain that I spend too much time doing the job!'

Matilda's podgy cheeks coloured under the layer

of powder. 'Don't you shout at me! Why *did* you agree to accept the crownership, then, if you're so set against it?'

'I didn't say I was against it . . . though, by God, it's a hard task sometimes. I did it to please you – or, at least, to avoid your endless nagging. It keeps me occupied as you're so set against me going off to fight – where any man with guts would wish to be,' he added, with a pointed look at his brother-in-law.

Richard's condescending good humour faded at this. 'You well know I've this old wound in my side, suffered in King Henry's service – it plagues me continually. But for that I would, of course, be following Coeur de Lion in Normandy.'

John had his own ideas on that, but even the heat of a family dispute was insufficient to bring it out now – he was keeping it for a more rewarding opportunity.

Matilda, however, was still in full spate. She had subsided heavily into her chair, but continued to wag a beringed finger at her glowering husband. 'I suggested the coronership for your own pride and status in Exeter, John. I had no intention of you taking on most of the county of Devon as an excuse for you to go galloping over hill and dale every hour God made!' John turned angrily and bent over his wife. 'You know well enough what happened, Matilda, and you were greatly pleased at the time, for it puffed up your image in the county as well as the city.'

The Article of Eyre had demanded that three knights and a clerk be appointed to form a coroner's service in each county. John de Wolfe had been summarily elected by the burgesses as their city coroner. His crusading connections with both the King and Hubert Walter had ensured that he was a prime candidate. In truth, the coronership was not much sought after, as it was unpaid. In fact, coroners had to have a private income of at least twenty pounds a year: a rich man would have no need to resort to corruption as the sheriffs had. As the job was so unattractive, only one other coroner had been found, and he, Robert FitzRogo, had fallen from his horse two weeks after his appointment and died from spinal paralysis. John had been left with the jurisdiction of the whole county until someone else could be pressed into service.

Matilda chose to ignore this. 'The devil with your excuses! The nub of the matter is that you are staying out all day and night, on some pretext about crowner's duties when I know that you're sitting in taverns or carousing with your old wartime comrades – and bedding as many dirty wenches as you can throw your leg over!'

John purpled again with righteous indignation, though what she alleged was not far off the mark. Today, however, he had been out in teeming rain since dawn, had ridden thirty hard miles and had barely spoken to a woman.

Richard de Revelle put in, 'You're a law officer, John, like myself. I don't go chasing around the countryside after every petty criminal, I let my sergeants and men-at-arms do that. Why not stay in Exeter, direct matters and come home each day?' Matilda took up the theme: 'Yes, send that Cornish savage to do the work – and your misshapen clerk. Have more dignity and less mud on your boots.'

John stared at them scornfully. 'Do I have a castle full of men-at-arms at my command, Sir Sheriff? And can I send my only servants to hold inquests for me in places thirty and forty miles away? If you find me someone to be coroner in the north and south of Devon, I'll gladly stay in this city and be home every noon and night!' His black eyes flashed. 'And when I get home, what welcome is there for me? If it were not for the maid, I'd go hungry, for I fail to see you bustling about, Matilda, to see that the kitchen finds me a meal when I get back wet, tired and famished. All I get is your nagging and the smirks of your damned brother.'

The others stared at him, surprised by the bitterness in his voice. Though they constantly bickered, this was stronger stuff than usual from John de Wolfe.

He wagged a long finger under his wife's nose. 'And if you falsely accuse me, woman, then I'll justify it by doing what you claim,' he threatened, thinking attack the best form of defence. Striding away from the hearth, he delivered a parting shaft. 'I'm going down to the inn, where at least I'll get a kind word, some ale . . . and possibly a cheerful wench!'

The heavy door made a satisfying bang as he slammed it behind him.

He sat near a large log fire, leaning on a scrubbed table, screened from the main room of the inn by a wattle partition that formed an alcove near the hearth. The bones of half a chicken, some pork ribs and the crumbs of a small loaf lay scattered on the boards of the table, the remnants of a good meal that his mistress had provided an hour earlier.

The Bush Inn was acknowledged as the best in Exeter, tucked away in Idle Lane, in the lower part of the town, not far from the West Gate and the river. For the moment he sat alone. Nesta was in the outhouse kitchen behind the inn, scolding the cook for being so long with another customer's supper. Edwin, the potman, an old cripple who had lost an eye and some toes in the battle for Wexford over twenty years before, washed pewter tankards in a bucket of dirty brown water, before filling them with ale from two rough barrels propped at the back of the room. Seven or eight townsmen, all well known to John, sat on benches, drinking and gossiping.

Something approaching contentment, born of the beer and the warmth, began to steal over him. His resentment and fury at his wife and her brother had been brimming over when he had stalked into the Bush, but Nesta's affection and common sense had soon calmed him down. The good food and drink and his draught-free seat before the crackling sycamore logs had pacified him and he was now slightly sleepy.

He took another long pull at the ale, bittered with oak-galls, and stared at the almost hypnotic leap of the flames. Was that damned woman right, he wondered. Did he really want this coroner's job hung like a millstone around his neck? Was it just a device he used to avoid his wife and and sit in taverns or visit his women? He had been coroner for only two months but, there in the firelight, John decided he enjoyed it.

'What's this deep thought about? Is my beer too strong for your brain?' She had come back from the kitchen and stood behind him, a hand on his shoulder.

John reached up to cover her fingers with his own. 'I was thinking that maybe I'm too old to go racing off to the wars, Nesta, my love. My sword arm is getting too slow and I'd be run through at the first skirmish.'

She squeezed his shoulder affectionately and came round the table to sit on the bench by his side. Twelve years his junior, the Welsh woman had dark red hair and, unusual in one of her age, a perfect set of teeth. A round face, a high smooth brow and a snub nose gave her prettiness rather than beauty. Small and shapely, she wore a high-necked plain gown that did nothing to hide her prominent bosom.

'You're a big handsome man in his prime, John. You're as strong as a horse and I can personally vouch that you rut like one! So shake off this "poor old man" nonsense, will you? It's just your usual gloom after fighting with that old bitch you call wife.' Nesta reached across and drank from his pot, while he slipped an arm around her and hugged her. 'I don't know where I'd be without you, sweet woman.'

Nesta smiled up at him, rather wistfully. 'You'd be with one of your other sweet women, Sir Crowner. I've no illusions about your faithfulness, though I think you like me best – so I'll settle for that, for it's all I'm likely to get.' She finished his ale and yelled at the one-eyed old soldier to bring a refill, then pointedly changed the subject. 'Was that chicken to your liking, John? This new cook had some daft idea of stuffing its belly with bread and sage herbs.' 'It was good, very good.' He ran a finger across the table top and licked at the grease appreciatively. The Bush had not taken up the new fad for platters, but served the food on thick bread trenchers, direct onto the scrubbed boards, walling in the gravy with crusts.

Old Edwin limped across and banged a brimming quart pot in front of John. 'Here ye are, Captain. Good health to you.'

He used the Coroner's old military name. Although

he had never served under him, he had a respectful admiration for John's record as a soldier.

'There's another who doesn't think you're past it as a warrior,' Nesta observed slyly, as Edwin shuffled across to the fire to load on more logs. 'Come on, John, cheer up. Tell Nesta what's on your mind.'

After six pints of ale he had to search for the root of his earlier despondency. He pulled Nesta closer to his side, so that his free hand could cup her breast, while he drank.

'My wife suggests that I took this crowner's appointment only as an excuse to escape her. But, damnation, it was she who encouraged it, to get a rung or two up the ladder of nobility.'

Nesta wriggled as his fingers played with her nipple. 'Forget her for a moment, John. Tell me what you've been doing today to make you look as if you could drop off to sleep, even in the company of the prettiest woman in Devon.'

He bent his head down to the crown of her curls, his black locks mingling with the red. 'We've been riding since dawn, out to Widecombe and back . . .' He told her about the body in the brook and the probability that it was that of a Crusader.

Nesta took a drink from his pot. 'Not bad ale, though I say it myself . . . Well, what about this Crusader? Was he young and handsome?'

John grinned, an uncommon lightening of his normally stern expression. 'That's all you flighty wenches think of, thank God!' he chaffed her. 'He might have been handsome once, but ten days or so dead takes the beauty out of any face.'

Nesta grimaced and pressed closer to his big body. 'And who do you think killed him, Sir Crowner?'

John emptied his pot before answering, and Nesta signalled to old Edwin to bring another from the best barrel.

'I don't know. The cause of most deaths in a village – or town, for that matter – is plain. Drunken quarrels, violent robberies, strangled rapes, beaten wives . . . Everyone knows the culprit and the hue-and-cry is hardly needed to catch the felon. But this one . . .' He fell silent as the old potman put a new jar in front of him.

Story-telling had taken John's mind off fondling her, and Nesta pulled back his hand to her bosom in mock annoyance. 'You think he's a nobleman, you said?' she asked.

'He was certainly no common soldier. Good clothes, fine boots, belt and scabbard – mostly Levantine made. No doubt he's come recently from Outremer.' She looked up at his profile, his long jaw pink in the flames from the fire.

'How did he reach the edge of Dartmoor? I've heard that Widecombe's an outlandish place.'

Like most town-dwellers, to Nesta the countryside was a remote, alien place. She had hardly set foot outside Exeter in the five years since she had come from South Wales. Her late husband, a Welsh archer named Meredydd, had returned from fighting in Touraine with an unexpected bounty and some loot. He landed at Exmouth, took a fancy to the area and bought the Bush Inn, sending home to Gwent for his wife. Within a year, he was dead of the jaundice and Nesta had carried on alone – with unusual success for a widow.

John pondered her question. 'He had marks of spurs on his boots, but even those had been stolen from him, along with everything else he possessed except his dagger. It was undoubtedly a robbery, probably by at least two attackers from the wounds he suffered.'

'So, a simple robbery – but why would a Crusader be riding alone along the edge of Dartmoor?' she persisted, partly to emphasise her interest in his doings and partly to keep his mind away from the spat with his wife.

'Depends where he was headed – some people take the moor track to Tavistock and Plymouth instead of the longer road through the lowlands. Or he might have been going to some manor near Okehampton, or even further into North Cornwall. And we don't know that he was alone. He may have had a companion or servant – also lying dead now in the forest.'

Nesta was becoming restive, but she sensed that her man needed to talk himself out of his mood.

'You think it was outlaws that killed him?'

'It seems most likely. The forest and moor abounds in fugitives. The two manor reeves each blamed the other, but I feel their sin is in trying to move the body from their land, rather than murder.' He thought for a moment, his beetling brows coming down in thought. 'A man called Nebba was there, too. Not a villager, he had been a soldier, I'll swear. Two fingers missing.'

This struck a chord with the shapely innkeeper. 'An archer, like my poor Meredydd! A barbaric custom, to cut off a man's fingers with a knife.'

'Not so bad as lopping off other parts, my girl,' he grunted, giving her thigh a suggestive squeeze.

After a short silence, his chin dropped on to his chest and he raised his head with a jerk, startling the auburn head next to him.

'Come, Sir Crowner, time you were in bed before you fall asleep across the table.' Nesta pulled herself away from him and stood up. 'You'll stay here this night, John, in my bed – though by the look of you, there'll be little action other than snoring. Come.'

She pulled him towards the wooden stair at the back, past the amused glances of the patrons and a chorus of 'Good night, Sir John.'

As he lumbered up the steps behind her, John was vaguely uneasy. 'I've not stayed a whole night with you before, Nesta.'

Holding a tallow candle high, she turned and grinned at him. 'Afraid I'll turn into a witch at midnight? You've spent many an afternoon and evening enjoying my hospitality, John.'

'They'll all know where I am,' he muttered.

But Nesta scoffed, 'It's no secret in Exeter, not even from your wife. So don't concern yourself, let her stew until the morning. She'll not petition the Pope for an annulment and lose being Madam Coroner for the county of Devon!'

CHAPTER FOUR

*In which the Crowner visits a lady,
then a corpse*

In spite of his lethargy, Crowner John roused himself
sufficiently to give a creditable performance in the
arms of his agile mistress before he rolled over and
fell sound asleep for the rest of the night.

Some hours before dawn Nesta was awakened by an
urgent tapping on the rough boards of the bedroom
door. The upper part of the timber hostelry was built
out over the yard, under which were the kitchen and
a shanty for the two servants. It was divided by a
partition into one small chamber, where Nesta lived,
and a larger room in which four crude beds and some
palliasses on the floor provided accommodation for
guests at the inn. This night, no one was staying at
the Bush, so Nesta knew that the tapping could not
be one of the guests wanting to creep into her bed,
as sometimes happened.

She climbed out reluctantly from beneath the woollen blanket and sheepskins. Pulling her nightrobe
tightly about her against the raw November morning,
she stumbled in the gloom to the door and put her
mouth to a crack in the planks.

'Who is it?'

'Edwin, missus. There's a man here for the Crowner.'

'Man? What man?'

Edwin shuffled outside the door and Nesta heard him mutter, 'Gwyn, his officer, he says. Wants a word with Sir John.'

'Wait there, will you?'

Sighing, Nesta groped her way back to the bed and shook John. The soldier in him rapidly threw off sleep and he stumbled to the door. Lifting the crude wooden bar that served as a latch, he stuck out his head and saw the figure of his man behind a flickering candle, old Edwin hovering nearby.

'Sorry to disturb you,' grunted Gwyn, without the trace of a smirk or even a glance into the room where Nesta was again submerged under the bedclothes. 'There's been a killing and a wounding during the night. Two fellows have been seized by the sheriff's men outside the Saracen.'

The Saracen was a rougher tavern than the Bush. Though not far away on Stripcote Hill, it catered mostly for sailors from the quayside and drovers up from the country.

'How did you know where I was?' demanded John.

Gwyn shrugged. 'Everyone knows where you are. It's no secret, nor anyone else's business.'

John shivered, the chill seeping through the under-shirt he wore in bed. 'How long to first light?'

'About two hours, by the cathedral bell.'

'I'll come to the castle at dawn. Is that where the corpse lies?'

'It is – but the injured man is still at the tavern. Eadred of Dawlish he is, in Exeter to sell his pigs at yesterday's market. He may die, he may not,' the Cornishman added philosophically.

'I'll be at the Saracen later. Gather enough men for

a jury, anyone who was witness to the fight.'

Gwyn nodded and turned away.

'And get that damned clerk out of bed. No reason for him to rest, if we've been roused.'

He slammed the door and dropped the bar into its slot. Slipping thankfully back under the bed-fleeces, he was immediately seized by a warm naked body: Nesta had peeled off her nightrobe while he had been talking to Gwyn. She pressed her lips against his and slid a sinuous hand up his thigh. 'One good thing about being woken so early, John, we've time for another tumble before the day begins!'

Nesta climbed on top of him and rode him as energetically as he cantered his grey stallion. When they had first become lovers, her fondness for straddling him had rather offended his masculine need to be dominant. However, she had broken him of the habits of a lifetime with good-humoured persistence until he had come to enjoy it – though often, with a roar of passion, he would roll the pair of them over and hammer her almost through the palliasse to the floorboards beneath. When exhaustion finally overcame them, they lay quietly side by side, his long arms wrapped tenderly around her.

There was silence for a time. Eventually he asked, 'Have you heard the Bishop's bell strike six?'

With no clock nearer than an inventive monastery in Germany, time was measured by graduated candles or a sand-glass in the cathedral and rung out over the city by tolling one of the bells.

'No, though with you panting in my ear, I'd not have heard the roof fall in! But I think we have time yet, until Edwin starts to throw logs on the fire for cooking.'

After a few more minutes of companionable silence, Nesta asked again about the man in Widecombe. She stroked his belly gently. 'And you've no idea who he is?'

'None at all. Other than he's Norman of good family.'

'How can you get further, then? The killing of a knight or someone of lordly rank cannot go unpunished. If it were a mere serf or villein, well, life is cheap, but not a gentleman.'

Sometimes John could not be sure whether she was teasing him or serious. Now he suspected the latter, as the Welshwoman had no love of the Normans' feudal system. If he had not been half Celtic himself, through his Cornish mother, he suspected she would have never let him into her bed.

'I'll have to make wider enquiries about the county, maybe even further afield. Gwyn and that poxy clerk can get the criers and heralds in each town to broadcast a description and seek any sighting of the man. But this affray on Stripcote Hill will occupy most of the day, God blast it.'

She bit his shoulder gently. 'This crowner's job seems too much for one man.'

Further conversation was interrupted by a crash below: Edwin had dropped a pile of wood on the floor. Almost immediately, they heard the clear notes of a bronze bell chiming in the distance. When they counted to six, Nesta cruelly threw back the covers and jumped out of bed, leaving John lying with his underwear around his neck. 'Come, Sir Crowner. By the time we get you fed and watered, it'll be light.'

With a good meal of ham fried in butter, three fresh

eggs and several large slabs of wheaten bread inside
him, the coroner marched complacently through the
streets of Exeter, from the south-west corner across to
where the castle stood on the edge of an escarpment.

He passed tradesmen putting up their stalls in the
dawn light, setting out baskets of fresh vegetables,
bread, meat and fish, ready to sell to the early risers
among Exeter's townsfolk. In the Shambles above Bell
Hill in South Gate Street, the butchers were felling
cattle on bloodstained cobbles and pigs screamed in
their death agony – all part of the morning sounds
of a city.

Everywhere he was met with a nod, a greeting or a
pulled forelock. Even though Gwyn of Polruan had
assured him that they all knew where he had spent the
night, he saw not a snigger or a smirk – which was just
as well, as he would have had little hesitation in felling
any offender with a smack of his brick-sized fist.

His tall, slightly stooped figure strode up the slope
to the castle's open portcullis. He carried his wide-
brimmed hat, his shoulder-length black hair lifting
as he walked. He wore a short black cloak over the
grey linen surcoat that came to his shins, tight black
breeches with cross-gartering below the knees and
pointed shoes. He hoped that Mary had cleaned his
riding boots, as he suspected that, come the afternoon,
he would be in the saddle again.

In the city, he felt no need to buckle on his heavy
sword, but his dagger was sheathed on his belt, though
in truth, these days, he used it far more for cutting his
food than any violent purpose.

The castle, called Rougemont after the red rock
upon which it was built, dominated the town from
the highest point. A small room had been allotted to

John on the first floor of the gatehouse, far removed in distance and importance from his brother-in-law, who lived and officiated in the keep. Unlike many Norman castles, there was no central mound, but a low square tower rose from the middle of the inner ward. It was the first stone keep that William the Bastard had built in England. It was said that in 1068 he had paced out the measurements for the foundations himself. Other fortified buildings were built into the curtain wall, the main ones on the edge of the low cliff that dropped down to Northernhay, the hedged fields below the city wall.

At the gate, two mailed guards banged the stocks of their spears on the cobbles in salute to him. Like most soldiers, they respected John for his military reputation, as well as for his new royal appointment as the second most important law officer in the county.

He passed under the outer arch of the gatehouse and turned left through a low door that led to the spiral stairs to his room. Little security was needed other than a couple of men to keep out beggars, children and madmen. The last time the castle had seen fighting was over fifty years ago, when for three months Baldwin de Redvers had held it for the Empress Matilda against the forces of the King, until lack of water had defeated him.

John's office was a dark chamber above the guardroom, lit only by a pair of arrow-slits looking down over the city and a narrow window-opening on the adjacent wall. The dawn light penetrated one of these and threw a pallid rectangle on a trestle table covered with parchment rolls scribed by Thomas de Peyne. The coroner sat on a hard stool behind the table and picked up the nearest roll, squinting at the penned

words on the outside without untying the cord that
held it closed. With difficulty, he slowly read the name,
mouthing the Latin laboriously with moving lips.

John knew the alphabet fairly well and was taking
secret lessons every week from a junior deacon in the
priory. He was too proud – or too arrogant – to ask
his own clerk for tuition, though Thomas knew that
his master was almost illiterate.

John identified the name on the document: he had
levied an amercement on a cottager in Cheriton for
burying the body of his wife, who had hanged herself
from an apple tree, without informing the coroner.

Feet were stumping up the stone stairway and
Gwyn's head came round the open door, bright eyes
peering through the forest of red hair and whiskers.

'The dead 'un lies in the cart shed, if you want to
see him.'

'What about the wounded fellow from Dawlish?'

'He's bleeding into a bed in the Saracen. Too ill to
be moved, they reckon. Willem, the innkeeper, is fit
to be tied over it, asking who's going to pay for a new
mattress and blanket.'

John followed his lieutenant down to the inner
bailey, the large area within the curtain walls that
was parade-ground, horse-corral and main street of the
castle. Around the inside walls, there were lean-to huts
of all shapes and sizes. Some, kitchens, blacksmiths or
forges, had smoke coming from their eaves. Others
were barracks for the constable's troops. Women and
children hung about, though the quarters for married
soldiers and castle servants were in the lower ward.

The ground had hardly a blade of grass left on
it, being mostly churned mud, horse droppings and
rubbish. Even at that early hour, the whole place

was a hive of activity, morning meals being eaten outside the huts, horses being saddled or coaxed into cart-shafts and other wagons trundling in and out of the main gate.

Used to such scenes all his life, John spared it hardly a glance but ploughed through the muck, following Gwyn towards a large, dilapidated shed inside the west wall. The doors had long since fallen off and been used for firewood by the castle residents. It housed the half-dozen big-wheeled carts that carried provisions and fodder. Right at the back, against the ruddy sandstone of the wall, lay an ominous long shape under an old cart-cover.

'I had the bailiffs bring him up here. No point in leaving him in the street for all to gawp at.'

'Do we know who he is?' asked the coroner.

'Willem the inn-keeper knew him. He's Osric, a carter from Rock Lane.'

Gwyn stooped and flicked off the canvas sheet to reveal a body with a bloody mass where the man's head had been.

John's black eyebrows rose. He was impressed by the destruction that had been wrought on the victim's face, scalp and skull.

'They used a ball on him?' he suggested.

Gwyn nodded, quietly proud of his master's instant and accurate diagnosis. 'A chain mace, with a ball the size of a turnip. Beat his head to a pulp.'

He tossed back the cover over the gruesome sight and wiped some blood from his hand on the weeds that grew at the foot of the wall.

They walked out into the grey light of the bailey.

'What about the other man?'

'He had a dagger thrust into the back of the

shoulder. But he's lost a mortal amount of blood. If it turns purulent, then he's a dead man as well.'

The coroner jerked a thumb back towards the shed and its cadaver. 'Get some of the inquest jury up here to view the body. No point in clogging the place up with half the town, ten men will suffice. And have the felons sent down to the Saracen – if the sheriff can find a couple of guards who'll not let them escape on the way,' he added ironically.

While he went back to his office to practise his reading, Gwyn went about his errands, one of which was to chase their clerk away from the food stall in the cathedral close where he was finishing his breakfast and up to the castle.

John sat for a time with a vellum roll in his hands, but his mind was not on deciphering the Latin script. He thought about last night and the calm companion-ship, as well as the healthy lust, of Nesta, both of which were so different from the petulant frigidity of Matilda. From there his mind wandered to the unknown man at Widecombe.

Virtually all coroner's cases were straightforward: any difficulties were due to the ignorance or obstinacy of the public, or obstacles raised by the sheriff and his men. During the first two months of his duties mysteries had been almost unknown, so this problem was new and intriguing, especially as the dead man seemed to be a Crusader. John began to assemble a plan of action and, not for the first time, wished that he could write well enough to list things with a quill, rather than have to carry everything in his head.

His reverie was broken by the shuffle of feet on the stairs and the head of his clerk appearing round the door. With an obsequious bow, the little ex-cleric sidled into the room and slid on to a stool opposite the Coroner.

'I've had a busy night, Thomas,' John snapped, with an ambiguity lost on the other man. 'A killing and a near-mortal wounding. There's an inquest at noon, but you'd better start entering details on your roll about the injured man, in case he doesn't die, so that his aggressor may be hauled up before the justices.'

Thomas scrabbled in the shapeless cloth bag he always carried for a new piece of parchment and his writing implements. As he arranged these on the table between them, the coroner stared at him steadily, as if seeing him for the first time. Though Thomas was the butt of scorn and often ridicule – not least from John and Gwyn of Polruan – John felt flashes of pity for him, in spite of his personal distaste for the man's character. He was ugly, too, and must have been the runt of his mother's litter, small and crook-backed with his chinless face and long nose below small beady eyes, one of which had a slight turn when he looked to the right. His lank dark hair was as lustreless as old rope and his face was pitted with the scars of cow-pox. No wonder, thought John, that he had been driven to rape, for surely no woman would ever give herself voluntarily to him.

'Put this in your best Latin. Use your own words, I'll give you the sense of it.'

He got up from his stool and paced the width of the small room.

'Whereas on the fourth day of November in Our Lord's year of eleven hundred and ninety-four, Eadred son of Oswald, freeholder of Dawlish, was found injured near to death, against the King's peace, by virtue of knife wound in the back, after an affray after midnight outside the Saracen Inn, Stripcote Hill, Exeter, in the County of Devon, allegedly by the hand of . . .' He hesitated and wrinkled his face in annoyance. 'Damnation, I forget who Gwyn told me was the attacker. Just leave a space, you can get it from him when we go down to the town.'

He carried on with a preamble to the wounding and the death, as recounted to him by his officer. He paused now and then, to let the clerk catch up with his words, which Thomas had to a translate into Latin. In the lower courts, run by the sheriffs and burgesses, English or Norman French was used in speech but anything written, especially for use in the courts of the King's justices, had to be in Latin.

Thomas worked slowly, but John had to admit that his rolls were a work of art, even to those who could hardly read the words. The regularity of his script, the faultless spacing and straightness of the lines showed that good could come out of even the most unprepossessing people.

By the time they had finished, some weak rays of early sun had struck through the rain-clouds and the narrow wall-slits into the chamber.

The ninth bell had sounded from the cathedral when Gwyn returned. He brought a large loaf from a street baker, and a slab of hard cheese. The three sat round the table and shared it, washed down with beer that John produced from a two-gallon earthenware jar kept in a corner under a cloth. For a time, there was peace, as the three men chewed the fresh bread and odorous cheese, and gulped ale from chipped pottery mugs that were part of the furnishings of the bare room.

Even Gwyn seemed temporarily to have forgotten

to bait the scrawny clerk while they enjoyed their simple snack. His huge body required refuelling at frequent intervals – there was too much of a gap for him between a pre-dawn breakfast and the midday meal. A fiercely independent Cornishman, married to a Cornish wife and with a score of relatives still in Polruan, he had become of necessity a mercenary soldier twenty years ago, and with John de Wolfe, who had had no true squire until Gwyn, he had travelled half the known world as far as Palestine. When his knight had run out of wars, Gwyn had stayed with him as his officer.

When the last crumbs had been swallowed and the empty pots returned unwashed to a niche in the wall, John returned to business. 'Did you tell the town crier to ask for information on our Crusading corpse?' he demanded of Thomas.

'Last evening time, Crowner. He will be shouting it about the city this morning. Five times today he'll cry it in various streets.'

'If we get nothing by tomorrow, I want you to ride to Cullompton, Crediton, Tiverton and Honiton to get the criers or bailiffs to put about the same message.'

The clerk groaned. 'Master, that's more than a day's ride for me on that poor beast of mine.'

The coroner was unsympathetic. 'That's your job, clerk. You get free lodging at the Archdeacon's expense and fourpence a week from me to live. Would you prefer destitution?' There was no answer to this and Thomas fell silent, though his backside ached already at the thought of a day and a half on a mule's back.

'If nothing comes of that within a few days, we'll enquire further afield. From Okehampton to Barnstaple, across to Yeovil, and maybe you'll have to travel to

Southampton, Gwyn, where the ships from Palestine berth.'

'What if he had come by sea to Plymouth?' asked the clerk, seeing a chance to extend Gwyn's travels.

'That may well be – so your nag may have to take you there as well, Thomas,' countered the coroner. 'But not yet. Let's see if the local criers get something for us.'

Gwyn hauled himself to his feet, pulling his frayed leather cape over his shoulders. 'We should leave for the Saracen to see this wounded man. Maybe you can get a declaration from him before he dies.'

CHAPTER FIVE

*In which Crowner John attends one
wounded man and two hangings*

As they shuffled on their outdoor clothes, for the sun
had vanished again in favour of cloud and cold wind,
Gwyn reminded him of another routine task for that
morning. 'I put the inquest back an hour as you must
attend two hangings at noon.'

John had forgotten, but now recalled it was Tuesday,
one of the two weekdays on which executions were
carried out. Sentences of death could be passed in
the sheriff's county court and the mayor's burgage
court of the city, as well as on the rare occasions when
king's judges were in the city. Baronial and manorial
courts, too, had power over life and death.

'Who is to be turned off today, Gwyn?' he asked,
as they walked down from the castle to the High
Street.

'An old beggar who knocked down a fishmonger
and stole his purse, and some lad of thirteen, who
made off with a pewter jug.'

John sighed, with no particular revulsion, for hangings were an everyday occurrence, but from irritation
that his presence was still needed, even though the
felons had no property to be recorded and confiscated
for the royal Treasury. 'A couple of paupers – not

worth a strip of Thomas's vellum to record the event. Still, the law's the law.'

They turned right into the High Street, the main artery of the city, a busy road thronged with stalls. Most of the buildings were wooden, but a few new stone-built dwellings and shops were beginning to appear, belonging to the wealthier burgesses. The many churches were also being reconstructed in stone as the city became wealthier. All the buildings had steeply pitched roofs to throw off the West Country rain, most of which ended in the street to form sludge with the rubbish from the food stalls and the refuse and sewage thrown out of house and shop doorways.

At least the High Street was cobbled, unlike St Sidwell's, where Gwyn lived. In the few paved streets, the mire tended to gravitate to the central gully and from there run downhill to the river Exe, but elsewhere the garbage and horse dung stagnated to form a glutinous ooze.

The tavern named after the Crusaders' enemies was near the West Gate, in a side lane parallel to the High Street. The lower storey was of stone, with an overhanging wooden upper structure, topped by a steep thatched roof. A low central door led from the cobblestones, flanked by two pairs of shuttered windows. A board nailed to the wall above the door had a crudely painted head supposedly representing a Mohammedan warrior, daubed in garish primary colours.

A small group of curious onlookers hung about outside and Gwyn pushed through them to enter the inn, bending almost double to pass under the low lintel. The coroner did the same, but their stunted clerk cleared the doorway with inches to spare.

Inside, the gloom was lightened a little by a roaring fire in the large room that occupied all the ground floor. In the middle stood the landlord, a rough-looking man of Flemish origin. Though he had been in Exeter for twenty years, he was still known as Willem of Bruges. He glared at the new arrivals, hands on hips, his chest and belly covered by a leather apron that protected him when he carried in barrels of ale from the back yard as easily as if they were flagons. Pouches of lax skin hung below his blue eyes, and much of the rest of his face was covered by a stubble of grey beard that matched his matted hair. 'Come to see my unwelcome guest, have you?' he grated. 'Who will pay for the bed he lies on, one that I could let to a traveller for a penny-halfpenny a night?'

John ignored his complaint. 'Where is the man, Willem? Has the apothecary seen him?'

The burly Fleming jerked a thumb at the wooden steps that led up to the floor above. 'Up there, bleeding on my palliasse. The leech came two hours ago, put some plaster on his wound, but said there was nothing he could do that God couldn't do much better.'

'Will he live?'

Willem shrugged indifferently. 'Ask me in a week, though I'll not suffer him here that long without payment. Find me his family, Crowner, for I must dun them for his keep.'

He turned to picking an empty hogshead and carried it to a door at the back. 'The criminals are out here, if you want them – unless de Revelle's men have let them run off.'

This was a stock local joke and, indeed, over most of England, for the expense of keeping prisoners fed and guarded in the gaols fell on the local community. Many would have preferred the felons to melt away and become outlaws in the woods rather than pay yet more taxes to house them until they were either hanged or brought before the judges at the General Eyre. Guards, gaolers and men-at-arms were often bribed to turn a blind eye and let prisoners escape.

Willem pushed through the back door with his load and let it slam behind him, leaving Sir John and Gwyn to clamber up the stairs, which were little more than a stout ladder set against a hole in the floor above.

Unlike the Bush, the upper floor was divided by rush or wattle screens into a series of cubicles. These were set against the walls, all open towards the centre of the large room. The more desirable ones contained a palliasse stuffed with dry ferns, and a few even had a low bed-frame. Most, though, had merely a pile of straw on the floor, at a penny a night.

Only one of the stalls was occupied and the coroner walked over to its entrance. On a pallet on the floor lay the still figure of a man, covered with a rough grey blanket. Sitting on a three-legged stool alongside him was an elderly nun, holding his pale hand and pressing a wet cloth against his brow. She looked up as John came near, her lined old face placid, resigned to a lifetime of dealing with man's cruelty.

'Good day, Sir Crowner. I don't know yet if this man will come to one of your inquests. It will be a near thing if he doesn't.'

John had great respect for the sisters of the healing orders, whom he had seen care for hundreds of sick and wounded in campaigns both at home and abroad. 'God be with you, Sister. How did you come to find this fellow so soon?'

'Your big man Gwyn there, he sent a pot-boy down to the priory soon after the fight. They called us straightway, but he had lost much blood even before I arrived.' She added, as an afterthought, 'He told me earlier that his name was Eadred, that he was a free-holder from Dawlish, here to sell his pigs.'

John went to the other side of the pallet. He bent down to bring his dark head nearer to the victim.

The man's eyes were closed, the skin of his face stretched over his pallid cheekbones.

'Is he awake, Sister?'

The man answered, not the nun, in a voice that seemed to whisper from the floorboards rather than from his throat. 'Who is that? Who are you?'

'The Crowner, come to see how you are – and if you can tell me anything. Who did this hurt to you, eh?'

The man made no reply, but panted almost silently.

'Can you show me his wound, Sister?'

Somewhat reluctantly the nun pulled down the blanket and exposed the man's left shoulder and upper chest. A pad of clean rags lay across the front of the armpit, the centre soaked with blood, which had run down into the pallet.

When the cowled nurse pulled away the dressing, a small, almost circular hole, the size of an acorn, could be seen in the bloodstained skin of the man's chest, below the fold of muscle across the armpit.

'It must have gone into the upper part of the lung. He has bled much outside, but I fear that a great deal has drained into the inside of the chest.'

The coroner looked at the wound with professional detachment. 'Gwyn, an unusual wound from a poniard. A round hole, not a slit.'

The big Cornishman leaned over his shoulder to

look. 'Like a sharpening steel, more than knife. Yet I have seen misericords like that, mostly Italian made.'

A misericord was a sheathed dagger, carried by noble warriors, for jabbing between the joints of plate-armour and also for administering the coup de grâce to vanquished opponents. Their interest was more than academic, as a characteristic wound from an unusual weapon could help to identify the offending knife and its owner.

'He's awake again,' observed the nun, as she covered up the injury.

John turned to speak to the man once more. 'You may die, fellow, though perhaps this good lady and the God she serves may save you. But in case they don't, your declaration to me may help bring you revenge and justice to the people . . . and reparation for your family.'

Weakly, the lips moved to frame words. 'Robbed, we were . . . as we left the inn. Two men fell on us.' Heaving breaths punctuated the story. 'One was hairy – black frizz of beard and long, ragged hair. Very hairy.' He gasped into silence. Then, 'He struck down my friend as we turned the corner. The one who stabbed me was younger and fair – must have been Saxon.'

John motioned to his clerk to write as they spoke. 'You knew them – or their names?'

'I have seen the hairy one around the town – but I don't know his name.' Again he sucked in air in a spasmodic gulp. 'The young one was a stranger to me.'

Exhausted, the man's head fell back and his eyes rolled up. His breathing grew laboured and the coroner could see that he would get nothing more from him. The nun pulled up the covers. With a farewell nod to the old lady, John moved out of the cubicle and waited for Thomas to finish his note. Then he said, 'Let us see who is downstairs.'

The Flemish landlord opened the back door for them and they passed out into a filthy yard, where chickens and a few ducks competed in the mud with the cook, who made meals for the inn in a lean-to shed with a tattered thatched roof. Opposite this was an open stable, where the hostelry guests tethered their horses, and a pig-sty, from which came a cacophony of grunts and a terrible stench.

Directly opposite the back door was a rickety gateway that opened into the lane behind the inn. Tethered to it were two dejected-looking men, their hands lashed behind their backs with ropes that were tied to the gatepost. At the other side lounged two castle guards, wearing round helmets with nose protectors, but no mailed hauberks in the relaxed military conditions of the town. They hauled themselves languidly upright when they saw the coroner emerge from the inn. They knew the man's office was held in mild contempt by Sheriff de Revelle, and rumour had spread of the rivalry and competition between the two men. They did not know what respect they should afford him.

John left them in no doubt. 'Is this how you stand guard?' he snarled. 'You are paid to be soldiers, so stand alert, especially when a King's officer comes among you.'

The pair glowered at him, but straightened their backs and rammed the stocks of their lances onto the ground in some semblance of a salute.

'You'd have had your throat slit by a Mohammedan on the first day in Palestine if you'd been as slack as this,' John grumbled, but his interest had already turned to the two wretches bound to the other gate-post.

One was a large, bulky man in middle age, with wild black hair and an untamed beard. His smock was torn almost to the waist and his barrel-like chest was a mat of dark bristle and John was reminded of the apes he had seen chained on the Continent, brought from Africa to be cruelly exhibited by mountebanks at fairs. The other fellow was much younger and, in stark contrast, a typical Saxon blond. They stared at him, like animals awaiting slaughter – which was almost certainly their eventual fate.

'I am the King's coroner, charged with investigating your crimes.'

The hairy one spat contemptuously into the mud, just missing Gwyn's feet. The Cornishman growled ominously, but John put out a restraining hand.

'The injured man swears you killed his companion. What have you to say to that?'

'I did not. I know nothing,' said the hairy one. With nothing else between him and being hanged, flat denial was the only option.

'Liar! I have six men who will say they saw you strike the victim with a chain mace!' Gwyn had little time for ruffians who spat at his feet so had no qualms about exaggerating the evidence: only two witnesses of the affray had come forward.

The bearded man looked away sullenly, tugging at his wrist bonds.

The coroner turned to the younger man. 'And you, what have you to say for yourself?'

Less truculent than his accomplice, the fair man trembled at the prospect of a noose around his neck, but tried to remain defiant. 'I know nothing of it. I was but one in the crowd outside the inn when a fight broke out.'

Gwyn pushed him roughly in the shoulder, making him stagger. 'A pair of liars, then! We have a dying declaration to say that you stabbed the man mortally in the chest.'

He was again stretching the truth, but it had the desired effect. The Saxon, who was no more than nineteen, sagged into the mud, held up only by his wrists bound to the post behind him. 'It was an accident,' he sobbed. 'The man was pushed on to my knife. I was holding it out to protect myself.'

Gwyn grunted. 'A likely story!'

The cathedral bell chimed in the distance and Gwyn reminded the coroner that other duties called.

John called to the two men-at-arms loitering beyond the gate, 'Take these prisoners to the castle and lock them up. Try not to lose them on the way.' Then he and his men made their way back through the inn, and walked back along Butchers Row towards South Gate Street, dodged down Milk Lane and thrust through the throng of shoppers, porters, carts and animals that congested the narrow streets.

'The hairy one will hang, no doubt,' squeaked Thomas, crossing himself in anticipation as he scurried behind the two big men.

'If Gwyn's witnesses so testify at the inquest I'll hand him into the tender care of my brother-in-law to appear before the royal justices who, no doubt, will condemn him.'

'What about the boy?' asked Gwyn.

'Depends on the holy sister's care – and her God's will. If he dies, the boy hangs. If he survives a year and a day, the lad may only be charged with assault.'

Thomas pondered this for a moment as they passed into the Serge Market, heading down to the South Gate. 'So he'll lie in gaol for a year?' he asked, crossing himself again.

John thought about this. 'I think I'll let him free, if he has a family to go surety for him. The best chance the injured man has of survival is if his assailant must provide for his care, for if he dies, so does the Saxon – at the end of a rope.'

Gwyn was doubtful about this proposed leniency. 'Let him out of the castle dungeon and he'll vanish into the forest within the hour – or else claim sanctuary in a church.'

John was philosophical. 'He may prefer to gamble that the man will live, rather than become an outlaw. In any event, the city burgesses will be saved the expense of keeping another prisoner in the castle gaol.'

Gwyn grunted. 'Cheaper still to cut their throats or drop them in the river.'

By now they were past Holy Trinity church and nearing the South Gate. A steady stream of townsfolk was converging on one of the main exits from the city, which led to the London and Winchester roads. They were not going far, only to the gallows site, which lay a few hundred yards outside the city walls. Beyond the gate, the road divided into Holloway and Magdalene Street, which skirted Southernhay, a wide strip of pasture, gardens and trees that lay on the slope below the town wall. The first part of the London road beyond Magdalene Street was known as Bull Hill and, after the few houses petered out, the hanging tree stood starkly at the side of the highway.

It was a chillingly simple structure, just two stout

posts twelve feet high, with a longer crossbar joining
the upper ends. Nearby were several single posts with
a short arm at the top, from which were suspended gib-
bets, hooped iron frames the size and shape of a body.
Inside, the rotting remains of previously executed
fellows wafted a foetid stench to remind the populace
of their mortality and the wages of sin, which meant
the theft of anything worth more than twelve pence.

By the time that John de Wolfe and his party arrived,
a crowd of a hundred or more was assembled around
the gallows. Hangings were a popular diversion for
those who had an hour to spare on Tuesdays and
Fridays. It was a social occasion, where people could
meet and gossip, even conduct business while waiting
for the felons to be dispatched.

Hawkers stood by with their trays of sweetmeats and
fruit, yelling their wares at the matrons with babies
at their breast. Old men and cripples fended off the
children and urchins who dodged about, yelling and
playing hide-and-seek in the bushes at the side of the
road. Only when the moment of death approached
did the crowd become silent, better to savour the
vicarious thrill of a life extinguished in the final agony
of strangulation.

John disliked hangings, though he was not sure
why this was. As he approached the foot of the empty
gallows, he felt a vague unease. Violent death was so
familiar to him that he gave it not a second thought –
men mutilated on the field of battle had been part of
his way of life for years, and he had killed more than
his share with his own hands, sword, mace and dagger.
Yet there was something about this cold-blooded ritual
of snuffing out civilians that bothered him, irrational
though he knew it to be. Justice must be done,

examples must be made of miscreants or the whole fabric of society would tumble about their ears . . . and yet . . .

He shrugged the mood off and motioned to his clerk to set out his pen and ink on a nearby cart, which would be used to turn off the condemned after the ropes were set around their necks.

'Thomas, take the names and dwellings of the felons – though today we are wasting our time. They haven't a pennyworth of goods between them.'

It was the task of the coroner to record all executions and make sure that the property of the hanged was collected, as it was forfeit to the Crown. But most criminals were penniless ruffians, whose only possessions were their tattered clothes, fit only to be burned or buried with them, if they avoided rotting in chains or on the gibbet.

Gwyn had wandered off to buy a pie, so the coroner sat on the edge of the cart to await the ceremony. Soon a small procession wound its way from the South Gate and there was an expectant buzz from the crowd, which parted on the road to allow another cart to trundle through, escorted by a dozen soldiers from the castle. As it came nearer, he could see a woman running alongside the wagon, throwing herself at its side every few yards. Nearer still and he could hear her screaming and wailing, as she tried to clutch its rough rails. The cart, pulled by a stolid mare, slowly rolled up to the foot of the hanging tree, the mob rolling in behind it like a human wave.

Standing inside, their hands lashed to the front rail to keep them upright, were the victims of today's ritual. An old man, grey hair falling in unkempt strands over his threadbare smock, slumped uncaringly, his chin on his chest, bereft of any hope. John sensed that his death might be a welcome release from a long, miserable life.

In stark contrast, the other was shaking with fear, worsened by his poor mother's hysterical screams as she scrabbled at the side of the wagon. He was a thin waif of thirteen, his red hair heightening the pallor of his face, a white mask with red-rimmed eyes, from which tears dribbled down his sallow cheeks.

The babble and screams of the woman, herself less than thirty years old, were almost incoherent, but John picked out repeated exhortations to God to save her only son.

As soon as the cart stopped, one of the soldiers walking behind it pulled her away. 'Come on, Mother, there's nothing you can do.'

She fell to her knees in the muddy earth and clasped his legs, her terror-racked face upturned to him in agony worse than that her child was soon to suffer.

'My son! Save him! Let him go, sir!'

More embarrassed than angry, the sergeant-at-arms pulled his feet away and she fell to her face in the wet soil. A yeoman, obviously her husband, pulled her gently to her feet and led her away towards the edge of the crowd, as she continued alternately to sob and howl.

The soldier motioned the carter to move directly under the gallows, while he walked up to the coroner and raised a hand to his chest in a perfunctory salute. 'You need the names of these felons, Sir John?'

'And their place of abode, if you know them, sergeant.' He turned to point at Thomas, who was still leaning against the other side of the unused wagon. 'Give them to my clerk there, to record on his roll.'

The soldier hesitated. 'There was also a message I was to give you, Crowner. The town crier may have some news of the man found dead in Widecombe.'

News travelled fast within the closed community of Exeter, where every citizen was a professional gossip. They all knew about the man lying stabbed in the stream, fifteen miles from the city.

'What news, man?' demanded John.

'I don't know, sir. But a journeyman mason told the crier that he wished to speak to you. He is working at the cathedral.' He turned on his heel and went about his business.

As John pondered the development in the Widecombe affair, the last act of the drama before him was being played out.

The hangman, who on days other than Tuesday or Friday, ran a butcher's trade in the Shambles, climbed a rough ladder resting against the gallows cross-bar and pulled down two nooses that had been wrapped around the timber. Then he slid a plank deftly across the width of the wagon under the side-rails and climbed aboard. John sensed the hubbub of the crowd damping down, as the man untied the ropes that lashed the two victims to the cart, leaving their wrists tied. The old man he urged up to stand on the plank and the boy he lifted on to it. The child was keening softly, staring at his mother and father on the edge of the crowd in mixed supplication and incomprehension.

With the soldiers had come a priest, and he now began to read some unintelligible dirge in Latin from a book held before him, his tone suggesting that this was an unwelcome chore with which someone from the diocese was stuck every Tuesday and Friday. The hangman slipped the rope over the old man's head and pulled it firm. Then he did the same to the boy, who began to screaming, his wails matched by heartrending cries from his mother. The crowd was silent, but as the executioner leaped from the wagon and smacked the horse's flank, a low animal growl rose from the throng.

The mare, as well accustomed as the priest to what was required, moved forward with a jerk. The noise from the crowd swelled and, as the two victims tumbled first from the plank and then from the back of the moving wagon as it cleared the gallows, an orgasmal groan spread across the meadows.

The screeching of the boy was strangled into a gargling croak as the noose tightened around his neck and he began to kick furiously, constantly at first, then in spasmodic jerks. With a cry of despair, his father broke from the crowd and raced to the gallows. He flung himself around his son's legs and pulled as hard as he could to shorten the death throes, oblivious of the collapse of his wife into a dead faint.

The old vagrant died as he had lived, quietly and inconspicuously. A few intermittent twitches lasted for several minutes as his soul left the unhappy body that had sheltered it for sixty years.

The coroner watched impassively, but with a return of the unease and foreboding that these rituals always generated. What sense could there be in publicly throttling a young lad who had run away with a pot worth twelve pence? Would there ever be a time in England when a better method of dealing with juvenile petty thieves could be devised? He motioned to Thomas and Gwyn as the two corpses made their last nervous twitches on the gallows.

'Come on, Thomas – and you, Gwyn. There's an inquest to hold, and on the way we'll hear what this journeyman has to tell us about our mysterious corpse from the edge of Dartmoor.'

CHAPTER SIX

In which Crowner John meets a mason

The crowd, their passions satisfied, drifted raggedly back to the town gates, the pedlars still trying to sell and the children still darting about in play.

The coroner strode out more robustly, overtaking the straggling throng on the muddy roadway, his small clerk almost running to keep up with him. Once in the town, they climbed the slope of South Gate Street and turned right into Bear Lane, which led towards the cathedral precinct. This part of Exeter was an island of episcopal independence, outside the jurisdiction of the sheriff and portreeves. A narrow entrance – one of six around the precinct – was known as Beargate and carried a door of blackened oak, studded with crude bolt-heads and iron bands. During daylight it lay open and led into the territory of Henry Marshall, Bishop of Exeter, whose diocese stretched from the edge of Somerset to the tip of Cornwall.

Beyond Beargate, there was a stifling clutter of buildings on twisting lanes. Here lived those of the twenty-four canons who were resident in Exeter, the other ranks of the cathedral hierarchy and the servants, families and hangers-on who made up the considerable population of the religious heart of the city. The lanes were as filthy as those in the rest of the town, composed of trodden mud and refuse. The coroner and his hobbling, skipping clerk pushed their way through the ambling pedestrians and walked past the dwellings that clustered against the cloisters to their right. This brought them to the west end of the cathedral and the more open area of the Close.

Between the north side of the cathedral and the jumble of buildings that lined the High Street beyond were several acres of grass, weeds and bare earth. Its saving grace was a number of large trees that provided welcome shade around the edges and along the many trodden paths. The coroner spared it not a single glance – he had been familiar with the Close all his life – but if he had been of a more aesthetic turn of mind, he might have thought it incongruous that such a beautifully crafted house of God should be so closely surrounded by a combination of rubbish-dump, meadow, cemetery, games arena and market place.

Shop stalls lined the outer paths and youths noisily threw and kicked crude leather balls about. Old and fresh graves lay haphazardly across the ground, with piles of red earth thrown up by the pit-makers and old bones from previous burials, which they took to the charnel house near St Mary Major Church on the further side of the Close. A trench ran across the area, carrying sewage from the canons' houses down towards the distant river. The all-pervading smell of garbage was as constant here as throughout the rest of Exeter. None of this reached John de Wolfe's consciousness as he marched the last few yards around the end of the cathedral and back to the North Tower, one of the two massive blocks that flanked each side of the nave and chancel.

'This man was to be here, was he?' snapped the coroner over his shoulder.

Panting with the effort of keeping up, Thomas nodded. 'Cenwulf, the sergeant said – a master-mason of Lincoln.'

They came to a halt at the foot of the tower, where a dozen men were working. Some were operating a pulley hoist to the dizzy heights of the parapet, taking blocks of stone to masons working a hundred and forty feet above them. On the ground, others were manhandling new unfinished stones from an ox-cart while yet others shaped blocks in various stages of completion. A few old men stood watching, but as the building process had been going on for most of the century – since 1114, when Bishop William Warelwast began replacing the previous Saxon church – there was little that was new to watch.

John approached the nearest man. 'Where would I find Cenwulf of Lincoln?' he demanded.

The craftsman rocked back on to his heels, resting his iron chisel and heavy mallet on the ground. A thick leather apron, scarred by tools and chippings, covered him from neck to knees. 'Who wants to know?' He was a middle-aged fellow, his face almost as leathery as his apron but relieved by a pair of bright blue eyes.

'The King's coroner,' said John bluntly.

The mason dropped his tools and rose slowly to his feet. Master masons were never a servile breed, they were sought-after craftsmen, well paid, with a strong guild behind them. But the mention of the King triggered respect and attentiveness.

'Look no further, Crowner, I'm Cenwulf . . . and I know what business you have with me.'

John liked his directness, sensing an honesty and a desire to assist that was absent in most folk, who would do all they could to evade any contact with the law. 'Then tell me what you know of this man who lies dead now in Widecombe,' he said, settled his backside against a large untrimmed stone block and folded his arms, ready to listen.

'It's little enough, sir. But I heard the town crier's messages this morning, when he paraded the close, wanting news of many things, including a man slain near Widecombe. It may have been the same fellow that I met just twelve days ago at Honiton.'

The coroner nodded encouragingly, his long hair swirling over the neckband of his grey tunic. 'Why do you think he was that man, mason?'

'Fair, and about the same age as claimed by the crier, but that is little enough. Yet he had a tanned skin and wore a Mussulman's sword in a curved sheath on his belt.'

'What was he wearing?'

'When I saw him, a moleskin rain-cloak, but under that, a green tunic or a surcoat – I couldn't swear to which. And a red cloth capuchin on his head. He had curious high riding boots, too.'

Thomas, lurking behind his master, whispered in his ear, 'Certainly sounds like our cadaver.'

Ignoring him, John continued, 'Where, then, did you see him?'

'We had harsh words, that fellow and me, a wonder we didn't come to blows.'

John's interest quickened. Was this another possible suspect, he wondered. Though it seemed odd that he volunteered in his first few words that there had been bad blood between them, considering that the other man had come to a violent end.

'I came by my pony from Salisbury, where my contract on the cathedral there had finished and I had arranged for three months' work here. On the last morning of the journey, I stopped for ale and meat at an inn in Honiton, some fifteen miles on the east road from Exeter. While I was taking my ease on the benches outside, eating and drinking, this man led his horse from the stable and then mounted. The innkeeper stood out to bid him a good journey, so no doubt he had stayed the night there.'

John scratched the stubble on his dark chin. 'Why did you dispute with him?'

The mason traced a finger almost lovingly along the huge stone touching the material that was his life's work. 'He got up on his steed and prodded its belly with a spur. The beast lunged forwards like an arrow from a bow and raced past me, splashing mud and horse-shit from the yard all over me. The bread I was eating was fouled and my clothing splattered.'

'It was an accident?' John prompted.

'Accident be damned! It was the sheer thoughtlessness of a young man with no respect for his elders.'

'So what did you do?' chipped in the coroner's clerk.

'I yelled after him and shook my fist. He looked back, wheeled his horse around and came back to me. I thought he was going to apologise . . . but he started to abuse me for shouting and gesturing at him.'

John was not interested in their quarrel – it seemed

hardly likely to lead to a murder. He wanted to know more about the other man. 'Do you know his name – or where he came from, or where he was bound?'

Cenwulf shook his head. 'I had no reason to be more curious than anyone sitting in the sun with some ale, watching the world go by, until he covered me with mire.'

There was loud crash nearby: a sandstone block had slipped from its sling on the hoist and fallen to the ground. Fortunately no one was standing underneath or the coroner would have had more work that day. Cenwulf, responsible for this team of workers, yelled an oath at then and muttered even more under his breath. 'Clumsy fools! Men are not what they were in years past.'

John was not to be distracted from his quest. 'You say he had a horse?'

'A grey, medium height, dappled in black. It had a black ring around one eye, not the other . . . and very muddy hoofs!' he added cynically.

'You're an observant man, Cenwulf,' said John appreciatively. 'Can you recall anything else?'

The man's forehead puckered in thought. 'I was too angry to take much notice. The man looked as if he might strike me with the bolt of leather he used to whack his horse but, thank God, he thought better of it.'

'Why was that?' asked John

'Because I would pulled him off his horse, gentleman or not, and given him a good hammering,' said Cenwulf truculently. 'As it was he muttered something, then turned his grey mare and trotted off. That was the last I saw of him. I asked the landlord who he was, but

he had no idea of his name, just said he'd taken a
night's lodging on the way from Southampton, but
didn't say where he was going.'

John scratched the dark stubble on his chin reflec-
tively. 'You said "gentleman". What led you to think
him that?'

'Good clothes, though foreign-looking. His voice
was not that of a common soldier. Though he spoke
English as good as me, there was no doubt that he
was a Norman.'

John, a half-breed himself, was unsure whether to
take this as a compliment or not.

'Can you recall anything else?'

'There were bulging saddlebags and two wicker
panniers across his beast's shoulders, next to the
rider's knees. I remember thinking this must be a
man going home after a long absence, with gifts and
his worldly goods.'

A few more minutes' questioning showed that the
mason had nothing else to offer, apart from the name
of the inn, the Plough at Honiton. He would be in
Exeter until the early spring, so John knew where to
find him if anything else turned up.

The coroner thanked Cenwulf civilly and left him
to his work.

As they walked back to the centre of the Close,
John gave firm orders to his clerk. 'Saddle up your
mule, Thomas, and go straight to Honiton. Even that
sad animal should get you there by nightfall. Here's
threepence for your board and lodging. Stay at the
Plough and learn all you can – and be back here
directly tomorrow.' He felt in the pouch at his belt
for the coins.

One look at his master's face convinced Thomas of

the futility of protest, so he took the money, crossed himself and slunk off to his lodging.

This left the coroner with no scribe to record the imminent inquest on the Saracen affray, but he decided to commit to memory the names of those involved and to dictate the proceedings to Thomas the next day.

The cathedral bell boomed once above him and he hastened his steps back towards the castle. He had to go past his own door, as St Martin's Lane led from the close into the high street. If Matilda was at home, there was no risk that she would see and delay him, as no windows opened on to the street. Her room, the solar, was at the back.

However, as soon as he turned the corner into the high street, he saw two familiar figures planted in his path. They were deep in conversation, but as soon as he approached, they turned to greet him.

'John de Wolfe, are you well? How are the dead today?'

Hugh de Relaga was a portly man, above middle age and with the benign joviality of a merchant blessed with more than average income. He was a wool merchant, with family in Devon and Brittany, and was one of the two portreeves of Exeter. John had purchased a share in his business with money he had acquired during the Irish campaigns and the income from this kept him in adequate, if not lavish comfort.

The other person was a different figure, but an equally staunch friend of John. A churchman, he was of lean, ascetic appearance, almost to the point of being haggard. While the plump portreeve was dressed in a brocade tunic and velvet short-cloak fastened at one shoulder with a large gold brooch, John de Alecon, Archdeacon of Exeter, wore a street cassock of dull fawn hessian, girded by a plain rope, a wooden cross hanging from a leather thong around his neck. His thin grey hair was combed forward to a ragged fringe across his lined forehead. As with Cenwulf the mason, though, the appearance of this sombre priest was relieved by a pair of darting bright eyes, this time of a darker, almost violet blue, a legacy of the Viking ancestors of the Normans. 'How many customers today, John?' he inquired. 'Is the corpse trade flourishing?'

Though his face was not built for much smiling, John grinned good-humouredly. These were his friends and he needed such in Exeter as enemies were to be had in plenty.

'Come with me now, if you want to see the crowner at work,' he responded. 'I'm on my way this minute to hold an inquest at Rougemont.'

Hugh de Relaga smacked him on the shoulder. 'I think I will, friend, to see how Hubert Walter's latest bright idea is working. What about you, priest? Will you join us?'

John de Alecon shook his head wryly. 'Some of us have duties to attend, Portreeve. Not all of us have time on our hands, like you burgesses.'

With a gesture of benediction, he moved off towards the cathedral close while de Relaga and the coroner set off up the slope towards the castle. They talked about the price of wool and the loss of a shipload going from Exmouth to Flanders. They passed through the gate in the curved embankment that cut off the north-eastern corner of the town and formed an outer ward to the castle, part quarry, part living space for soldiers and their families, who had erected huts against the walls.

'Is this about the killing in the Saracen last night, John?' asked the portreeve, as they climbed the steep incline and then the drawbridge into the castle gate-house.

'It is indeed – and a wounding where the fellow may die.'

De Relaga puffed a little at the exercise, his short legs not matching the long stride of the coroner. 'This used to be sheriff's business. How does he take your meddling in his functions?'

John made a sour face. 'Not happily, but he has to put up with it. He's torn between dislike of me and my appointment and the wishes of his sister, my dear Matilda, who likes the idea of a law officer for a husband.'

De Relaga shook his head sadly. 'Be careful of Richard de Revelle, John. He can be a devious, spiteful man, as I know to my cost.'

'I'll watch him, never fear,' John replied grimly. 'He'll not get the better of me – since the Holy Land campaigns I have some powerful friends.'

'But they are not in Exeter, John.'

By now they had entered the busy inner ward and passed the little chapel of Mary on the right of the gatehouse. Straight ahead was the Shire Hall, a plain building with a roof of stone slates. It had one large room with shuttered window openings each side and two wide doors. There was nothing inside except a wooden dais at one end, on which were a few stools. Here the sheriff held his county court every two weeks. The borough court of the burgesses, under the portreeves, was held in the Guild Hall in the high street, and the ecclesiastical court was held in the old wooden chapter house of the cathedral, signalling the jealously guarded divisions that held sway in the town.

Inside the bare hall, people were already milling around. Gwyn of Polruan was marshalling them as best he could, with a voice that could shatter a clay pot at twenty yards. He had assembled all those who had been within sight of the Saracen the previous evening, together with half a dozen men and boys from each of the four quarters of the town. Several burgesses had also turned up, partly out of curiosity and partly from a sense of civic duty. One was the other portreeve, Henry Rifford. He was a large, red-faced, self-important fellow, with a town house and a large manor out at Clyst St Mary, on the Exmouth road. A crony of the sheriff, Rifford had been hostile to John's appointment and the coroner was as wary of him as he was of the Bishop, another of de Revelle's men. In fact, as far as John was concerned both town and cathedral seniors were split down the middle.

The crowd parted as two soldiers trundled a two-wheeled cart through the door, on which was a body, covered with bloody canvas. This was for the numerous jurymen to view, according to the new legal procedure.

John stepped onto the platform and the two portreeves, though they had no official function, followed him and sat on two stools to observe the proceedings.

Through the other door, four soldiers, wearing conical iron helmets with nose-guards, dragged the two miscreants, hands bound securely behind their backs. To ribald jeers from the jury, they frogmarched them to stand below the centre of the dais.

Just as John was about to begin, there was a blast outside from a horn and two sergeants strode in, followed by Richard de Revelle and another two soldiers as a ceremonial rearguard. Just behind the Sheriff walked Ralph Morin, the constable of Rougemont, appointed by the King. He was a large man, with a mane of grey hair and a flowing beard to match. John had fought alongside him in Ireland and knew him to be fair and impartial.

The sheriff, though not in armour, wore his bright armorial surcoat, white linen with a crimson griffin front and back. He climbed onto the platform and stood centre stage, almost pushing the coroner aside.

The crowd fell silent. The sheriff was by no means a popular figure, neither for his office nor his personality. He represented authority as a tax collector, a harsh judge and the fount of fiscal and capital punishment.

Richard de Revelle looked at his brother-in-law and smirked, his thin, handsome face conveying a mixture of amusement and contempt. 'Pray carry on, Sir Crowner!'

John scowled at him, but said nothing. The sheriff had the right to be present if he so wished, although his attendance was not necessary to the proceedings.

As Gwyn finished bellowing his introduction, the coroner and sheriff subsided on to stools, mainly to mark their status as everyone below the dais had to stand. Ralph Morin waited unobtrusively at the back of the platform, his eyes missing nothing.

As at Widecombe, the multitude of the jury had to view the corpse. They jostled and stumbled past the cart, where one of the guards had whipped off the canvas from the body, displaying the mangled remains of the head. Though late in the season, a few opportunist bluebottles had already yellowed the eyes and mouth with clusters of eggs.

John stood up and briefly set out the events of the previous night. The injured man, Eadred of Dawlish, was too ill to be brought to the castle even on a litter, so the coroner described his injuries. Gwyn had previously picked one man from each of four town wards to act as spokesmen for the large jury and had taken them to the Saracen to inspect the wounded man. They had reported what they had seen to the rest of the jury.

Two men from St Sidwell's, a cluster of houses beyond the East Gate, swore that the corpse was that of their brother Osric, a carter who had lived in an alley off Rock Lane, near the Watergate. The whole family was obviously Saxon and thus no question of a murdrum fine arose. Then several witnesses gave their account of the affray, and Gwyn gave the deposition of the injured Eadred that the hairy one had struck the deceased to rob him.

Within minutes, the jury had given their unanimous verdict that Osric the carter had been slain against the King's peace by Tostig, the fellow now in front of them.

John summed up. 'There is no doubt that he was killed by a mace blow to the head, and equally little doubt that this Tostig is the culprit.' He pointed down at the hairy rogue gripped by the two soldiers. The man struggled, swore and spat defiantly towards the dais, and received a crack on the head from one guard's spear shaft for his insolence.

'However, it will be the King's judges who finally decide on his guilt and his fate at the next Eyre.

Until then, I will commit Tostig to the gaol in the safe keeping of the town.'

Before he could continue, Richard de Revelle rose to his feet. 'Crowner, this is unnecessary. The Eyre was here only three months ago and may not return for a year or two – perhaps more. Why on earth should we waste money on keeping this – this creature, in my gaol for that length of time?'

John stared at his brother-in-law angrily. 'The new law says that the coroner must keep the Pleas of the Crown, which means that he must document and then present malefactors before the King's justices. Would you just take him out now and hang him?'

The sheriff brushed imaginary dust from the red griffin on his breast. 'It would be far more efficient, given his obvious guilt. But no, I am a just man. I would have him brought before my shire court in this hall next week – and then hang him.'

There were a few muffled guffaws from the crowd, which were silenced by a glare from the coroner, who then addressed the sheriff again. 'By the King's command, relayed by the chief justiciar through the justices in Eyre, such cases recorded by the coroners must be brought before the royal judges.'

Henry Rifford rose from his stool. 'I agree with the sheriff. It is ridiculous to commit every common thief and murderer to the castle gaol, which would be full within a month. It costs almost a ha'penny a day to feed these vermin, a drain on the finances of the town.'

Before John could open his mouth, de Revelle chimed in again. 'It is a matter of chance as to who seizes these criminals first. If my sergeants and their men came across a fatal affray and arrested the wrongdoers, they would come before my court and be dealt with speedily. Even the manorial courts and, of course, your burgage courts, Portreeve, have the power to try and hang felons. So why should we be plagued by the cost and delay you coroners claim is the new law?'

Rifford, face flushed with righteous indignation, nodded vigorously, but John refused to be swayed. 'Because the new law *is* the law. We are here to carry it out, not to bend it as suits our convenience. If there's a death, then, Sir Sheriff, your men must not usurp the coroner's function. It must be reported to me and I will take the steps laid down by the King. They may be new, they may be inconvenient – but they are the law.'

Richard de Revelle made a gesture of impatient dismissal, but Hugh de Relaga joined in to back up the coroner. 'I agree with Sir John. Progress may be unfamiliar and sometimes irritating, but better brains than ours in Winchester have devised this new system and it is up to us to carry it out.'

The sheriff threw up his hands in despair. 'Very well, we shall see. The Shire Hall is no place for us to debate politics. In any event, this dog must be thrown into the gaol until somebody hangs him!' He motioned to the guards to take away the hairy man, stepped from the platform and marched away towards his castle quarters, followed by the silent constable and Henry Rifford, who made it plain that he had no wish to remain with his dissident colleague or the coroner.

When the murmurings of the jury and onlookers at this high-level bickering had settled, the fair young man was dragged by his guards to stand before John. The coroner described Eadred's injuries and called on the jury foreman to confirm that they had seen the wound in his chest. He told them that the injured man had, while in fear and solemn expectation of imminent death, accused his assailant of the dagger thrust.

No verdict was required in this case, but John addressed the young man sternly.

'First, the mace and knife are declared deodand, as they caused the death and injuries. I therefore confiscate them and they will be sold for the benefit of the family of Eadred. Secondy, there is no doubt you harmed Eadred of Dawlish with intent to rob, even though you gained nothing from it. He may die, he may not. If he does not survive for a year and a day, you will be brought back before me and committed for murder, just as your accomplice was a few moments ago. If he lives, you will be brought back and charged with wounding, but may escape the gallows.' He pointed a long finger at the young man. 'I therefore commit Eadred into your care and the care of your family, as being the best way of providing him with a chance to survive. I attach you and your kin in the sum of five marks to appear at the next General Eyre – and if Eadred dies I have little doubt that the sheriff will delight in throwing you back into Rougemont gaol.'

Shaking with relief, the young man was released by his guards and returned to an anxious group of his relatives at the back of the hall. They were pleased at the survival of their lad, yet appalled at the enormous sum of money they would have to find if he ran away to become an outlaw in the forest.

As the jury and spectators melted away, Hugh de Relaga came across to John. 'There's trouble brewing over this new law,' he said. 'The sheriff has been used to seizing the property of felons, confiscating the deodands and raking in the amercements and attachments. Though much of that found its way to the county treasure chest, I'll wager some got lost in his purse.'

As they walked back across the castle ward towards the gatehouse, John agreed with him. 'It's why he wanted a tame creature appointed, like Giles de Mandeville, whom he could easily manipulate.'

De Mandeville had been the favoured nominee of de Revelle, the Bishop and Henry Rifford, and they had been exasperated when John de Wolfe's connections with the chief justiciar and the King himself had foiled their plans.

At the gatehouse, John took leave of his friend, anxious to join Gwyn in his chamber for beer, bread and cheese.

'Look out for yourself, John. Avoid dark alleys at night, in case our rivals are lurking there!' A mischeivous grin spread over the portreeve's chubby face as he strolled down the drawbridge to the town.

John watched him go with some affection, then turned to climb the steps to his gloomy office.

chapter seven

In which Thomas de Peyne rides to Honiton

The mule was a game little animal, which kept up a steady trot. Though punishing to the clerk's backside, it covered four miles each hour. This respectable speed was helped by a good road, as Thomas's route took him along the main track to the east, the most frequented out of Exeter.

A day without rain had dried up all but the largest puddles, so the bare surface was, for once, neither a morass nor a dust bowl. Part of the road was still paved, as it followed the old Roman road, still in use after almost a thousand years.

Well before the November daylight faded, the former priest had reached Honiton, where the road branched to the old Roman towns of Ilchester and Dorchester. Accustomed to travellers, the village had several inns, which provided food and lodging for those who journeyed between Exeter, Cornwall, Southampton and the flesh-pots of Winchester and London. One of these was the Plough, in a dip of the road near the centre of the village. It was a single storeyed, wide building with a high thatched roof, an untidy ramble of stables and huts lying on each side and at the rear. A crude model of a wooden plough hung on a bracket over the central front door.

The clerk jogged on his steed to the inn yard and slid off. He handed the bridle to a ten-year-old stable-boy, then took his saddlebag inside and negotiated a penny bed for the night, which included a meal.

By the time he had finished some fat mutton, bread and cheese and was sitting by the fire with a pot of cider, his earlier annoyance at having been sent out of Exeter had subsided. As his master had, at the Bush the previous evening, Thomas sank into a warm reverie, full of food and cider. With luck, he thought, if he avoided the cost of breaking his fast next morning, he might be twopence better off, thanks to Sir John's unthinking generosity. For the moment, he forgot this errand, preferring to sit on his corner of the bench and enjoy his drink and the atmosphere around him.

After an hour or so, he moved reluctantly from the roaring log fire and went to the back of the main room. Here the innkeeper was knocking the plug out of a new barrel of beer, then pushing in a wooden spigot before more than a few cupfuls gushed away into the leather bucket held underneath. Thinking it best not to reveal his official interest, the clerk began to ask about the dead man, as if he had been a friend.

It was in vain, as the burly landlord, more intent on not spilling his ale, seemed to have no recollection of his former guest. 'This is the busiest inn between Exeter and Bridport. I can't recall a quarter of the folk who call here,' he replied, with conviction.

'Not even a man with a curious Saracen sword, curved within its sheath? And a dappled grey horse with a black ring around its eye?'

The man thought for a moment, holding the barrel firmly on its chocks. Then he shook his head. 'No, I've seen a few like that in my time, swords and horses, but can't recollect one lately. Best ask the lads in the stables – they see more of the guests and their beasts than I do.'

With that, Thomas had to be content. With a sigh, and resisting the urge to cross himself, he went to the door and stood on the threshold. It was pitch dark, and though there were no cathedral bells here to toll the hours, he guessed it must be a few hours before midnight. As his eyes grew accustomed to the dark, he could make out a flickering glow around the right-hand corner of the building, from a bundle of tarred rushes burning in a bracket in the stable-yard. He decided to take the innkeeper's advice and set off for the yard.

Other men would have been more wary of walking alone around highroad inns at night, but the years of sheltered life in a cathedral close had left Thomas oblivious of the risks. The moment he turned the corner, an arm came from nowhere to hook itself around his neck and simultaneously he suffered such a punch into the belly that most of the cider and his dinner shot from his mouth like an arrow from a bow. Though dazed, shocked and terrified, he realised from the cursing that his stomach contents had scored a direct hit on one of his assailants, but any triumph was short-lived.

'You dirty little bastard,' snarled a voice in English, and retribution came swiftly by way of a punch in the face, which split Thomas's lip and made his nose gush blood like the innkeeper's spigot.

Disoriented, but aware that he was about to be killed, the little clerk would have slumped to the ground but for the arm that was still half throttling him. Then he felt another hand tearing away the scrip at his belt, which held several quills, a lucky stone and all his worldly wealth, which amounted to three whole pence and several clipped halves and quarters. The man tipped the contents of the scrip into his palm and squinted at it in the poor light of the flaming torch across the yard. He gave Thomas another buffet, this time across the side of the head. 'Three bloody pence! Why d'you always pick paupers to rob, you great fool?' he yelled at his accomplice.

Before the villain who held Thomas could reply, the situation suddenly and dramatically changed.

There was a roar from a different voice and through the haze of pain and fear, the clerk heard the metallic scrape of a sword being pulled from a scabbard and a vague flash as the blade shone in the dim light. Then there was a howl of pain from the robber with his purse, the arm around his neck was abruptly removed and Thomas slid to the ground.

'Stand and fight, you scabs!' came a harsh bellow from the wielder of the sword, but the footpads had vanished into the night.

As his sight and hearing slowly returned, Thomas was aware of a large shadow standing over him. Another scrape told him that the sword had been slammed back into its sheath.

'Bloodied one of the swine, at least. If he'd stayed, I'd have cut his head off!' said the shadow, with some regret. He bent down and pulled Thomas none too gently to his feet. 'Let's have a look at you – nothing broken or missing by the looks of it. But we'll get you into the better light inside. We could both do with a pot of something to drink.'

A quarter of an hour later, when the clerk's teeth had stopped chattering with fright and he had swilled the blood and filth from his face, he sat at a rough table opposite his saviour, who was unconcernedly champing his way through a meal. He was a broad, muscular man of about thirty, tanned from the Levantine sun. A rim of brown beard surrounded his face, surmounted by a thick moustache like Gwyn's. He wore a conical leather cap with earflaps and a thick leather cuirass, the outfit midway between ordinary clothing and armour. A huge broadsword clanked at his belt, as well as a formidable dagger. On his feet, Thomas was intrigued to see, were a pair of patterned boots similar to those on the mysterious Widecombe corpse. As he watched the other man eat, he was puzzled by the nonchalant way in which he had dismissed the violent robbery.

Indeed, the landlord of the Plough seemed equally unconcerned about such crimes being perpetrated in his backyard. 'What d'you expect me to do?' he had retorted. 'The forest is full of outlaws, who live by murder and theft. I have an inn to run. I can't be going out every five minutes to chase off criminals.'

Though the shaken clerk tried to thank his champion, the other seemed unconcerned. As the gratitude of one with only threepence in his purse seemed inadequate, Thomas disclosed that he was the agent of the King's coroner, from whom appreciation might be of more substance. At this, Alan Fitzhai, for that was the name he gave, seemed more interested. 'Sir John de Wolfe, you say? He who was with the King at Acre and on the march to Jerusalem?' He whistled through his teeth. 'I arrived there later, just before the Lionheart left for home, but I remember seeing de Wolfe several times. He was much thought of in Palestine, especially by Hubert Walter, who commanded the English army after the King sailed away.'

As Thomas had suspected, Fitzhai was another returned Crusader and, as such, might have news of their anonymous corpse. He plunged into the story of why he had come to Honiton and the Plough.

In the middle of hacking off the leg of a roast fowl with his dagger, Fitzhai stopped to stare at Thomas. 'A fair man with a green jacket and a Mussulman sword?'

The clerk nodded. 'He had a grey horse with a black ring around one eye. He stayed here at this inn.'

'Ten days or so since?'

'About two days short of a fortnight, yes.'

Fitzhai took the chicken leg almost to his lips, then paused. 'I know him. And you say he's dead?'

'Stabbed in the back during a sword fight.'

Thomas sensed that the other's attitude had changed. From being careless and self-confident, he was now cautious, looking warily at the clerk over his meat.

'You say you knew him?' Thomas persisted.

Fitzhai threw the stripped bone onto the table. 'Well, I might have seen him somewhere,' he replied evasively. 'Your description makes him a Crusader, like myself – no doubt about that. There are hundreds like us.'

'But you know his name?'

'Not at all! How am I to tell one knight from another among all those coming home in dribs and drabs ever since the King left three years ago.'

Thomas knew that Fitzhai was avoiding the truth.

'When did you come back yourself?' he asked.

The broad man seemed on firmer ground here. 'Five weeks back. I sailed into Southampton from Harfleur in early October. Took two months to get across France from Marseille.' He thought for a moment. 'Long before your man got himself killed,' he added.

The clerk wondered why he had seen fit to add that. He tried further questions, hinting that maybe Fitzhai had known the dead man either in the Holy Land or on the long journey home, but Fitzhai became surely, and even annoyed.

Eventually, he threw down the last of his ale and stood up so abruptly that his bench fell over with a clatter. 'Look, I saved your hide out there, but that's the end of it. I want nothing to do with any affair of the law or to waste my time as juryman or witness. I want to keep clear of sheriffs and crowners and the like. So I'll say goodnight to you, and advise you to stay indoors on dark nights.' He grabbed his sword belt from the end of the table and buckled it on as he pushed his way to the door.

CHAPTER EIGHT

*In which Crowner John disputes
with the sheriff*

By noon next day, John had been told of the events at Honiton. He had been to one of his reading lessons in the cathedral cloisters and, on his return at mid-morning, had found Thomas and Gwyn waiting for him in the gatehouse chamber.

The clerk, who had timorously waited for full daylight before setting foot outside the door of the inn, had examined the scene of his ordeal before leaving Honiton. To his joy, he had discovered his pathetically few coins trodden into the mud alongside an ominous patch of blood from the wound Fitzhai's sword had inflicted on the arm of one of the attackers.

John sat silently behind his trestle table while Thomas related his story, in which he made much of his assault and the valiant resistance he had put up against at least four desperadoes. He ended his tale with the sign of the cross and waited expectantly, hoping for some expression of concern.

The dark, hawkish figure behind the table glared at him. 'And you let this fellow get away knowing nothing but his name?'

Thomas tried to look hurt, but his wry neck and squint spoiled the effect. 'He got up and left as soon as I questioned him. Said he wanted nothing to do with the law. But I'm certain he knew the dead man – he had said so at the outset.'

Crouched on a box across the small room, Gwyn gave one of his meaningful grunts. '*I* should have gone to Honiton, not him. But I remember there was a Fitzhai at Ascalon, in the last weeks before we left Palestine, though I can't recall what he looked like.'

John rose impatiently and walked to the slit in the boarded window to peer down at the inner ward of the castle.

'Why was this Fitzhai in Honiton? Was he staying at the inn?' The clerk fidgeted on his stool. 'I asked that of the innkeeper. He was loath to tell me anything, except that every man's business is his own.'

John came across the room and towered over the diminutive Thomas. 'So we have lost him, have we? Our only witness and he walks out of the door.' He swung round to Gwyn, whose red hair was glinting in a rare ray of sunshine. 'Are there any Fitzhais in that area?'

Gwyn shrugged his massive shoulders. 'Don't know of any hereabouts. But I'm no expert on Norman families.' His slight emphasis on 'Norman' was a subtle token of the resentment that still lingered among the native population, Saxon and Celt alike.

John rested his buttocks on the edge of the table, which creaked ominously. 'Then I'll have to ask the sheriff for help. He should know all the manorial holders in his own county. I thought I did too, but Fitzhai is new to me.' He jerked away from the protesting trestle and stalked to the door. 'I've given you those names from yesterday's inquest, Thomas. Get them down on a roll, with the usual style of words.

Tostig is committed to prison to await trial and Eadred of Dawlish is placed in the care of his assailant, once the holy sister says he can be moved.'

At the head of the stairs, he turned with an after-thought. 'And record that the innkeeper, Willem of Bruges, can distrain on the family to get his board and lodging for the wounded man. Now I'm off to see Richard de Revelle.'

John was tempted to divert to the Bush to see Nesta and take an hour's ease with some beer and a meal. Yet the prospect of having to negotiate again with his brother-in-law, who would be sure to put every difficulty in his path, decided him on a less invit-ing diversion. On his way down the high street, he turned into St Martin's Lane and entered his own front door.

At least he had slept in his wife's bed the previous night and attended his reading lesson – which had been her idea to improve his mind and social status – so their recent frigidity had warmed slightly. He walked through the entry passage and out through the back door into the yard, where Mary was throwing washing over some bushes to dry. He tickled Brutus's ear and pecked the girl's cheek before he climbed the outside wooden staircase at the back of the house to the solar. At the top, a heavy door led into the square room supported on timber stilts.

Inside, Matilda was working at her embroidery, the usual pastime for a woman of her standing. She was sitting near the window, which was the only one in the house to have glass in it – a useless luxury, John thought, as the distorted view it gave through its thick, curved surface was merely that of their back yard and the roofs of nearby houses. A large low bed, a table and two chairs completed the furnishings. Sombre tapestries hid most of the timbered walls except where, on the wall opposite the window, a shuttered opening looked down into the hall below.

After some strained but civil words of greeting, John lowered himself on to the other chair. 'I need your advice,' he began lamely.

Matilda's eyebrows rose and she looked up from her needle. 'Since when have you needed my opinion? You've gone your own way these sixteen years.'

Swallowing both a retort and his pride, he tried to look conciliatory. 'About your brother, Matilda. We have to work together, for the sake of the King's peace, if nothing else.'

'And for the sake of family peace, I should hope,' she snapped, conscious that, for once, she had the upper hand over her husband.

'I don't enjoy these futile squabbles with the sheriff,' he lied. 'It's a question of jurisdiction between us, you see.'

Matilda stared at him suspiciously, her needlework forgotten. 'What d'you mean, jurisdiction?'

John stretched out his long legs, the back flap of the grey surcoat falling to the floorboards. 'The new Articles say that all violent and uncommon deaths be investigated by the coroners.' She grudgingly nodded agreement. 'And, furthermore, we are strictly to record all such happenings – and many more besides – to present to the King's justices when they visit.'

'Of course. Everyone knows that.'

He silently disagreed with her, but kept his peace. 'Your brother seems to think that the new law is a personal intrusion into his powers.' And into his purse, thought John, but kept that to himself too.

His wife put her needle to the linen and fiddled with the thread. She was in something of a dilemma, as although she was devoted to her brother she had ardently supported her husband's elevation to the coronership. But both she and the sheriff had assumed that his appointment had been to a sinecure and had never dreamed that John was going to pursue his duties with such unrelenting zeal.

'So what advice do you want from me?' she asked uncertainly. He leaned back and locked his hands behind his head, his fingers buried in his thick black hair. As he told her the story of the dead Crusader and the trail that led to Honiton, she listened and watched him covertly.

What did she feel for this hawk-like man, who had been joined to her for almost half her lifetime? Love was for the young and for illicit dalliance after marriage, and the purpose of marriage was to weld together family lands and fortunes, to produce sons, to gain political advantage. Love was the last consideration. She and John had been joined by their parents for mutual links between two Norman families – even though John's mother was Cornish, which still rankled with Matilda.

The de Revelles were a well-known, moderately wealthy clan, and Simon de Wolfe, John's father, had had the best part of the marriage bargain when he had arranged to join his son to Matilda. True, the de Wolfes had two manors at Stoke-in-Teignhead but they were far from notable county figures. As for getting him sons, she had failed miserably – unless the fault lay with him. Their sporadic and unenthusiastic coupling in the first years of marriage had produced no offspring and had declined from lack of interest to their current celibacy. She was well aware that he satisfied his appetites elsewhere, as did most men, and she herself had had several liaisons when John was away at either the Irish wars or in the Levant, but it had been several years since she had bothered to trail her skirt at anyone.

And here he was now, her tall, dark man, telling her some interminable tale about a rotting corpse in a Dartmoor brook. 'Matilda, I need de Revelle's help to find Fitzhai.'

His wife failed to see the problem. 'Well, just ask Richard to seek the man out.'

With difficulty John concealed his impatience. 'Only yesterday we had a public shouting match about who was to hang a felon. Richard and his miserable portreeve declared that coroners were a waste of time and money and that the sheriffs should continue to have total jurisdiction, in spite of the royal command.'

Matilda could see that if her brother had his way her husband's new role would be short-lived. 'What do you want him to do, then?' she asked, briskly.

'Seek out this Alan Fitzhai in or about Honiton. I can't do it, with only Gwyn and that poxy clerk at my command. Thomas ferreted him out, then lost him. No use sending him back.'

'So send that lout of a Cornishman instead,' Matilda snapped.

'He can't drag the fellow back alone, if he refuses to come, as the clerk claims he will. A sergeant and two men are needed to flush him out and bring him here. That's sheriff's business.'

His wife looked at him with distrust, her pale hair showing stiffly under the white linen coverchief around her head. 'So what help do you want from me?'

'Richard will undoubtedly refuse me when I ask so come with me and shame him into doing what the King's law directs him to perform. Otherwise this crowner's appointment is worth nothing.'

Matilda's needle was still for a moment. But she did not doubt that she had to support her husband or lose face over her championship of his appointment.

Suddenly she stood up and laid her work on the table.

'Right, husband, no time like the present.'

CHAPTER NINE

In which Alan Fitzhai identifies the dead Crusader

At noon on Friday, the seventh day of November, almost two days after the coroner's meeting with the sheriff, a sorry procession climbed the drawbridge of Rougemont Castle and halted just inside the inner gate. Three soldiers slid from their horses and one, the sergeant, moved to the fourth to untie a rope from the saddle pommel, the other end of which was wound around the waist of Alan Fitzhai. His hands were free to hold the reins, but he was astride the poorest horse, lashed to the saddle, and had had little chance of escape.

His mood was of disgruntled outrage, rather than a desperate will to escape. A twenty-seven-mile trot from Lyme, most of it in rain, had dampened most of his anger to simmering indignation. They had slept overnight in a stable of the Plough at Honiton, where the sergeant had checked with the landlord that their prisoner was, indeed, the man who had stayed there a few nights earlier.

Fitzhai slid to the ground and looked about him. 'Three days and I'm back in damned Exeter again,' he complained ruefully. He had exhausted his extensive vocabulary of curses and blasphemies during the first five miles out of Lyme and had settled into a resigned, cynical acceptance.

The sergeant, a hard-bitten soldier with thirty years' service, sympathised with Fitzhai, whom he recognised as a fellow warrior. They had talked on the journey, and although Fitzhai was a cut above the sergeant in the social scale, their shared experiences of campaigns in France forged a bond between them. The sergeant learned that Fitzhai had been to Plymouth that week, to find hiring for a local war threatening in Brittany, but he had been too late: the ships had sailed and he had been making his way back to Bridport to visit a woman, before moving on to Southampton, to try his luck there.

'Let's get you up to the Crowner's office. There should be a bite to eat and some ale there, if I know Gwyn of Polruan,' said his benign captor. 'And de Wolfe wants you to identify this belt and scabbard from the dead man.'

As they entered the gatehouse, he sent a soldier across the inner ward to notify the sheriff that they had returned, and the other went hot-foot to St Martin's Lane to fetch John.

Upstairs, Gwyn recognised Fitzhai as the man he had seen at Ascalon. He showed him the Levantine leather-work that they had taken from the corpse in Widecombe. The mercenary seemed positive abouts its close similarity to that worn by the man in Honiton, but they all knew that many men returning from Palestine had acquired such Moorish-looking accoutrements.

As the sergeant had forecast, he also produced beer, bread and cheese and the three military men swapped stories and reminiscences while they waited for the sheriff and the coroner to arrive.

Thomas de Peyne skulked in a corner on his writing stool, ignored by the trio of burly warriors, and watched with his customary fascination as their powerful masculinity brought the bleak chamber alive. Alan Fitzhai was talking animatedly, his rim of brown beard spiky from the rain and his full moustache waggling as he talked and chewed.

After some twenty minutes, a sudden hush fell on the occupants. The sheriff and coroner had met downstairs and John had followed de Revelle up to the room. The sergeant pushed himself away from the wall and held himself erect, furtively brushing the crumbs from his grey beard.

De Revelle walked to the rough bench behind the trestle table and sat down, John standing in his own office. Thomas slid off his stool to allow his master to sit, but the coroner moved to the end of the table and hooked a thigh over its corner.

'Alan Fitzhai, sir, as you commanded,' said the sergeant steadily. Although he disliked the sheriff, de Revelle was his master: loyalty and respect were due to his rank.

'How did you find him, sergeant?' demanded Crowner John.

The old soldier pulled at his moustache. 'It was easy, sir. The landlord at the inn in Honiton told us that he had left, saying that he was making for the coast at Bridport. So we rode there and in an hour looking in the taverns we turned up Alan Fitzhai.'

'And a damned aggrieved Alan Fitzhai, Sir Sheriff!' said the whiskered warrior loudly. 'I was half-way to Southampton and got dragged back here, lashed to a lousy nag like some common criminal'.

De Revelle looked up at the coroner, and raised an

eyebrow. John understood the signal: certainly Fitzhai could not be pushed around like some villager or town serf. He was a Norman and obviously had aristocratic blood in his veins. He was also a recent Crusader and men who had taken the Cross were popular and deserved respect. He was entitled to be treated as their peer, at least until some skeleton was found in his cupboard.

John began with an apology for the manner in which Fitzhai had been brought to Exeter, rather unfairly giving the impression that the sergeant had exceeded his authority is lashing him to his saddle. 'But this dead man was a Norman and almost certainly a Crusader like ourselves,' he continued, in his sonorous voice, 'so I'm sure that you would wish to do all you can to help us give him a name and a decent grave.'

Fitzhai nodded slowly. 'No one wants a fellow soldier dead – unless he's on the other side of our lances.'

'So who was this man?' John demanded bluntly.

Fitzhai looked from him to the sheriff and back again, reluctant to commit himself irrevocably to a situation that might bring him nothing but grief.

'Come on, man!' snapped de Revelle. 'What evil are you hiding?'

This stung Fitzhai into a retort. 'No evil at all, Sheriff – but wagging tongues never did any man good service,' he added obscurely.

The sheriff glared at him. 'Your silence might condemn you, Fitzhai. If you persist in obstructing the law, you can expect to be treated with suspicion.'

The mercenary's cheeks flushed even deeper, but he held his ground. 'Why should I help dig a hole for myself to fall into, Sir John? I'm not involved in this matter – that's why I shied off answering the questions of your nosey little clerk. If I'd not saved his miserable skin from those footpads outside the inn, you'd never had heard of me, would you?'

He was pugnacious and aggressive, but John felt an undercurrent of anxiety, even fear, in his voice. He guessed that Fitzhai had seen too many hangings to want to become involved in a murder investigation. He had some sympathy with this, but he knew he must ignore it.

The sheriff was less tolerant. 'You know more than you've admitted, fellow. Either you tell us what you know or you'll spend the night in the cells under my castle keep. Which is it to be?' John saw that Fitzhai was weakening, and, sure enough, he said, 'All right, I'd seen the fellow before somewhere.'

'A name, for the Virgin's sake!' exploded the coroner.

Fitzhai looked from one face to the other. Stony stares met his gaze and he capitulated. 'It was Hubert de Bonneville, if the description is right.' The words came out in a defiant rush.

John looked at his brother-in-law, their animosity temporarily forgotten in their mutual interest at this revelation. 'De Bonneville? Are there not de Bonnevilles near Tavistock?' he asked.

De Revelle was better versed than John in the Norman occupancy of the county. 'At Peter Tavy, where old Arnulph de Bonneville holds the manor from the de Redvers. The last I heard of him, he was sick near to death.'

John stared hard at Alan Fitzhai. 'How well did you know this man? Were you with him in Palestine?'

The mercenary shook his head, but said nothing.

Suddenly Gwyn spoke up, jerked out of his usual gruff silence. 'Alan Fitzhai! I recollect that name now. You were in trouble at Ascalon, after the retreat from Jerusalem!' Richard the Lionheart had twice come almost within sight of the Holy City, but had failed to reach it. The coastal city of Ascalon had been refortified before the King sailed for Europe as a base for the remaining English troops.

'What trouble was that?' demanded the sheriff.

John answered him without hesitation. 'There were all kinds of scandals and rackets going on there. Twenty thousand men-at-arms and knights, all with little to do, while the King and Saladin thrashed out their peace treaty. A recipe for trouble, idle hands with nothing to occupy them.'

Gwyn went on, 'Two hundred Moorish prisoners had their throats cut, after being promised as exchange for our men taken captive. You were accused of being party to that – and of looting and raping local families in Ascalon.'

'It was all damned lies,' protested Fitzhai, his present problems suddenly overshadowed by old rumours.

Gwyn supplied more details. 'There was a trial of the ringleaders by Hubert Walter. Twenty men were hanged on the testimony of other Crusaders.'

'But maybe this Hubert de Bonneville laid testimony against you, eh?' asked the sheriff.

The mercenary looked genuinely astonished. 'Nonsense! I never laid eyes on the bloody man in Palestine. There was trouble, I admit, but I was judged free from all blame. What the hell has all this to do with me now, eh?'

The argument went on for a few moments, but Fitzhai stubbornly denied that he had had any dealings with de Bonneville in Palestine, or even that he had ever set eyes on him there.

'So how could you recognise him in Honiton if you never knew him in the Holy Land?' demanded de Revelle.

'It wasn't like that, at all!' yelled Alan Fitzhai.

'Well, how was it, for God's sake?' snapped the coroner.

'I met him not there but on the journey home,' said Fitzhai. 'Three months ago I landed in Marseille by ship and joined a party of English Crusaders making their way back up to the Channel ports. De Bonneville was one of them, though I didn't know him well – there were more than forty of us in the band.'

The sheriff looked suspiciously at him. 'You say "not well", but how well? Were you friends, comrades-in-arms?'

Fitzhai was now evidently uncomfortable, under the gaze of two senior law officers, a stolid sergeant, a coroner's officer and a curious clerk. There was a heavy silence.

'Well, were you?' barked de Revelle, his lean face and pointed beard pushed forward agressively.

Fitzhai shifted from one large foot to the other and folded his arms. 'If you must know, I heartily disliked the man, God rest his soul. He was too fond of pushing his nose into other people's business.'

The sheriff, for all his many faults, was a shrewd judge of men and felt vindicated that he had indeed smelt a rat. 'So! You fell out with de Bonneville, this man you hardly knew. Perhaps you killed him?'

Fitzhai leaned forward and indignantly punched the table with his fist. 'For God's sake, of course I didn't kill him! I hardly knew the man. I kept clear of him in France, and when we arrived at Harfleur, I never saw him again, live or dead.'

'You left him in Normandy?' asked John.

'Yes, I took ship for Southampton within two days, as the wind happened to be favourable. The devil knows what he did. Why should I care? He was nothing to me.'

As the coroner digested this, Richard de Revelle asked, 'If you knew him so slightly, how can you be sure that he is the dead man, on such a slight description?'

'I've seen the belt and the scabbard, haven't I?' retorted Fitzhai.

'Those may have been stolen from him – and they're common enough.'

'Well, he always dressed in green, either his surcoat or his cloak. And he had that hairy mole. How many other fair-headed men have such a distinctive blemish on their neck as your officer described?'

John tried another approach. 'Do you know anything about de Bonneville? His family, where he came from, where he was going?'

'I've told you, I do not! Neither did I want to know. I'm sorry the poor fellow is slain, but I couldn't abide him, what little I knew of him.'

De Revelle steepled his fingers together, elbows on the table.

'Why this dislike of Hubert de Bonneville, eh? There must have been bad blood between you?'

Alan Fitzhai shook his head obstinately. 'It was a personal matter, Sheriff, with respect, none of your business. He put on superior airs and acted as if he was the soul and conscience of our party as we came up through Burgundy and Aquitaine.' He wiped a hand across his luxuriant moustache. 'He was a sanctimonious prig, with an attitude far above his station.'

'You sound as if you know him better than you admit,' observed the sheriff, but a few more minutes of questioning showed that Fitzhai either could not or would not tell them anything more.

'You will not leave Exeter without my consent, Fitzhai,' commanded the sheriff. 'Your sword and your horse will be impounded and you will stay within the city walls until I give you leave to go. Is that understood?'

The spiky beard bristled with indignation. 'Am I arrested, then? And under suspicion?'

John slid off the end of the table and looked down at him. 'You are the only one who knew and can name the dead man. You confess yourself that you had no love for him, and in due course we will pursue that further – much further. Can you wonder that we wish you to remain within our sight?'

De Revelle added his own warning: 'If you were not a Norman soldier recently returned from Palestine, you would be thrown into the castle gaol, so be grateful for our clemency.' He gestured to the sergeant, who stepped forward and touched Fitzhai's arm to motion him out of the chamber.

As he went to the narrow arch at the head of the stairs, the man turned for a last indignant complaint. 'And what am I supposed to live on in Exeter, while you decide what to do? I need bed, bread and beer.'

John grinned at him cynically. 'If I know anything about returning Crusaders, they'll have a few gold coins sewn into the hem of their clothing. You'll not starve!'

The sergeant urged Fitzhai out, and left John and his brother-in-law to take stock of the new situation.

'Well, John, I have to say that our joint venture certainly turned up something, though I could have done just as well without your new-fangled coroner's business.'

John bridled. 'Without my inquiries in the first place, you'd never have heard of Alan Fitzhai. It was my initiative in sending my clerk to Honiton that flushed him out for us!'

The sheriff chose to ignore this obvious truth. He rose from behind the trestle table. 'Is this our man, I wonder? I wouldn't trust him beyond a sword's length.'

This gave Thomas the courage to enter the discussion. 'Until I told him that the man in green was dead, Fitzhai was quite happy to talk about him. Surely if he had been involved in his killing, he would never have mentioned him?'

John nodded at this. 'I'll not prejudge him, Richard. The first thing is to confirm that our dead man is, indeed, Hubert de Bonneville. For all we know, Fitzhai is spinning us a pack of lies.'

'I doubt that, Crowner. Why should he involve himself in this affair if the corpse is not de Bonneville? Fitzhai was reluctant, but he admitted that he knew him. A pound to a penny that he's responsible for his death, too.'

John scowled. 'I'll not presume in any inquest that the dead man is this Hubert until some relative confirms it. That will be the next step.'

Richard de Revelle pulled on an elegant pair of broad-cuffed gloves, ready to leave the chamber. 'I care nothing for your inquests, John. All I need is a culprit, a trial and a hanging.'

John grunted, a habit he was catching from Gwyn. His opinion of the sheriff's sense of justice was low, even in an age not renowned for the concept of fair play.

De Revelle had decided that he had given enough of his valuable time to humouring the coroner and marched out, followed by his sergeant, leaving John and his retainers to their own devices.

The taciturn giant from Cornwall stirred himself to pour them what was left of the pitcher of ale, and settled back on the window ledge with his mug.

John slid on to his stool, still warm from the sheriff's backside. 'We must go out to Peter Tavy to see these de Bonnevilles. They'll have to come to Widecombe to view the corpse.'

Thomas shuddered into his ale and crossed himself. 'But he's buried and he'll be putrid by now,' he squeaked, with an expression of disgust. 'How can a brother, or anyone else, be asked to look at a loved one in that state? And, anyway, could they tell who it was after he has become so corrupt?'

'He'll not be too bad after being in the ground for only a few days – keeps them cool, does moist earth.' Gwyn seemed unmoved by the prospect of other folk's revulsion.

The coroner agreed with him. 'It's been cool wet weather and a grave is the best place to slow putrefaction. Even if they can't recognise his face, his build, his hair and, above all, this birthmark on the neck should satisfy them once they've seen his clothes and weapon.'

The clerk looked unconvinced, but no one cared much what he thought.

Gwyn sank the last of the beer in his jar and wiped the back of his hand across his luxuriant moustache. 'There's a lot more truth to be squeezed out of that Alan Fitzhai. He was telling us only half a story.'

Thomas nodded, like a bird pecking grain. 'He's keeping back something that's to his disadvantage.'

John shrugged and rose again from his seat. 'You may both be right, but we must move one step at a time. First thing in the morning, we ride across Dartmoor. You can stop off at Widecombe, Thomas, and organise the digging out of the cadaver. Gwyn and I will ride on to the Tavy valley, break the bad news to the family and bring someone back to identify the body.'

As the coroner left the chamber, the clerk was uncertain whether to feel relief at being spared the extra mule-ride across the moor or having qualms at seeing the rotting corpse hauled back to the surface at Widecombe.

CHAPTER TEN

In which Crowner John crosses Dartmoor

Sir John's truce with his wife was short-lived. Though she had co-operated with him in persuading the sheriff to recover Alan Fitzhai from Honiton, her annoyance was still simmering at his continued neglect of her in favour of his duties. When he arrived home in the early afternoon and announced that he would probably be away for the next two days, Matilda's mood reverted to abrasive sarcasm. Sitting, as usual, in her solar, as the acid-faced Lucille braided her hair, she glowered at her husband from under her heavy eyelids. 'Yet another excuse to leave me alone while you go jaunting around the countryside! I've said it before and I'll say it again. Why can't you send that great oaf of a Cornishman in your place or that perverted clergyman?'

John's patience, ever parchment-thin, broke. 'Jaunting about the countryside, you call it! An eight-hour ride across Dartmoor in the mist and rain, to visit an old, sick knight, then five hours back to Widecombe with a grieving family to view a putrefying corpse. Some jaunting, wife!'

Matilda was unmoved. 'Alehouses, rough soldier comrades and whores – those are your main interests as I know from years of bitter experience.'

Her husband stood over her menacingly, a black hawk hovering above a fat pigeon. 'What would you have me do, woman? Sit and embroider linen like you?' he snarled.

'Be like other men of substance!' retorted Matilda. 'Sit by the fire, have friends among the influential men of the town. Invite them to eat with us and be offered more invitations to their own halls and guild meetings. Play your part in the life of the town.'

John flung away from her. 'Oh, yes, talk endlessly about the price of mutton or the latest scandals from Winchester! No, thank you, Matilda. I might do that in my dotage when I've lost my hair, my teeth and my wits but not yet, while I can still ride a horse and lift a hunting spear.'

Matilda threw down her needlework. 'Riding, hunting, spears and swords! There's more to life than those, husband. Why do you never go to holy service, except when forced? You never pray, you ignore the scriptures and treat the priests with scorn.'

John kicked a stool and sent it spinning across the room. 'Untrue, Matilda! John of Alecon and John of Exeter are good friends of mine, as well as being among the most senior of the cathedral priests.'

His wife made a rude noise meant to convey her scorn. 'The Chapter Treasurer and the Archdeacon! A fine pair, well known to everyone always to be at cross purposes with the Bishop and Precentor. Typical that you should ally yourself with the dissidents!'

In a reverse of logic, Matilda was referring to the fact that the Bishop, the Precentor and her own brother, the sheriff, were sympathisers with the attempt of Prince John to seize power in England when his royal brother was at the Crusades and imprisoned in Germany. True, few expected the King ever to return alive, but John's rash anticipation of taking the throne was little short of revolt and treason in the eyes of loyalists like John de Wolfe, and the two Johns in the cathedral. When the Lionheart had unexpectedly landed in Kent last March, he had rapidly extinguished the rebellion – and foolishly, as many thought, forgave his younger brother for his treachery.

With her words ringing in his ears, John lost whatever remained of his temper.

'To hell with it, wife! You do nothing but criticise and scold me. Why in God's name I ever agreed to marry you, I'll never fathom.'

She snapped back, without a second's hesitation, 'You married me because your father wanted advantage for you – and a poor way you've repaid fulfilling his ambitions for you.'

'At least it wasn't for love – you've spared me that!'

'No, you get what passes for your love at The Bush tavern – and many other places, I suspect!' spat Matilda. John cast about for some other stone to hurl at her. 'For all my faults, as you see them, at least I don't come from a family that's forever looking to line my purse by whatever means possible – legal or corrupt!'

'And what might you mean by that, sir?' shrilled his wife. Her face was now almost puce under the layer of powder that Lucille had not long dabbed on her cheeks. The maid was standing back against the wall, trying not to smirk at this hottest episode yet in her employer's long-standing feud.

She was a fit companion for her mistress, a gossip with rarely a good word for anyone. A sallow,

unattractive woman of about thirty, she had project-
ing yellow teeth and lank dark hair. Of Frankish origin
from the Vexin, north of Paris, she was a refugee from
a village desolated by the endless wars between the
Normans and the French that had flowed back and
forth over that region. She savoured Matilda's present
wrath against Sir John, being as partisan against him
as Mary was in supporting him.

'Come, what are you insinuating?' repeated her
mistress belligerently. 'Is this another slur against my
brother?'

'He's always seeking ways to divert silver into his own
pocket at the expense of the King's Exchequer.'

Matilda was rocking back and forth on her chair in
fury. 'That's vile slander with no foundation!'

John gave the footstool another kick, sending it back
across the boards of the solar floor.

'Where did the property of many convicted felons
end up during this past year? Where did much of the
deodand sale money go before I became coroner? And
why was your precious relative ejected from office last
Lady Day, eh?'

Richard de Revelle had been nominated as sheriff
the previous year, through his partiality to Prince John
and his support for the Bishop, who was brother to
the Marshal of England. By the time he had taken
office at Christmas 1193, John's rebellion was already
tottering, as his mother, the redoubtable old Queen
Eleanor, had set forces against him. Within months,
many of the sheriff's sponsors were in disgrace, and
after the King returned in March and massacred the
last rebels in Nottingham castle, de Revelle's number
was up. He had been relieved of his duties and Henry
Furnellis had become a caretaker sheriff.

Partly because Henry was even more corrupt than Richard, but also because the Lionheart had pardoned his brother John, Hubert Walter had reinstated Richard de Revelle when John de Wolfe became coroner.

'He was restored at Michaelmas. It was all a misunderstanding,' said Matilda, defensively.

'Some misunderstanding! If the King wasn't so lenient, and your brother so supported by the Bishop and his brother William the Marshal, he'd have swung at the end of one of his own ropes.'

Matilda hissed, 'Are you accusing my brother of corruption?'

'Corruption! That's his lesser sin. It's common knowledge that he was part of Prince John's treachery. Only powerful voices at Winchester and Rouen keep him in office.'

John was reckless now, the breach with his wife having cracked open wider than ever before.

'It's treason to accuse the King's officer for this county. You're a bigger fool than you are a liar, John!'

'Treason be damned!' he yelled at her. 'I know what Coeur de Lion thinks of your damned family, supporters of Prince John's underhand conniving!'

This was too much for Matilda, who was almost gibbering with rage. She stood up and hurled her embroidery, wooden frame and all, at her towering husband.

'Get out, you blasphemer! Go to your bloody inn and your painted strumpet and ride the moor tomorrow until your arse-bones stick to the saddle!'

Her uncharacteristic descent into coarseness betrayed the height of her passion, and even through his own anger, John saw that it was time to let her cool off.

With a last muttered curse, he stamped out and clattered down the outside stairway, to seek his solace and refuge in the Bush tavern.

Even though he had precipitated the worst quarrel yet with his wife, John decided not to spend the night in Nesta's bed. Although, after beer, food and sympathy, he spent a couple of consoling hours with her in her bedroom, intuition told him to go back to the house in St Martin's Lane for the night. When he arrived, the dog greeted him warmly and Matilda ignored him, pointedly leaving the hall for the solar the moment he walked in.

He had a late supper alone at the long table in the gloomy chamber, Mary fussing over him with cold bacon and hot bread straight from the oven. As she cleared the wooden platters and set a large cup of warm spiced wine before him, she rolled her eyes in the direction of the upper room. Her voice low, as the high window slit could carry voices from below, she said, 'You've really done it this time. Your lady's lips are as hard and thin as the edge of your sword – and will be as sharp when she opens her mouth!'

John, whose few hours at the Bush had restored his spirits, winked at her. 'I can no longer do anything right in her eyes, so I've nothing to lose. Matilda and I must go our own ways in future, Mary – but I can take that as long as I've still got you to feed me and give me the occasional kind word.'

She gave him a quick kiss on the back of his neck and took his empty wooden platter and pewter mug back to the kitchen.

John blew out the solitary candle and crept up to the solar, where he spent the night on the edge of the wide hay-stuffed palliasse, with Matilda, wakeful but silent and studiously ignoring him, on the other side.

Next morning, she was snoring heavily when he rose before daybreak and left the house after one of Mary's huge breakfasts. Collecting his massive stallion, Bran, a prematurely retired warhorse, he rode through the West Gate as it was opened at the first glimmer of dawn. Pushing past the crowd of early traders clustered outside with their produce, he met Gwyn outside the city walls, near the ford across the river. The new stone bridge was still under construction by Nicholas Gervase, but money for its completion had again run out and the old narrow wooden bridge was strong enough only for pedestrians and pack-ponies. Carts, wagons and large animals had to splash across the stony river-bed, which was impassable when the Exe was in spate.

The two men sat side by side on their horses, looking around at the influx of people into the city.

'Where's that cretinous clerk?' growled Gwyn.

The weather was dry now, but had turned colder with the first hints of winter creeping into the November air. Gwyn was enveloped in a huge, tattered brown cloak that had seen service over half the known world. With his wild red hair poking from under a conical leather cap and the fiery whiskers half hiding his face, he looked like one of the mythical beasts often portrayed on the roof bosses of churches.

John was dressed in his usual black and grey uniform but today sported a light grey capuchin wound around his head, the end trailing over his shoulder. He turned in his saddle to look back through the gate. 'Here he is, on that miserable mule of his. Maybe I should spend some of the next wealthy felon's forfeit on a decent pony for him.'

The little clerk was forcing himself ineffectually between the crowds of peasants jostling through the narrow gate, jamming it with baskets, boxes and squawking live poultry. At last he broke free and trotted up to join them.

The trio set off westwards across the ford and past the buildings outside the protection of Exeter's walls. The houses and shacks straggled on for a few hundred yards along the road that led away from the city towards the Cornish lands. The mud from the recent rains had now dried in the cold wind and the going was relatively good. Even Thomas's much-maligned mule kept up a steady trot and they covered a better than average five miles each hour.

Although the woods and forests came to the road edge for much of the way, this lowland was fertile and villages were frequent. Soon, whenever there were gaps in the trees, the barer hill-tops of Dartmoor could be seen, some surmounted by tors, the strange outcrops of granite rock.

They passed the hamlets of Kennford, Little Bovey and Ashburton before they struck north-west to the flanks of the wilderness that, together with Exmoor, covered almost half of Devon.

Near Buckland, a somewhat apprehensive Thomas was detached from the group to make his way towards Widecombe, while Sir John and Gwyn continued towards Tavistock and Peter Tavy, almost on the border with Cornwall.

The most direct way was across the moor and along

the bleak track between the hills and tors of the bare plateau. The higher slopes were either dotted with scrub or were bare grass, heather and rock.

The coroner and his guard rode silently for the most part. These two had journeyed together for thousands of miles over the years of their acquaintance and, both being of a taciturn nature, found little left to say, apart from the business of the day. Yet it was not a strained silence: it was a mutual acceptance of each other's reserved personality. Though they were master and servant, their relationship was one of fraternal comradeship: John stated what needed to be done and Gwyn carried it out, usually without demur. Occasionally, the Cornishman would answer an order with a direct stare when John knew that discussion was needed of an alternative strategy. If the coroner persisted in his demand, Gwyn would carry it out to the letter, but with an almost palpable air of disapproval that usually caused John concern about the wisdom of his decision.

At noon, under the glint of weak autumn sunlight, they stopped on a patch of coarse grass and winberry bushes to have their meal, using a flat slab of lichen-covered rock as a table. From Gwyn's saddlebag came a stone bottle of rough cider, which they passed from mouth to mouth, and a loaf of coarse horse-bread made from a mixture of grains. The coroner contributed a small crock of yellow butter and a lump of boiled ham, part of the provisions provided by Mary, as Matilda – never much concerned with domestic issues – was now indifferent to his welfare.

A long silence was broken as they sat on the mottled rock to eat and drink. Gwyn passed the cider bottle and wiped his moustache with the back of his hand.

'I asked among my neighbours last night, some of them carters often in Tavistock. But about the de Bonnevilles they knew little, except that they held the manor of Peter Tavy from the de Redvers and rent some more pasture from the Abbey of Tavistock'.

John took a long swig of raw cider and set down the bottle on the stone. 'I also inquired about them, in the Bush. Nesta seems to know every soul between Dorchester and Bodmin. It seems that the old lord Arnulf is in his seventieth year. He suffered an apoplexy some six months ago and now hovers between his bed and his grave.'

'What of this son who may be your dead man?'

John cut a thick slice of ham with his dagger and looked at it contemplatively. 'The sheriff said that the old man has three sons, two still at home to manage the estate – they have another large manor at Lamerton, as well as Peter Tavy.'

'And the eldest?' demanded Gwyn.

'He went to Palestine two and a half years ago, taking the cross against his father's wishes.' He slipped the ham into his mouth and, through his chewing, continued, 'Nothing else seems known of them, but that they are prosperous and keep out of trouble and the public eye.'

There seemed little else to say and, after finishing the food, the two men climbed aboard their horses and trotted off again across the deserted moor. The only persons they saw were shepherds tending the great flocks that were England's economic strength, providing the wool that was virtually the only fabric used throughout Europe.

The clouds remained high and the mist held off until twilight. Before dark they dropped down from the moor into the broad valley of the Tavy. This marked the western edge of Dartmoor and separated it from the similar, though smaller, plateau of Bodmin moor in Cornwall. Their tired horses entered the little town of Tavistock and came to rest in the stables of the abbey, where John and his officer claimed the usual traveller's one-night hospitality from the monks in return for a donation to their funds. After a simple but substantial meal in the guest-hall, John paid a courtesy call on the prior. The abbot was absent, which was usual among senior clerics, who spent far more time elsewhere on administration and politics than in religious duties in their own houses.

Prior Wulfstan was a benign, rather unworldly fat monk, with a vague manner and speech full of meaningless platitudes. He knew little about the de Bonnevilles, apart from their location and their prosperity. John was beginning to feel that the family was so ordinary as to be almost invisible in the social structure of the county.

After the meal, John went wearily to his hard pallet in a cubicle of the great dormitory and sank into a deep sleep, oblivious to the midnight perambulations of the monks to matins, and the bells and chanting of their nocturnal routine.

Both men and horses were refreshed when they saddled up after a simple breakfast and trotted out into the cold November mist. Peter Tavy was a couple of miles up the valley, spread across the slopes on the right that climbed back up to the moor.

'Good land here. They must have a decent living, these de Bonnevilles,' observed Gwyn, looking at the extensive new clearings in the river-bank woods. Turning off the main valley track that led to Okehampton, they took a well-beaten lane that slanted up the valley side. They passed a cowman with a fat herd, who told them that the manor house was another half-mile further on, and in a few minutes they entered a wide open space on the slope of the hillside. An oval earthen embankment, with a stout timber fence on top, stood inside a deep muddy ditch. It was a hundred and fifty yards in diameter, but the wooden walls were dilapidated, some stakes were missing and one section was cracked and blackened by fire. The drawbridge across the ditch in front of the only gate looked embedded in the earth and could not have been lifted for years.

The eyes of both visitors took it all in at a glance. 'They seem seem to care little for defence – too many years of easy living,' Gwyn grunted.

John looked at the few villagers passing by and had to agree: they looked plump and content. 'I suppose there's little fear of warfare here – unless you Cornish come rampaging across the Tamar and the Tavy.'

The later years of the reign of Henry II had brought stability and peace to much of England, other than the north and the Welsh Marches, so the fortifications raised in the troubled times of Stephen and the Empress Matilda had often fallen into disrepair. True, the recent intrigues of the scheming Prince John after the capture of King Richard had stimulated many to repair their defences, but such concerns had evidently not reached such a backwater as Peter Tavy.

There was no guard on the gate and they dismounted to lead their horses through to the manorial compound. A well-built fortified stone house occupied the centre, with an undercroft at ground level and wooden stairs leading up to the entrance on the upper floor, pierced by a single arched doorway and a number of narrow slits in the walls.

'At least the house is defensible, even if they have let their bailey wall decay,' said John. He looked up approvingly at the castellations surrounding a pitched roof.

'And they have slated it with stone, not thatch,' commented Gwyn. 'No use shooting fire-arrows at that.'

Within the palisade, the bailey contained the usual motley collection of frame and wattle huts and sheds, as well as two barns from which a few labourers gave them curious glances. The arrival of two men of menacing and rather military appearance was never likely to be good news to a placid rural manor like Peter Tavy.

No one challenged or greeted them as they walked across to the foot of the steps leading to the door. The undercroft had open bays for stores and stables and, as they approached, a boy ran out to take their horse's bridles. The coroner and his henchman slid out of their saddles and the boy led away the beasts to feed and water them.

Simultaneously, a figure appeared in the arched doorway above and strode to the top of the steps to look down on them. He was a powerfully built, short-necked man of about thirty, soberly but well dressed as if he was about to go hunting, with a dark brown surcoat, slit back and front over a heavy woollen tunic. He carried no sword, but a quiver of arrows was slung over his shoulders. John was immediately reminded of Alan Fitzhai in his stocky solidarity but, unlike Fitzhai, the man's hair and beard were as black as those of the coroner. He came down the steps to greet them at the bottom.

'Good day to you. Have you come to visit our lord de Bonneville?'

The words implied that he was not one of the family and John guessed that he was a squire to someone – he was too well dressed and self-assured to be a mere bailiff or seneschal.

'We have indeed, though I understand that Sir Arnulph is gravely ill.'

Blackbeard nodded sadly, and spoke low. 'He is, and never will recover.' He glanced up quickly at one of the window embrasures above, as if to make sure that his pessimism had not carried to the bedchamber.

'I am Sir John de Wolfe of Exeter, the King's coroner for this county, and Gwyn of Polruan is my officer. May I know who you are?'

The man's attitude was immediately more deferential yet, at the same time, wary. The arrival of a senior royal law officer was never to be a matter for rejoicing, and these new coroners were said to bring bad news for all and sundry.

'I am Baldwyn of Beer, squire to Gervaise de Bonneville, the second son, who has had the burden of ruling this honour of Peter Tavy since his father fell so sick. May I learn the reason for your visit, sir?'

John pulled off his heavy gloves and tucked them under his baldric. 'It is a grave and personal matter, which I must urgently discuss with the family.'

Baldwyn hesitated a moment, as if he was unused to being bypassed with any business that affected the de Bonnevilles, but the uncompromising attitude of the stern man who stood before him made it clear that the matter was not negotiable. He stood aside and waved a hand towards the steps.

'Please come into our house and take some refresh-
ment. Gervaise is with his father, as is his younger
brother Martyn. I will tell them at once that you have
arrived.'

They entered the hall, a well-built chamber that
took up more than half of the entire building. It
was almost empty, apart from a couple of servants
removing the remnants of the morning meal. John
and Gwyn were led to a table where meat, bread and
ale were placed before them. The swarthy Baldwyn,
whose name indicated that he came from the small
coastal village of Beer near the Dorset end of the
county, vanished through a curtained doorway into
an adjacent bedchamber.

Gwyn fell on the meat with appetite but John could
only pick at the food for the sake of courtesy: it was
only a couple of hours since they had breakfasted at
the abbey. 'Baldwyn seems to hold considerable power
for a young man's squire. Perhaps he is also the lord's
steward.'

The curtain parted and two men emerged, followed
by Baldwyn. John was immediately struck by their
resemblance to the Widecombe corpse: they were both
fair-haired and long-nosed. They were also dressed for
horse and hunting, and seemed apprehensive at the
sudden arrival of the county coroner. John and the
de Bonnevilles made stiff-necked bows, both Baldwyn
and Gwyn standing back.

Introductions were made and John guessed that the
brothers were within a few years of each other in their
twenties. Martyn had an air of innocence, seen in some
monks and friars, as if he was only half aware of the
world in which he walked. Gervaise seemed more
brisk and efficient and, no doubt, would manage the

manors well in the absence of their elder brother and the disablement of the father. He had slightly darker hair than Martyn and took the lead in conversation.

'I am my father's middle son, Sir John. My elder brother, Hubert, is away at the Crusade.'

The Coroner nodded gravely. 'It is he whom my visit concerns. First, I would like to speak with your father or does his disability make communication impossible?'

Gervaise's pleasant face creased into sadness. 'Since his stroke last midsummer he has been paralysed in his right arm and leg and has lost all sensible speech, as well as control of his bodily functions. But sometimes he seems to understand what we say to him.'

His younger brother cut in, 'He varies greatly from day to day. It seems unpredictable, but sometimes he nods or shakes his head.'

John looked from one to the other. 'I feel I must try to speak to him first, as a matter of courtesy to the head of the household.'

Gervaise de Bonneville could rein in his anxiety no longer. 'Sir John, please tell us what this is about. My father is sick near to death and I would prefer to spare him whatever troubles you bring to us.'

John put a hand on his shoulder in an almost avuncular manner. 'Your father has the right at least to my attempting to inform him about a grave matter that might concern his eldest son.'

Startled, the de Bonnevilles stared at each other, then at the coroner.

'What has he done this time? He was always a hot-head!' exclaimed Martyn.

John stored this in his memory for further digestion, then took both brothers by the arm and led them towards the inner doorway.

'If he is as sick as you say, I'll not trouble him, but I must set my eyes on him, as a token of my duty to him.'

With a warning glance at Gwyn to stay behind with Baldwyn, the coroner passed into the inner room, which was much darker than the hall, lit only by a single window slit in the outer wall. The chamber smelt of stale urine from the incontinence of the pathetic figure huddled in the bed. An elderly woman hovered in the background with a bowl and some rags. As if reading John's thoughts, Gervaise murmured, 'Our mother died five years ago.'

They approached the bed, a large palliasse spread on the floor, covered with a heavy bearskin. Crouched diagonally across it, his head pulled down to his left shoulder, was an emaciated figure with grey hair and a stubbled beard. One corner of his mouth drooped and saliva ran from the lax lips. The left arm was above the bed coverings and the thin fingers twitched and picked constantly at the fur.

Arnulph de Bonneville, a shadow of his former self, lay dying in his own excretions. John thought that it would be a Christian mercy if one of his retainers were to hold a pillow over his face finally to extinguish the miserable mockery of a life he now endured. 'Leave the poor man in peace,' he murmured, and they moved back into the hall.

Gervaise led the way to benches set near a smouldering fire, where hurrying servants brought them cups of heated wine.

'Our parish priest spends much of his time here,

waiting to shrive him in case he suddenly stops breathing.' Martyn sighed unhappily.

John sipped his wine. 'I have a sad duty to carry out. Until I saw you both, I thought there might be room for doubt, but the similarity of your features tell me that almost certainly your brother is dead.'

There was a stunned silence.

'You have heard from Palestine, then?' asked Gervaise, in a hollow voice. 'But why didn't the news come straight to us?'

The coroner shook his head. 'He died not in Palestine but in Devon, not twenty-five miles from here in Widecombe.'

The younger brother looked bewildered, his fresh, ingenuous face uncomprehending. 'But Hubert is abroad. We had news of him last Eastertide when a soldier returning to Plymouth from Jaffa called upon us with a message from him.'

'Yes, he said that he was alive and well,' added Gervaise, 'and that he hoped to be home within a year or so.'

'You've heard nothing of him since?'

'Not a word,' replied the elder brother, sombrely. 'But neither did we expect to. None of us has the gift of reading or writing, so any message from such distant lands can only come by word of mouth.'

'But what has happened to him?' Martyn persisted. 'What is all this about Widecombe?'

Crowner John explained the whole story as he knew it, the stricken brothers listening silently and Baldwyn edging closer, as if both to hear better and to offer support to his master and to Martyn.

This sudden news was more of a shock than a reason for overwhelming grief but, even so, John realised that it had hit the family hard. Gervaise moved closer to his younger brother and put an arm around his shoulder and they stared silently into each other's eyes. The squire Baldwyn came nearer, as if to console them with his powerful presence. After a moment, Gervaise turned back to the coroner. 'What would you have us do about this, sir? As you saw, it is useless trying to tell our father. Unless he improves, which is unlikely, he is incapable of understanding.'

The coroner spread his bony hands in a gesture of regret. 'I must have a positive identification of the murdered man. We must be sure that it is your brother before I complete the inquest, though I am afraid that I have little doubt. You must ride back with us to Widecombe to view the body, distressing though that might be.'

The brothers murmured together, Baldwyn also putting his head into the discussion. Then Gervaise turned back to John. 'I will ride with you, together with my squire. Martyn will remain here as, with our lord so sick, someone must be on hand in case he dies, as well as having to attend to the daily business of running the manor.'

John nodded. 'I must be back in Exeter by the morning, so we should leave for Widecombe now, to have enough light left for what we have to do there. You are already dressed for the saddle, so nothing need delay us.'

CHAPTER ELEVEN

*In which Crowner John attends
an exhumation*

In the churchyard at Widecombe, a heap of fresh earth proved that Thomas de Peyne had carried out his master's instructions. By the time the coroner and his small party arrived in the mid-afternoon, the clerk had ordered Ralph the reeve to complete the digging and two serfs had removed all the soil from the new grave.

Before he took Gervaise de Bonneville and the squire into the churchyard, John adjourned to the large hut on the other side of the village green, which did service as a tavern. Here, the widow of a freeman crushed to death two years before by a bull supported her three children by brewing beer and selling oat-cakes. Her thatched wattle hut stood in the dip of the track that came down from the moor and led on towards Dunstone. The green was humped, as was most of the land around the village: the church was on one side of the slope and the tavern on the other, the green hillside rising steeply behind.

The travellers sat outside the door on a large log that served as a bench, while the toothless young widow brought them bread and ale, to which John added the remains of Mary's ham and some hard cheese.

For a few moments they ate and drank, Gervaise and Baldwyn uneasy as they anticipated the moment of truth at the graveside.

John looked across the open green space to the low dry-stone wall of the churchyard, from where he could hear the final sounds of the raising of the coffin. The rise of the land prevented him seeing their activities and, as he chewed the rough bread, his eye fell instead on three straw mats, held up vertically on poles stuck into the ground at the further end of the green.

'They seem keen archers in this place,' he commented to Gwyn.

The woman, refilling his beer mug, grinned a gummy smile. 'Good for my business. Shooting at those targets is thirsty work. The lord of our manor, FitzRalph, insists that every man above fourteen practises with the bow at least once a week. He wants plenty of good shots if he has to raise men for an army.'

When the food was finished, the coroner got down to business. 'Show them the effects of the dead man, Gwyn,' he commanded.

The cornishman went to his tethered horse and took a hessian-wrapped bundle from a pannier. He unrolled it on the ground before then and displayed the ornate sword belt, the empty scabbard and sheathed dagger.

The two men leaned over to study and then handle the objects. Gervaise sank back on to the log. 'I've not seen these before, but they are undoubtedly foreign so it means little. If they were Hubert's then he must have obtained them in the East.' Baldwyn nodded in silent agreement.

'What about this, then?' asked John, unrolling a green surcoat from the bundle. It had been washed, but the tear in the back was still obvious.

Gervaise and Baldwyn looked doubtfully at each other. 'Certainly Hubert had some green clothing – he was fond of the colour. But so are half the men in England,' Gervaise said.

'There's nothing special about this one,' added Baldwyn. 'It would be about his size, but there are thousands of men it would fit.'

John motioned to Gwyn to roll up the artefacts again, and they all rose to their feet. 'Then it remains only to view the body, painful though that might be to you.'

He led the way across the green to the church. It was a poor structure of old wood, with peeling whitewash, dating back to Saxon days, but a new tower had been built in stone during the past decade, presumably a gift from the manorial lord.

Thomas was waiting at the gap in the wall, standing with bowed head, his hands together before him, and turned to lead the procession solemnly to the graveside, as if he was still a priest and conducting a funeral. At the heap of earth – grey here, not red like Exeter – Thomas turned and crossed himself. 'The box is ready to open, Crowner,' he said sonorously.

The two village men, one of whom habitually acted as sexton, stood by the crude coffin, which rested at the end of the hole. The parish priest, a thin soul with a furtive, hunted look, stood well back against the church wall, as if to distance himself from these unwelcome goings-on in his churchyard.

'Open it, man,' snapped John, as they stood in a ragged half-circle around the gaping grave.

The sexton took an old rusty sword with a broken blade and rammed it into the joint of the coffin lid. He levered up and, with some cracking and splintering of wood, the two rough planks were torn off. Thomas hopped back like a frightened sparrow, his hand to his mouth, while the others looked on impassively, Gervaise's face pallid.

An aura of sweet-sour corruption wafted from the box, but soon drifted away on the slight breeze. Within the coffin was a crude cross, made of two sticks lashed with cord. This lay on a length of soiled linen that covered the body, the fabric marred by greenish yellow patches where it lay over the face, chest and belly. Without ceremony or hesitation, Gwyn stepped forward, took out the cross and whipped off the cloth, revealing the victim's naked body.

In spite of Thomas's apprehensions, the corpse was not much changed from the day of the inquest. The skin was more tense, moist and slimy, and was beginning to peel in places. Along the flanks were large blisters filled with bloody fluid and the abdomen and genitals were grossly swollen and green. The face, though, was only moderately puffy and blurred.

'Cover him, for decency's sake!' grated Baldwyn tensely. Gwyn spread the linen over the lower half of the cadaver and turned to look inquiringly at Gervaise de Bonneville. The coroner's eyes also swivelled to the young man. 'Well, sir, is this your brother or not?'

Gervaise stood transfixed, staring at the putrefying body in the splintered box. For a long moment he was as motionless as the corpse, then he turned slowly to the coroner, his face even paler than it had been before.

'It is Hubert, God rest his soul.' His voice cracked and his squire took his arm.

Thomas edged forward, made the sign of the cross

in the air over the open box and began to mutter some incantation in Latin.

The coroner turned to Baldwyn of Beer. 'You must have known him well. Do you agree that this is your master's kin?'

Baldwyn dropped his hand from Gervaise's shoulder, stepped forward and bent to look more closely at the cadaver. Like John and Gwyn, he seemed immune to the sights and odours of death.

'There is no doubt, sir. Though the face is swollen and the eyes squeezed shut, it is certainly Hubert. The build, the hair, the features and, above all, that disfigurement he was born with, they all prove it.' He pointed at the raised brown mark on the side of the dead man's neck, its colour and hair virtually unchanged, though it now sat on a slimed waxy bed of mottled skin.

John waved a hand imperiously at the sexton. 'Seal the box and put him to rest.'

He turned to Thomas. 'See to it that everything is done decorously – and tell that lurking priest to say a few words over the grave.'

As the party turned from the graveside, Gwyn nudged the coroner and pointed into the crude coffin. 'Those bruises on the arms have come out since we last saw the corpse,' he muttered.

John squatted to looked at the greening skin between each elbow and shoulder. On either side, three or four reddish purple marks, the size of a thumb-nail, were now prominent on the shiny, peeling surface.

'Grip marks, where fingers have pinioned his arms,' he said.

'Held by one man, while another stabbed him in

the back, already disarmed by a slash into his sword arm,' completed the Cornishman.

The coroner rose and shrugged at his henchman. 'Nothing we didn't know before, but it confirms that he was ambushed by more than one assailant.' He led the way out of the churchyard and back to the ale-house, his black cloak billowing behind him.

Waiting for him was Ralph the reeve, who had been out in the fields when they arrived. He had been supervising the villeins as they ploughed some of the harvest stubble ready for next year's crop, leaving the rest fallow as part of the rotation system that he had to organise.

Immediately John put him to work again. 'Collect as many men from the village as you can muster for an inquest jury. Especially find those who were at the first inquiry a few days back.'

Ralph's mouth opened in surprise. 'What, now?'

John dropped heavily on to the log outside the tavern door and sat with his hands planted aggressively on his parted knees. 'Yes, now! And hurry, it will be dark in a couple of hours, too late to ride back either to Exeter or to Peter Tavy, so we must sleep here tonight. We may as well use the remaining daylight to complete the inquest formalities and make an early start in the morning.'

Muttering under his breath, Ralph hurried off, shouting at every villager he saw to assemble at the tithe barn, set just beyond the church. As he went, Gwyn's bright blue observant eyes lit on something else, this time at a distance. He tapped John's shoulder. 'Look over there, in the reeve's croft,' he said.

John followed his man's pointing finger to where a horse was contently cropping the thin winter grass in the fenced plot of land that lay behind the hut. He yelled after the reeve, in a voice that could be heard up on the moor, 'Come back here, damn you!'

Ralph, who had been giving orders to a couple of villagers to gather up a jury, plodded back to the coroner and his officer.

John grabbed him by the arm of his coarse tunic and turned him round, none too gently, so that he faced his own house. 'Is that your dwelling there?' he boomed, gesturing with his free hand.

Ralph looked surprised. 'Of course it is – you ate and rested there last week.'

'And is that your croft behind it?' John indicated the patch of grass between the back of the house and the cultivated strip that stretched towards the field system.

'It is . . . yes.' The reeve was more puzzled than ever and apprehension crept into his voice.

'And is that your horse?'

There was a slight hesitation, but Ralph had to admit that the beast tethered to a peg in the plot behind his house belonged to him.

'A dappled grey mare with a singular black ring around her right eye!' said John, with a rising note of triumphant accusation in his voice.

'What of it? It's just a horse,' retorted Ralph, with tremulous defiance.

'What of it? What of it, man?' roared John. 'That horse belonged to the dead man, as can be tes- tified from when they were last seen together in Honiton.'

Gervaise de Bonneville and Baldwyn listened intently to this exchange, as did Gwyn, Thomas and the group of inquisitive jurymen. Village reeves were as unpopular as sheriffs or coroners: they were the agents of the manorial lord and chivvied the serfs from dawn to dusk.

Ralph turned this way and that like a cornered fox, but the coroner allowed him no escape.

'I don't know where the beast came from,' he muttered desperately.

John sneered, 'It just walked into your croft and tied itself to your peg. Are you going to have the audacity to tell me that a dead man turns up in the village and a horse, identified as his, also appears by sheer coincidence?'

Ralph stared at the ground.

'I found her,' was all he could manage to mutter.

'Speak up, man! Let's all hear what you have to say!' shouted the coroner.

'I found her, I tell you! She was wandering the woods between here and Dunstone, grazing among the trees. She was without an owner – I thought he may have been thrown and injured or killed, maybe miles away, so I brought the mare back here for safe keeping until she was claimed.'

'Ha! A likely story. Did you make any effort to find the owner? This man who may have been thrown from his horse and injured or killed?'

The reeve was silent.

'When did you "find" this animal?'

'Er, about a week ago . . . a week last Sunday. I was taking my ease and walking to Dunstone to visit the reeve there.'

'To visit your fellow reeve, eh? The last time I saw you two together you almost came to blows!'

The sullen Ralph had no answer.

'So did this horse have any saddle or harness?'

'No, nothing – she was just wandering, I tell you, cropping the grass here and there among the trees. God knows how far she had roamed.'

'And you made no connection between the singular arrival of this unusually patterned horse and the finding of a soldier's body in your stream?' asked John sarcastically.

'Why should I? I found the beast days before the body appeared. I had no cause to connect the two.'

'Of course not. Widecombe is such a busy place that a murdered nobleman and a valuable stray horse are everyday occurrences, I suppose.'

Again the reeve could devise no answer.

'You lie, Ralph,' thundered the coroner, 'and I will check your story. First, though, I'll talk to that other rascal, Simon, the reeve from Dunstone, to see what he has to say about it.'

Ralph crumbled. 'He'll know nothing of this. It wasn't me that found the mare, it was Nebba. He sold her to me for six shillings. He wanted the money to leave the village.'

'Ha, so Nebba's name crops up again, eh?' said John, sharply. 'And where is he now? Are you telling me he's left?'

'He went the day you held the inquest, Crowner. Just up and went, we didn't know where he came from and we don't know – nor care – where he's gone. The village has had nothing but bad luck since he walked in from the forest.'

John turned to be Bonneville and his squire. 'That mare is forfeit to the Crown, as a chattel of a slain man – but I think you should take her home with you to Peter Tavy. Though in no way compensation for the loss of your brother, she may be some living reminder of him.' He turned back to Ralph. 'As for you, you've not heard the last of this.'

The reeve stared sullenly at the ground. 'I'm tempted to drag you back to Exeter gaol as a suspect for the murder, but the city won't thank me for another mouth to feed at public expense. I know where to find you and I amerce the village in the sum of a further ten marks to ensure that you don't vanish into the forest as soon as my back's turned.'

Gervaise de Bonneville and his squire had been talking together in low voices, their heads close together, when John interrupted them again. 'I regret this, but the law must be observed. I will take down your depositions on my rolls. The murder of a Norman gentleman is a serious matter, as well as being a sad one for your family.'

Gervaise's face was drawn, but he had recovered some of the colour he had lost during the exhumation. John realised that he had never been involved in any fighting or war campaign, which made violent death an unwelcome novelty.

'Who could have done this terrible thing?' he asked. 'And how am I to explain it to my father? And to Martyn – he was devoted to his eldest brother.'

John clasped his shoulder in sympathy. 'As to the perpetrator, we have much to do to investigate – the inquest is but a starting point. The forest is full of outlaws, as you well know, some of them dangerous and desperate men, yet your brother was a fully armed campaigner, well able to take care of himself unless he was outnumbered.'

Thomas returned and the sullen reeve assembled more than a dozen villagers to act as jury.

At the barn door, John took the evidence of Gervaise

and Baldwyn as to the undoubted identity of the slain man, all of which Thomas scratched down on his parchment roll. As no other witness came forward, at Gwyn's stentorian invitation, the coroner declared that death had been due to a murderous knife attack by persons unknown, and the formalities were concluded.

Before the jury dispersed to go about their business, Ralph had a blunt question for the coroner. 'What about this amercement you put on the village last time, Crowner?' There was a murmur of assent and much nodding by the surrounding peasants, who would have to find the money if the fine were collected.

'It stays, of course,' John asserted. 'You failed to present Englishry at the first inquest and now that we know the dead man was a Norman, your manor is in more trouble even than before.' He glared round at the ring of faces. 'That amercement is now converted into a murdrum fine, for having a slain Norman on your land and not bringing forth the culprit.'

The village crowd dispersed with much grumbling and Gwyn noticed that the reeve received some jostling and more than one hard dig in the ribs.

After he had ensured that Thomas had inscribed everything on his parchment roll, John led his party up the valley to claim a night's lodging from Hugh FitzRalph, the manorial lord who, though he must have heard about the murdered Crusader on his land, had until now kept aloof from the proceedings.

Next morning, soon after dawn, the two from Peter Tavy left, anxious to reach home and break the sad news to Martyn.

After their early-morning meal, the coroner and his men prepared to ride in the opposite direction. John had given his thanks to FitzRalph for his hospitality. However, if he had had any hope of getting home quickly to avoid further friction with Matilda, it was soon dashed. Just as a their horses and the mule were being led out from the pasture behind the stables, a solitary horseman, dressed in the conical helmet and leather cuirass of Rougemont Castle's soldiery, came up the track at a fast trot and swung himself agilely from the saddle right in front of the coroner. John recognised him as one of the men who had brought back Alan Fitzhai from Honiton. He saluted and fished inside his belt-pouch.

'The reeve in the village said you would be here, Sir John. The sheriff sent me last evening. I slept the night at the roadside.' He held out a crumpled piece of vellum, which John, rather self-consciously, passed to Thomas to read.

The former priest unrolled it and scanned the few sentences. 'It's written by the sheriff's scribe, at his direction. It tells of another body found by shepherds on Heckwood Tor, up on the moor, apparently another murder by knife. It was known about for some time, but a carter only brought news of it to Exeter yesterday. The sheriff wishes to know if you will deal with it as you are so near or . . .' He trailed and looked somewhat furtively at the coroner.

'Well, go on! How does it end?' John was impatient.

Thomas cleared his throat. 'It says do you want to deal with it or shall it be handled properly by the sheriff's men?'

John spat on the ground, as if to rid his mouth of the taste of Richard de Revelle. Then he put a foot in his stirrup and hoisted himself up to Bran's broad back. 'I'll show him "properly", damn the man!' he muttered. 'Gwyn, find out exactly where this place is – and you, soldier, you've travelled all night so get some food and rest here at the manor house. Tell the bailiff that you're the sheriff's messenger.'

Within minutes, John, Gwyn and Thomas were moving off, back down the valley to Widecombe and then westward on to Dartmoor, following the track of the two who had left an hour before. Gwyn had discovered from the manor bailiff that Heckwood Tor was half-way to Tavistock, just off the road they had travelled the day before. The nearest village was Sampford Spiney.

It was three hours' ride, especially as Thomas's mule seemed less inclined to keep trotting than it had when they left Exeter. John wondered if he should have confiscated the grey mare for his clerk, instead of rashly returning it to the family – but he doubted that the puny Thomas could have handled it.

When they reached the place described by the bailiff, it seemed certain to the trio that the most prominent tor must be the one named in the note, but not a soul was in sight to confirm it.

'What now?' asked Gwyn, looking around the bare moor.

John was angry that the local population seemed so unaware or heedless of the new royal office. It was not that he felt a personal slight at this indifference, but that his unfailing devotion to King Richard interpreted this widespread apathy as a mild form of treason. He was silent, so Gwyn suggested, 'Let's get up there and look for ourselves.'

They turned their mounts about and plodded up the prominent hill to the south of the track. As they rose, they could see over the crest of the right shoulder of the tor into a deep dip where a flock of several hundred sheep was being guarded by two shepherds and their dogs.

'Go down and see what they know,' John commanded. Gwyn urged his horse over the crest, and a few moments later, John saw him haul one shepherd on to the back of the big mare. The pair came back to where the coroner waited with his clerk.

'He knows where the body lies. It's still there, above us in the crag.'

With the young shepherd clinging on behind and giving directions, they all climbed almost to the top of the tor, where granite boulders lay in tumbled disorder. The shepherd, clad in shapeless woollen garments little better than rags, slipped from the horse and ran the last few yards, vanishing into a cleft between two grey rocks that were each the size of a small hut.

The others had dismounted and John left Thomas to hold their mounts. By the time the coroner and Gwyn had caught up, the shepherd was crouched over a bundle lying at the foot of a rock face. He was prodding it with a piece of stick and muttering to himself, which suggested to John that he was simple.

'What have we got here, boy?' growled Gwyn, pushing the lad aside with his leg.

It was the badly decomposed body of a man in a sitting position against the rock. Unlike the one in Widecombe, it was partly mummified. The skin of the face was almost black, and leathery, stretched tightly over the cheekbones like a mask on a skull. The eye-sockets had collapsed to deep holes and the lips had dried to an open circle, as if the corpse was uttering an eternal cry. The hands, protruding from a brown leather jacket, were like bundles of sticks, the skin dried tightly around spidery finger-bones, with loosened nails on the ends.

'The sun and the wind have shrivelled him instead of the usual corruption,' observed John, with his usual detached interest.

'How long has he been dead, I wonder?' ruminated Gwyn, tapping the hard skin of the forehead with his knuckle.

'In the desert, in the burning sun and dry air, they can stay like this for months – even years,' said the coroner, veteran of Palestine. 'But here the maggots, the foxes and the rats would see him off in a few months, so I reckon on five or six weeks.'

He turned to the shepherd, a slack-jawed lad of about fifteen who was crouching nearby, gaping at these visitors from another world. 'When did they find this, boy?'

'Bout two weeks back, sir. I can't reckon time very well, but it was past a couple of church days ago. Will Baggot found it, looking for a missing ewe up here. He told the reeve a few days after, back in Sampford Spiney.'

'A few days!' exploded John. 'No hue-and-cry, no one telling the sheriff or myself? I despair of these idle people.' But it was no use railing against the shepherd, who had no idea of what went on outside his little world.

'Let's have a proper look at him, Gwyn. Surely we have another soldier here.'

They examined his tough leather jerkin, with reinforced shoulder covers and studded sides. He still wore a tight-fitting cap, like a bowl of tough leather, with a deep flap to protect his neck. His legs were encased in strong linen breeches with boots coming above the ankles, spurs still in place.

'He has no baldric or sword belt, but the waist-loops of his breeches are snapped through,' said the Cornishman. 'I reckon his belt, with sword, scabbard and dagger, has been wrenched off.'

The coroner was looking at the man's boots. 'Eastern work again, I'm sure. That traced stitching is a Mussulman design, just like Hubert de Bonneville's. This is another Crusader.'

Gwyn stood up and regarded the corpse from head to toe. 'Yet he's no gentleman. His clothing is coarser and of less value. He'll be a squire or perhaps even a mercenary soldier.'

John nodded. 'But the great question is, how did he die? And why is his body up here, in this God-forsaken place? And how long has it been here?'

Gwyn had no answers. Then he spotted something and bent again to put a hand inside the front opening of the corpse's jerkin. He pulled out a small crucifix, made of some base metal like tin or pewter but of a complex design and good craftsmanship. Thin wires were wrapped around the shank of the cross, like crude filigree work. It was held on a leather thong around the neck and Gwyn tried to lift it free from the body for a better look. The shrunken head was flexed with the chin on the chest and Gwyn lifted it to free the thong.

'Look there, at the neck,' said the coroner.

Gwyn took off the thong, but held back the head to expose the front of the throat. The skin there had been protected from the elements and was white with a tinge of green. Across the throat, almost from ear to ear, was a wide slash, exposing the Adam's apple, the muscles and vessels of the neck.

'A cut throat, for a start,' said John sombrely. There was a strong bond between all those who had made the arduous journey to the Holy Land to fight the defilers of Jerusalem, and it saddened him to think that two had survived the often lethal rigours of the journey and the campaign only to be slaughtered like beasts on their return to their homeland.

With the shepherd boy watching, wide-eyed, John and Gwyn struggled to undress the body to examine the clothing and the skin surface for other clues. On both arms, and across the chest, were thin lines of hard scar tissue, typical of long-healed war wounds – both Gwyn and the coroner carried similar signs of sword and lance combat on their own limbs.

When they moved the body, they found beneath it an empty sheath, but there was no sign of the dagger it had once held. They rolled it over, an easy task as it had shrivelled to half its original weight. On the brown wrinkled skin of the back, there was something that raised the eyebrows of both the coroner and his attendant. Just to the left of the spine, whose knobs corrugated the stretched skin, was a one-inch slit, sharp at the lower end, blunt and slightly notched at the upper extremity. John stared at the wound, then at Gwyn. 'Same wound, same place,' he observed.

They let the body slump back to the ground, as Gwyn made a cautious response. 'Many a man gets stabbed in the back – and most knife blades are much of a muchness, so the slits are similar.'

John stood up straight and stretched his aching back. 'Two men on Dartmoor, both with Levantine accoutrements, both stabbed in the back within a few weeks of each other. Is that coincidence?'

Gwyn held his peace.

Unlike de Bonneville's, this man's clothing seemed intact, although the inside of the leather jerkin, the undertunic and shift were blackened by dried blood, which had poured from the arteries and veins of the slashed neck. A small slit in the back of the clothing corresponded with the stab wound, which did not appear to have bled much.

Under the cap, they found an area of crushed, bloodied scalp, though the cap itself had not been penetrated. The blond hair was cropped short.

'He was struck a heavy blow with some blunt object,' was John's opinion. 'Enough to make him lose his senses and not resist having his throat cut . . . though maybe, by then, he had also been stabbed in the back.'

'Another unexpected, cowardly attack?' suggested Gwyn.

John raised his stooped shoulders in a gesture of doubt. 'That Fitzhai fellow said that de Bonneville was travelling alone in Honiton. And we have no idea how long this corpse has lain here, though I have no doubt that he died weeks before de Bonneville. So what connection can there be?'

The ginger-whiskered Cornishman looked again at the gaunt cadaver. 'No one could identify this fellow by his face, that's for sure. And if his clothing and property are from Outremer, they will be unfamiliar to anyone here at home.'

'There's this crucifix, though . . . It looks like Cornish tin.' The coroner rolled up the thong and placed the ornament in his pouch. 'It's the best we have.

Someone may recognise it. You had better bundle up his clothing and that dagger sheath as well – at least they don't stink like the last one.'

As they walked to where Thomas was holding their horses, the coroner dwelt on his administrative duties. 'We must get an inquest over with today, I can't ride all the way out here again tomorrow.' There was no sun, but he looked up at the sky to see where the clouds were lightest, reckoning that it was not yet noon. 'Thomas, go down straight away with those shepherds to that village – what was it called?'

'Sampford Spiney, according to the North Hall steward.'

'Get them to send a cart up for the body – take it to the church there. Tell the clerk to raise a dozen souls for a jury and we'll get the man's pathetic remains put underground after a quick inquest – although with idiots like these living around here, it seems a waste of time. We'll learn precious little from them.'

CHAPTER TWELVE

In which Crowner John meets the Bishop

The coroner spent that night sleeping on the floor of his own hall in the house in St Martin's Lane. He got home just before the city gates were closed at dusk, having ridden hard from the futile inquest on the second body. When he got back, Mary fed him at the long table in the hall, whispering to him that the mistress had been shut in her room all day.

Dog-tired, he trudged up the outside stairs, resigned to facing Matilda's icy sulks, but when he pushed the door of the solar, it would not budge. He shoved harder, but it was barred on the inside. He hammered on the door, getting angrier by the second. He called and battered so hard on the stout panels that his neighbour, Godfrey Fitzosbern, a silversmith and master of his guild came out on the step of his own upper chamber.

Fuming, John reluctantly climbed downstairs and sought out Mary in the kitchen. 'She's locked me out, damn her eyes!'

The serving woman shrugged. 'She's been working up to it for days. You not coming home for three days and two nights has tipped her over the edge.'

'Am I to leave her, Mary?'

The maid shook her head calmly. 'No, it'll all blow

over. She's too fond of being the wife of the King's Crowner. She'd never survive the sneers of the other fine ladies. Sit tight a while and she'll come round.'

'So where can I sleep tonight, now that she has deprived me of my own bed?' he complained.

Mary stood with her hands on her hips and spoke to him like a mother to her whining child. 'Not with me, that's for sure! You've got a choice. You can go to the Bush and creep under the blanket with your mistress or you can bed down in your own hall. At least it's a roof over your head. Given the state your wife's in, I'd suggest staying here, unless you want another week or two banned from your own bedchamber.'

John saw the sense of this and Mary brought him a spare straw palliasse from the store and laid it in front of the hearth. She stoked the fire with large logs, and threw a blanket over the mattress and a rolled-up cloak for a pillow. 'I expect you've slept in worse places in Palestine and Austria,' she declared, with what John thought was a lack of feeling. But he sank gratefully into the makeshift bed, pulled the blanket over him and was snoring within ten minutes.

Next morning, he felt obliged to report to the sheriff. Much as John disliked him, he knew that he must keep the man informed of this most recently discovered killing, especially as it might concern another Crusader. After a solitary breakfast, he trudged up to the castle and squelched across the ever-muddy inner bailey to the keep. He climbed the steps above the undercroft to reach the central doorway, men-at-arms and sundry hurrying minions stepping aside respectfully for him.

The sergeant on guard at the inner door to the sheriff's chamber told John that Sir Richard was already closeted with someone from the cathedral, so with ill grace he paced the flagstoned floor.

In the crowded main hall, business was as brisk as usual, clerks at tables around the edge writing at dictation for supplicants who wanted some cause heard before the county court or some personal favour from the sheriff. Knights ambled about, looking lost without a local war or even a Crusade to divert them, and their squires, local landowners, merchants and guild masters sought contracts, curried favours or gossiped. One of these was his neighbour, a dissipated middle-aged man with a reputation for drink and wenching. John disliked him heartily and avoided him, to the annoyance of Matilda who was flattered by Godfrey Fitzosbern's lewd compliments when they met outside their house-fronts. He was a person of substance and influence in Exeter, being Master of the Guild of Silversmiths. His first words did not endear him to the coroner. 'What the devil was all that shouting on your stairway last night, de Wolfe? Did your buxom wife have her lover in there, eh?'

John muttered something under his breath and turned his back on Fitzosbern, a coarsely handsome man, now going rapidly to seed. He wandered off, impatient at the continued delay, pushing through the crowd until he saw Ralph Morin, the constable. John approved of him as a sensible, moderate man. Morin had been appointed by the King, not dependent on local politics for his office. Rougemont Castle was under the control of the Crown, a wise move made years ago when all the West Country was rashly given to Prince John as his own private kingdom. The castle was retained outside this grant and when Coeur de Lion over-generously forgave John for his sins the previous year, the Justiciar persuaded him to keep the major castles in his own hands.

As he waited on de Revelle's pleasure, John chatted to Rougemont's constable, which at least helped pass the time. Then Morin said something that jolted the coroner's attention. 'That fellow our sergeant brought back from Honiton a few days ago. I see you have him already in the castle gaol.'

John stared at him. 'You mean Alan Fitzhai, the man from Palestine?'

'Yes, I assumed it was your order that committed him.'

'Not at all. I've been in the countryside these past few days.'

The constable shrugged. 'Then it must have been the sheriff. You can ask him yourself – it looks as if he's free at last.'

Grimly, John strode to the door of de Revelle's chamber, where the guard had beckoned him to enter.

He was already talking as he walked up to the table, behind which sat his brother-in-law. 'Why have you clapped Fitzhai into gaol?' he demanded.

'Because he is the prime suspect in this foul killing,' replied Richard smoothly.

'There is no evidence of that,' snapped the coroner. 'Nothing further has come to light since we spoke with him the other morning. Why lock him up now?'

De Revelle sighed dramatically and toyed with a sheet of vellum on his table. 'My dear John, you are basically a soldier, no doubt a very good soldier but naïve in the ways of politics.'

The coroner scowled and brought his dark head

nearer the sheriff. 'Don't patronise me, brother-in-law. What are you trying to say?'

'That running a county – or even a country – is like a game of chess or a dance. There are certain set moves and gyrations that have to be made, according to the situation.'

'What the devil d'you mean? Speak plainly.'

Richard smiled superciliously. 'Yes, you're a plain man of plain speech, John. I mean that when persons with power want something done, it is as well at least to make a gesture in that direction.'

'What's that to do with Fitzhai being in chains?'

'He's not in chains – yet. Just enjoying our hospitality beneath this building.' The sheriff stroked his narrow beard. 'The truth of the matter is, which I did not know until yesterday, that the stricken Arnulph de Bonneville is an old and close friend of our bishop. Although Henry Marshall is usually away from the city, he happens to be here this week to conduct ordinations. He has heard of the murder and is pressing strongly for the malefactor who killed Arnulf's son to be found and hanged speedily.'

Light dawned on the coroner. 'Ah, I see. You need a scapegoat and Fitzhai is the nearest at hand.'

De Revelle shrugged delicately. 'He's the best we have.'

John threw up his hands in exasperation. 'There is not a shred of evidence against him.'

The sheriff smiled gently, as if humouring a child. 'That need be no obstacle to satisfying powerful men. I need not remind you that our Bishop Henry is brother to William, Marshal of all England . . . and there are ways of obtaining evidence that I feel inclined to employ.'

John saw that it was useless to argue with Richard, so he delivered his other news, telling the sheriff about the other murder they had now to investigate. Though it was the sheriff's own men who had passed on the news of a body on Heckwood Tor, they had not known that the man's throat had been cut and the matter had been too trivial to report to him. Now he seemed mildly interested, and asked when the man was likely to have been killed.

'Four to six weeks ago, I should say. Impossible to be accurate,' John replied.

'About the time that Alan Fitzhai came back to England and travelled to Plymouth, maybe across that Dartmoor track. Perhaps we can get him to confess to both murders.'

John was uneasy: the same thought had occurred to him, but in the absence of any pointer to Fitzhai's guilt he was not ready to offer up the man as a sacrifice to county politics.

But the sheriff was not yet finished. 'I'm glad you came in, John, it saves me the trouble of sending for you.'

'About what?' John said gruffly, smarting at the sheriff's still patronising manner.

'I said that the Bishop was concerned about the murder of his friend's son. Well, he has summoned us both to attend on him to discuss it, at the end of the chapter meeting today. We will be at the cathedral three hours after noon.'

John's scowl deepened. 'Are you going to dance so readily to the tune of these damned clerics?' he demanded.

The antipathy of town against Church was never far under the surface. The burgesses of Exeter resented the autonomy of the cathedral Close within the city. Even the sheriff and coroner had no jurisdiction other than to police the roads that traversed it.

But in this case Richard de Revelle seemed willing to toe the line, for the sake of his own political agenda. The Bishop and the Precentor had supported Prince John against King Richard and the coroner knew that de Revelle's sympathies had also lain strongly in that direction. John de Wolfe considered them traitors and could not understand why Richard had distributed pardons so readily, even rewarding his brother with favours, instead of throwing him into gaol.

'I trust that you will be there, John,' the sheriff continued. 'The Bishop confers regularly with our Archbishop from Canterbury.' This was a crude reminder that Hubert Walter had appointed John to the coronership.

'I'll be there, never fear,' he ground out. 'If only to see that you don't show too excessive zeal in prosecuting the law.'

Henry Marshall, Bishop of Exeter, lived in the shadow of his more famous brother, William, yet he had many worthy attributes of his own and was undoubtedly a more godly priest than many who wore the mitre. He was not primarily a fighting prelate, as was Hubert Walter, who had distinguished himself with a sword at the Crusades. Henry Marshall was an ascetic, who hankered after the true style of priesthood that had existed in Celtic times. Though he lived a life of comparative luxury, it was modest by the standards of most bishops. An example of his deep feelings for the Church was his introduction of the compulsory gift that had to be made every Whitsun by all the households in Devon and Cornwall of a halfpenny to the cathedral – a charitable act that was as popular as snow in August.

This was the man that Crowner John and his brother-in-law came to visit that afternoon. When they arrived the chapter meeting had just finished and the prebendaries were dispersing. When they, their vicars and acolytes had scurried away, the tall figure of the Bishop emerged, followed by Archdeacon John de Alecon. Behind him was Thomas de Boterellis, the Precentor. They processed from the chapter house to the adjacent cloisters, and the Archdeacon beckoned the coroner and the sheriff to join them in the calm, colonnaded quadrangle.

The usual greetings were made and both visitors knelt to kiss the Bishop's ring. Richard de Revelle did this with flourish and drama, the coroner with grudging resignation.

Bishop Henry, dressed in his informal robes of a dark cloak over a white cassock, a skull cap on his head, stopped between two arches to look out over the grassy plot. Unlike the close outside, this area was kept clean and tidy.

'This is a bad business, Richard,' he said, in his thin, high voice, ignoring the coroner for the moment. 'Arnulph de Bonneville was an old friend. Our families came from the same town in Normandy and we both have interests still in estates there.'

De Revelle exuded sympathetic concern. 'Indeed, your grace, it is sad for all concerned. The lord Arnulf is near death, so I understand, and to have his eldest son murdered in this foul way is a cruel blow to a dying father.'

Hypocrite, thought John. You've no concern about

the family. All you want is credit for hanging a suspect – any suspect.

John de Alecon turned to the coroner, determined to bring him into the conversation and to the notice of the Bishop. 'I understand that you saw Arnulf de Bonneville when you visited Peter Tavy. How did he seem to you?'

'He was half dead – and it would be a mercy if the other half came quickly. Mindless, paralysed and lying in his own mess – that's no way to delay in leaving this world.'

'God's will be done,' said the Bishop piously. 'None of us can choose the manner of his passing.' John stayed silent, thinking it indiscrete to mention his idea of a merciful pillow over the face.

Henry Marshall changed tack abruptly, again speaking directly to the Sheriff. 'What's to be done, Richard? It's intolerable that Norman gentlemen can be massacred in their own county. We need to teach the people a short, sharp lesson.'

De Revelle tapped the side of his nose. 'I have a suspect already in the gaol, your grace. I think we need look no further for the culprit than that.' He omitted to add that his culprit was also a Norman.

'Has he confessed?' snapped the prelate.

'Not yet – but I intend to put him to the Ordeal to settle the matter rapidly.'

At this the coroner bristled. It was the first he had heard of it. 'Wait a moment, Sheriff. The death of Hubert de Bonneville has been enrolled by a coroner, officially to be presented before the Justices in Eyre when they come next to Exeter. You may not take such a serious case outside the King's courts.'

The Bishop turned his cadaverous face with its

large watery eyes on John, as if seeing him for the first time.

The Sheriff put on his familiar martyred expression. 'My dear Crowner, you may have this odd interest in dead bodies, treasure-trove, wrecks, royal fish and the like, but you have no jurisdiction over suspects.'

'What's all this about?' asked the Bishop suspiciously.

De Revelle stepped in again. 'John de Wolfe thinks that he can investigate all deaths himself, since Archbishop Walter set up this pointless coroner system. Well, he can amuse himself by recording dead bodies, but the apprehension and punishment of felons remains my responsibility.'

The Bishop nodded. 'Of course, you represent the sovereign in Devon. I cannot see how anyone can think otherwise.'

Here the Archdeacon interjected craftily, 'Yet, my lord Bishop, our brother in Canterbury specifically introduced coroners into every county in the land only two months ago. We cannot lightly put aside what has been instituted so recently.' Henry Marshall twitched his cloak around him and scowled at John de Alecon – their antipathy, mainly due to opposing political allegiances, was well known. The Bishop had been appointed only that year, long after the Archdeacon who had been a member of the chapter for eight years and an archdeacon for four. If the Bishop had been there first, John de Alecon would never have been elevated and Henry Marshall would have liked to get rid of him now, but no excuse to do so had yet presented itself.

'In matters of investigating crimes, it is the Sheriff who has the first and last say,' he bleated. 'If he thinks this man in custody should be put to the Ordeal, then although I have no secular authority, I certainly give it my moral approval. This murder must be solved – and speedily, for the sake of my old friend, mortally sick though he be.'

'I shall see to it without delay, your grace,' said de Revelle increasingly. 'Perhaps you could appoint one of your priests to be present at the castle an hour after dawn tomorrow.'

The ritual of the Ordeal had religious origins, both Christian and pagan. It consisted of subjecting the suspect to physical challenge, usually a torment which often proved fatal, in order to seek a supernatural sign of guilt or innocence. Formerly, the Church had officiated at such ceremonies, usually on sanctified ground, but latterly it had been content to send a cleric to bless the proceedings – indeed, there had been murmurings from the Vatican that this barbaric ritual should be banned.

Bishop Henry had another warning to deliver. 'This bickering and schism between you custodians of the law must end. I would remind you that Archbishop Walter, who set up these recent matters, is due to visit the diocese soon. I'm sure that, as well as seeing to the spiritual health of his flock, he will want to know how his legal system is faring, so you must put a better face on your relationship. Is that clear?'

Without waiting for a response, he turned and walked solemnly away. The interview was over. With a smirk from the sheriff and a face like a thundercloud on the coroner, the players went their separate ways.

CHAPTER THIRTEEN

In which Crowner John attends an ordeal

Much against John's will, the Ordeal went ahead and, whether he liked it or not, he had to attend. His antagonism to the procedure was not due to humanitarian distaste – or even his healthy scepticism about its usefulness – but because it rankled with him that his brother-in-law could so easily interfere with the coroner's work. Unfortunately, as he had complained to Gwyn during their ride back from Dartmoor, there had been as yet no firm ruling from the royal justices as to how the jurisdiction of coroner and sheriff interlocked.

Reluctantly, John had to admit that the sheriff's task was to arrest suspects, investigate their crimes and either try them at the county court, or keep them in custody for the royal judges. It was clear enough that for theft, assault, treason and the like the sheriff had sole responsibility – but where there was a body, the coroner was obliged to record all the facts for the Justices in Eyre, even though he could not try the cases. He also had to examine rapes and serious assaults and record the facts – but it was not clear whether this should prevent the sheriff from trying these cases, as he had been doing for centuries, at least since the time of the Saxon king Aethelstan.

Whatever the rights and wrongs, de Revelle was intent on putting Alan Fitzhai to the Ordeal, and tomorrow morning was the soonest it could be staged.

After he had walked the short distance from the cloisters to his house, the coroner learned from Mary that his wife was still locked in her solar so, not in the mood for another confrontation, John took himself to the Bush, seeking beer and sympathy. Rather to his surprise, he found Gwyn sitting at one of the benches, tucking into a mutton knuckle and onions soaking into a slab-like trencher of bread.

'Has your wife thrown you out as well?' he asked, sitting on a stool opposite.

Gwyn stopped chewing on the bone to shake his head. 'Her brother, the one that's a carter, came through from Taunton on his way back to Polruan so she and the children have taken a ride on his wagon to see her mother. Won't be back for two weeks or more, when he makes the next trip.'

Nesta bustled up to give the new arrival a quart jar of ale and a quick squeeze on the shoulder. 'You've come at a busy time, John. I'll be with you when I've settled these folk in their penny beds.'

Half a dozen pilgrims, with wide-brimmed hats and tall staves, had just arrived on their way from Truro to Canterbury, and the businesslike innkeeper was hurrying about, shouting at her chambermaid to bring extra pallets for the upstairs dormitory and yelling at the cook to throw more meat into the pot.

John threw his black cloak on to a bench and took a deep swallow of his beer. 'So we're both temporary widowers, Gwyn. Thank God for taverns or we'd both starve and go mad with boredom. What that poxy clerk of ours does with his time I can't imagine. He never goes into an inn unless we're travelling.'

Gwyn gave one of his grunts and returned to tearing meat from his knuckle. When this was done, he wiped the fat from his moustache with the back of his hand.

'I heard about Alan Fitzhai,' he said. The fraternity of sergeants and men-at-arms in Rougemont seemed to have an almost instantaneous method of communicating gossip.

'That he's in the gaol or having to undergo the Ordeal?' asked John.

'Both. But I don't know if it's supposed to make him open his mouth wider – if he has anything to tell – or to prove his guilt or innocence.'

The coroner sank a good half-pint of ale in one swallow. 'It's supposed to determine guilt. These things were dreamed up by priests long ago, so they say, but I can't see the sense of it myself.'

Gwyn began to tear the gravy-soaked bread into lumps, which he stuffed into his mouth before answering. 'It's like this business of murder suspects touching the bier of a dead man, I reckon.'

John frowned, his craggy face furrowing. 'But that happened to our King when old Henry died at Chinon in 'eighty-nine.' The story went that when Richard the Lionheart had approached the body of his recently dead father in the abbey of Fontrevault, the corpse began to bleed from the nose and mouth. Richard had fallen to his knees and wept tears of guilt for having contributed to his father's death.

John wasn't ready to dismiss all such beliefs, even when they were to the discredit of his hero, Richard Coeur de Lion.

'But Richard didn't kill him, did he?' persisted Gwyn.

'Helped break the old man's heart when all his sons turned against him. I'd have expected it of that bastard John, but not my lord Richard.'

They were silent as they both played over old battles in their minds. Then John returned to practicalities. 'If the sheriff forces Fitzhai to prance across nine red-hot ploughshares or whatever he plans for the Ordeal, then we must try to get as much information out of him as possible beforehand about Hubert de Bonneville.'

Gwyn vigorously wiped the last of the onion gravy from the scrubbed table with the final crust and thrust it between his lips. 'And as quickly as possible, too,' he said, through a mouthful. 'Half the people I've seen go through the Ordeal die of shock or burns the same day.'

Nesta, her duties finished, bustled across and tried to push Gwyn from his stool. 'Go on, you've been fed well enough now. Go and sit by the fire with your pot and let me talk to John.'

Gwyn ambled away amiably to talk to a group clustered near the roaring logs, leaving Nesta alone with the coroner.

'Can you stay tonight?' she asked, directly.

He looked into her attractive, open face and wished that he could. 'It isn't politic, according to my maid,' he said, with a lopsided grin.

'The hell with her!' exploded the red-head, who had a temper to match her colouring. 'Since when has she decided who you sleep with?'

Patiently, John explained his domestic crisis, and his mistress's wrath subsided as quickly as it had arisen. She even laughed at the thought of him sleeping in his cloak on his own floor and gave him a quick kiss on the cheek.

'Well, unless you're thinking of leaving home for good and moving in here as a crowner-cum-innkeeper, you'd better toe the line, my lad.' Her advice was virtually identical to Mary's. Edwin, the one-eyed potman, limped over with a fresh jug of ale from a new barrel and leered at the pair.

'Good to see you back, Captain,' he croaked, with a wink at Nesta.

She kicked his lame leg hard and told him sharply to get about his business. 'What's the latest on this dead crusader, John?' she asked. 'Like your dear wife, I've not seen you these past few days.' Nesta was anxious to keep abreast of all the county gossip. Usually she was a one-woman intelligence service, thanks to all the comings and goings at the tavern, but she was not up to date on this case.

John told her of all that had transpired and of the torment that Alan Fitzhai would suffer next morning.

'Do you think he did it?' she demanded, taking a mouthful of his drink.

'How can I tell? He's hiding something, that's for sure. Something was between Fitzhai and the dead man, but that falls far short of suspecting him of murder.'

Nesta nodded sagely. 'You need a motive, that's what you need,' she said, profoundly. 'And what about this other corpse up on high Dartmoor? D'you think there's any connection?'

'They've both been in Palestine, obviously, and though he was corrupt, this last corpse had healed sword wounds not a year old. But that's not to say he was anything to do with de Bonneville, though he did have a similar stab wound in the back,' he added, thoughtfully.

John could almost hear Nesta's astute brain ticking away.

'Why not enquire in Southampton?' she said. 'Maybe to see if anyone was with the Widecombe man when they arrived from France. This Fitzhai knew him, so maybe someone else saw something. Did he say he was alone in Honiton?'

John agreed to send Gwyn next day to see what could be discovered at the various ports along the Dorset coast and on to Southampton, the main entry-point from Normandy.

'There! You need a woman's touch in this,' teased Nesta. 'You men don't have enough imagination.'

John slipped a hand under the table and squeezed her thigh. He was suddenly beginning to feel that there was more to life than discussing violent crime.

'Let's go up the ladder and discuss it in private, my girl,' he said quietly. 'I can't stay all night, but I won't be missed at home for a few hours.'

Next morning, an hour after dawn, they assembled in the sinister chamber below the keep of Rougemont Castle. It was half-subterranean, reached by a flight of steps leading down from the muddy bailey – a gloomy place, made ruddy by a few flaming torches stuck into iron rings set in the walls. Beyond it, on the same level, was the gaol. A passage left the main chamber, with a series of heavy doors leading off each side into cells furnished only with chains and dirty straw. John de Wolfe came down the steps with Thomas behind him. Gwyn had already set off eastwards to tour the ports.

In the dank, shadowy chamber, the sheriff, his

bailiff and the constable Ralph Morin were gathered together with Thomas de Boterellis, the cathedral Precentor, sent by his bishop to represent the Church. The guard sergeant and several men-at-arms stood watchfully around the walls.

As John walked in, he saw that they were grouped around a large iron bucket about three feet high, set on four big stones on the earthen floor. A fire of logs and charcoal burned in a clay-pit underneath, tended by Stigand the gaoler, a dirty, grossly obese man, who crouched on the floor feeding firewood under the bucket to keep the water boiling.

Richard de Revelle greeted his brother-in-law with false joviality, as if they were meeting for a pleasant breakfast rather than preparing to inflict a maiming torture on a healthy man. If the sheriff had heard of the quarrel between John and his sister, he avoided any mention of it and went straight to the business of the morning.

'You'll agree that this Fitzhai, though he be Norman of sorts, is a damned liar?' he said.

John agreed unwillingly that the fellow was almost certainly holding something back. 'But that doesn't make him a killer. Why should it?'

Richard, elegant as ever in a bright blue tunic, gestured his indifference. 'Let's see what he has to tell us when his mind is concentrated by our little ceremony, eh?'

The coroner scowled. 'Then give him a chance to divulge it all first. He may tell us all that is necessary without maiming the fellow?'

The sheriff tapped his nose, which he did almost as often as Thomas de Peyne crossed himself. 'We may get a confession as well. Kill two birds with one stone

– a very hot stone!' He laughed at his own joke and the Precentor, an overfed priest with a round, waxy-white face, joined in his amusement.

'It will fix his guilt or innocence as well, so that's three birds for us.' He sniggered.

John was not amused, but any more badinage was ended by the squeal of the gaol's barred iron gate.

Two soldiers pushed a bedraggled Alan Fitzhai into the big room. His hands were free but his ankles were shackled with rusted metal bands so that he could only shuffle and stumble as he was prodded by the guards. He was in a poor state, compared to the last time John had seen him. His clothes were the same, but they were crumpled and filthy, his hair and beard were tangled, his cheeks were hollow, and he blinked in even that poor light, which was bright compared to the Stygian gloom of the cells. As soon as he saw the sheriff, coroner and constable, Fitzhai began to shout his indignation and innocence, until one of the guards gave him a shove that sent him staggering over his manacled ankles.

De Revelle stepped forward to stand in front of the prisoner. 'Everything points to you as the man who did this foul killing,' he lied, 'but now you have a chance to prove your innocence, before the Church and officers of the King.'

Alan stared at him in amazement. 'King Richard! If he knew of my condition now, he would vouch for me to the hilt. I fought for him at Acre and Arsuf and Jaffa . . . and this is the reward I get!'

The sheriff, who had been no nearer to the Holy Land than Aquitaine, dismissed this. 'That's not the issue, Fitzhai. A fellow Crusader lies dead, as well as

another man back from the Holy Land – and you are
the best candidate for the crime.'

Fitzhai was frightened, but still pugnacious. 'Another
Crusader dead? Who is he? I know nothing of this.'

John moved to face the prospective victim. 'It's
plain there are things you did not tell us the other
day when you were brought from Honiton. If you
give us all the help you can, it may go better for
you.'

The mercenary soldier looked from the coroner
to de Revelle and back again. 'About Hubert de
Bonneville?'

John nodded. 'Everything you know . . . now!'

Fitzhai hesitated, then looked at the gaoler stoking
the fire under the boiler and decided to speak. 'If I
had told you a few days ago, you'd have taken it as
extra proof that there was more bad blood between
de Bonneville and me.'

John thought that telling it now was hardly going to
improve matters, but held his tongue and let Fitzhai
continue.

'When we landed in Marseille, I said that a group
of English and Welsh Crusaders decided to band
together and we made our way up through France
to take ship to Southampton.' He looked down at
his feet and shuffled them, making the fetters jangle.
'Well, like all soldiers, we did plenty of drinking and
carousing . . . and there were girls, of course. We
hadn't seen women for months – even years. Spirits
and passions ran high some nights.'

De Revelle became impatient. 'Come on, man, what
are you trying to say?'

'All of us had a girl or two on the journey, a tumble
in a tavern or a hay-barn. All except that prig Hubert,

of course. He should have been a priest.' He looked sourly at the Precentor.

'How did this get you at odds with him?' rapped the sheriff.

'Somewhere in Touraine I got drunk and took a girl in an inn. We were all the worse for drink, including the women. Afterwards the girl came to me with her father and accused me of raping her.' He raised his voice almost shrilly. 'It was no such thing! She was eager for it, then got scared of being with child and lied to her family.'

John had heard similar stories many times – sometimes they were true, sometimes not.

'Hubert de Bonneville became sanctimonious and sided with the father, demanding that I admit my guilt and pay off the girl and her father with gold. I told him to mind his own damn business and a fight started.' He stared truculently at the two law officers. 'Naturally, I won. I hammered the fool into a pulp. It started a wholesale mêlée in the tavern, between his friends and mine. Next day he went, cursing me and swearing that he'd get even one day. I never saw him again until Honiton. It was just a common fight, I forgot all about him afterwards.'

There was a silence, broken only by the crackle of the burning firewood.

'A likely story!' sneered the sheriff. 'He probably hammered you and it's you who waited for your revenge.'

'Who is there to support this tale?' asked the coroner.

Fitzhai shook his head. 'All concerned are long melted to the four corners of the kingdom. But it's true, I tell you . . . and I wish by the Virgin Mary that

I'd never clapped eyes on the man in Honiton, even at a distance.'

John was somewhat inclined to believe him: the story rang true, of a typical squabble among travelling soldiery. But there was no proof either way and he saw no logical way of finding it. He turned to the sheriff. 'There's nothing more he can tell us. What point is there in doing more – or even holding him in custody?'

De Revelle stuck a thumb in his ornate belt. 'I think he's lying. But what does it matter? We have the means to determine the truth.' He pointed his other thumb at the boiling water.

Fitzhai roared and tried to shuffle backwards, but another a blow from one of the guards caused him to trip and fall full length on the beaten-earth floor.

The Precentor, who wore his white surplice under a long black cloak, placed an embroidered stole around his neck, produced a prayer book and began to intone an endless dirge in Latin, incomprehensible to all but Thomas de Peyne, who began to cross himself furiously.

John lost patience with them all. 'This is a pointless ritual, which serves no purpose but to show the Bishop that something is being done to satisfy the de Bonneville family.'

Abruptly de Boterellis stopped his Latin monologue and glowered at the coroner. 'Have care, de Wolfe. What you are saying is perilously near sacrilege. The ceremony of the Ordeal is hallowed by Christian usage and sanctioned by the Holy Father in Rome, as well as all our bishops. To call it a pointless ritual could be construed as blasphemy.' He resumed his reading and the sheriff stalked to the tall bucket over the fire.

'Is the stone already at the bottom?' he demanded of Stigand.

'It is, sir, a full two-pound weight, a pebble from the river bed. The one we always use for the test.'

Ralph de Morin, as constable of the castle, was the commander of the guard and now signalled to the men-at-arms to start the proceedings.

Alan Fitzhai struggled violently against the grasp of his two guards, but they dragged him towards the vat of boiling water. As the steam billowed about his head, he screamed, 'Why are you doing this to me? I've told you what you wanted to know.'

Richard de Revelle and the Precentor looked on impassively, but the coroner was more than uneasy. 'The man has nothing more to tell us!'

The sheriff rounded on his brother-in-law. 'Whatever you claim your duties to be, your business here is as a witness only, so hold your tongue.'

John could not dispute this, so he watched reluctantly as Fitzhai was manhandled to the tall bucket.

The Precentor mumbled another Latin passage from his book, then closed it and held up his right hand, two fingers together pointing at the roof, the others folded in his palm. He chanted some unintelligible exhortation in a high falsetto, while the sheriff addressed the still struggling and cursing Fitzhai. 'You are fortunate, partly because we acknowledge that you are a Norman and have taken the cross to fight in the Holy Land.'

Fitzhai spat contemptuously at the vat, his spittle hissing into vapour as it hit the hot metal. 'Fortunate! A bloody strange way you have of regarding my virtues.'

De Revelle ignored this. 'You could have been made

to carry the hot bar or walk the ploughshares. This ordeal of boiling water is the mildest of all.' He pointed at the bubbling surface. 'You must know well enough what is to be done. You will reach to the bottom of the bucket, using your right arm to your armpit, to seek the stone that lies on the bottom. You will take it out and drop it upon the ground.'

Fitzhai went pale as time ran out without reprieve, but when hope had gone, he was brave enough, except for one thing. 'I beseech you, not my right arm! Let me use the left.'

Richard de Revelle stared at him in surprise. 'What difference does it make, man?'

The priest stopped chanting his dirge to say, 'It must be the right arm. It is always the right arm.'

John de Wolfe, a soldier himself, knew well why the victim made the request. 'He's a fighting man, he makes his living by battle. Ruin his sword arm and he'll have no means of livelihood.'

Fitzhai looked gratefully at the coroner, who seemed to have a trace of sympathy with him.

The sheriff was impatient with these trivia. 'Use whatever damned arm you please! Now off with your tunic and shift.'

The imminence of agony again broke his self-control and, against his struggling, the guards pulled off his upper clothing, leaving Fitzhai's torso, rippling with muscle, naked in the flickering torchlight. He stood shivering with fearful anticipation while the priest again stopped chanting and began to speak. 'You will remove the stone from the water, as is ordained by the usage of the Holy Church. Your guilt or innocence of the crime with which you are suspected will be determined by the preservation of your arm. If you are innocent, God will protect it, if not, the signs of scalding will be apparent.' Though John had witnessed ordeals before, the futility of the ritual was too much for him to remain silent.

'How can the signs not become apparent, if the fellow has to grope around in a bucket of boiling water?'

De Boterellis looked coldly at him. 'Are you questioning the wisdom of the Holy Father's pronouncements on a Christian purpose that has existed since time immemorial?'

Fortunately, John had the sense not to pursue the matter – even the King's coroner was not immune to charges of sacrilege.

'That's enough of this delay,' snapped the sheriff. 'Get on with it.'

He stood aside and the Precentor made the sign of the cross over the bucket, mirrored by Thomas who skulked in the background.

The guards shoved Fitzhai to the edge of the bucket, where he had a final spasm of cursing and shrinking back from the rim of the vat. One of the soldiers grabbed his left arm and forced it towards the water. At last, accepting the inevitable, the Crusader screamed, 'Let me be, I'll do it my way!'

With a wild shout of defiance and despair, he plunged his arm into the bubbling, steaming liquid. Screaming in agony through clenched teeth, he bent so that his shoulder was almost in the water, groping desperately at the bottom, circling the base to find the rock.

With a great cry of agonised triumph, he threw himself sideways to hurl the stone out of the bucket. It flew across the dungeon and bounced off a wall, to lie steaming on the muddy floor.

Fitzhai crumpled to the ground, keening in pain and attempting to shield his scalded arm with his good one. Thomas de Peyne was quietly vomiting against the wall, until John curtly told him to pull himself together and make a record of the event.

The sheriff and the Precentor murmured together in low voices while the men-at-arms, as sympathetically as they could without attracting the attention of Ralph Morin or the sheriff, lifted Fitzhai from the floor. They supported him while the gaoler shuffled across with a few handfuls of fresh hay and some rags. Well used to these mutilating ordeals, he studied the burned arm with clinical interest, inspecting the fiery red skin, the early swelling and loosening of the surface layer.

Spreading the hay over the limb, which worsened the excruciating agony of the victim, he wound the grubby rags around the arm to hold it in place.

Thomas de Boterellis stopped muttering to the sheriff and addressed Fitzhai, who was now dead white in the face and leaning heavily against one of the soldiers. 'Your fate will be judged at noon, when the arm will be inspected. A ruddy hue is to be accepted as inevitable and will not deny your innocence. But if Almighty God causes the arm to blister, peel or suppurate, then your guilt is proven.'

'And you will be hanged!' added the sheriff robustly.

'After a trial before the Justices in Eyre,' snapped John, 'because the death for which you accuse him of murder was recorded in my rolls before you took him into custody.'

De Revelle gave one his patronising sighs. 'He goes back into the gaol, whatever is decided about when he is to be hanged.'

'Prejudging it again, Richard?' boomed the coroner.

'The arm has not yet been examined. The miracle of innocence might take place, for all we know.'

The look that the sheriff gave the coroner in response to his jibe suggested strongly that he had as much faith in the Ordeal as John and was looking forward to the hanging.

'We shall see, Crowner, we shall see.'

CHAPTER FOURTEEN

*In which Crowner John receives
news from Southampton*

The long palisade of turreted wall brooded over the busy quayside. Ships of all sizes, their yards carrying furled sails tilted up against the masts, berthed end to end against the wharf. Barrels, bales and boxes were being hurried up and down a host of gangplanks that levelled off gradually as the tide went down in the Solent.

Gwyn of Polruan ambled from tavern to inn, from inn to lodging house along the half-mile of rambling dockside. Huts, shanties and storehouses were built against the landward bank, amid the more solid houses of ship-owners and wool-traders. He had arrived the night before, after coming along the coast through the smaller ports of Lyme, Bridport, Weymouth and Poole. None had turned up any sightings of Hubert de Bonneville and Southampton was now his main hope. It seemed unlikely that the returning Crusader would have crossed the Channel further east, if the group that contained Fitzhai had intended to make for the Normandy coast at Harfleur.

By mid-morning the massive Cornishman had visited a dozen drinking places on the quayside and even his iron constitution was beginning to feel the effects of a jar of ale in almost all of them. He sat for a moment's respite on a bollard, a tree-stump set in the stone wharf, grooved by the hawsers of a thousand ships that had been tied to it. One such vessel was straining at it now, the ropes creaking as the hull moved slightly on the swell that flowed in from the sea beyond the Isle of Wight.

It was a Flemish boat and was being loaded with bale after bale of English wool, squeezed into hessian bags and tied tightly with cords. A succession of labourers trotted up the gangway in pairs, each holding one end of a large sack.

After a few moments, Gwyn's head cleared and he suddenly discovered that he was hungry, needing something solid to soak up the lake of beer swilling around in his stomach. He left the tree-stump and went diagonally across the crowded quayside, dodged by handcarts, jogging porters, sailors and merchants. Wagons drawn by bullocks and dray-horses creaked slowly along the wharf, heaped with bales of wool, or barrels and jars of wine, kegs of dried fruit from southern France and dried meat and fish to victual the King's army in Normandy. The air was redolent with a hundred smells, from the spices of valuable cargoes to the ubiquitous stench of dung that dotted the ground from the draught animals.

Gwyn picked his way through the odorous puddles and stepped over ropes, heading for the next tavern, a large wood-framed hut with plastered wall-panels and a roof of bark shingles. Over the single door swung a crude gilded metal crown. Inside, the smoky, noisy interior was bustling with as much activity as the docks outside. Gwyn used his bulk to shoulder a way to a vacant space on a plank bench under a window, which was merely a hole in the wall with wooden bars set vertically.

Eventually a slatternly girl with a strange accent that Gwyn thought might be from the distant North, understood his Cornish *patois* well enough to bring him horse-bread, cheese, mutton and more beer. As he filled himself, he looked into his purse to see how his funds were lasting. He had been two nights on the road and would need another two to get back to Exeter. The whole trip would cost at least eightpence and he wondered again where Master John found the money.

He knew the knight had a fair income from his wool partnership, but Gwyn assumed that he also kept back some of the deodand and felony confiscations for working expenses.

As he was chewing and meditating on his master's finances, the man next to him drank up and left. Almost immediately the space was claimed by a bigger fellow, who dropped heavily on to the bench and bumped against Gwyn, jolting the arm that was just pushing a piece of cheese beneath his red moustache.

'Sorry, mate – crowded in here, by God.'

As he had had the grace to apologise, Gwyn mumbled something neutral, then noticed that the man, who had cropped hair and a bull-like neck, had the appearance of a soldier. He wore the same type of thick leather jerkin as Gwyn and a heavy belt carrying a curved dagger of distinctly Eastern pattern. As the newcomer waved hopefully at the serving girl, he displayed a wide gold ring with a crescent-moon motif carved into it.

Using the camaraderie of the militia to start up a

conversation, Gwyn struck a rich vein of information. The fellow was Gruffydd, a Welshman of Gwent, so he could converse with him well enough in his own Cornish. Gruffydd had been in Palestine for almost two years and his service as a mercenary archer overlapped the period that Gwyn had spent there with John de Wolfe. They had places, people and battles in common.

'I came back only two months ago and am now hired to recruit more men for the King's present campaign against Philip of France.'

Gwyn asked if he knew any other returning Crusaders, especially Hubert de Bonneville or Alan Fitzhai. Gruffydd let out a bellow of affirmation and slapped Gwyn's shoulder. 'How the devil do you know those two?' he demanded cheerfully. 'They were both through here at different times. I offered Fitzhai a new contract to fight in France, but he said he had to visit his woman first and if he could find no fighting work down West, he would come back here to me – but I never saw him again.'

Gwyn shook his head over his beer. 'Nor will you, unless you have use for a one-handed swordsman.' He told the story, ending with Fitzhai's appointment with the ordeal.

The Welshman was concerned; he had a soft spot for the extrovert Fitzhai. 'And all this was over de Bonneville? And he's slain?'

'Fitzhai is in gaol as the prime suspect – on very little evidence.'

Gruffydd shook his big head. 'I can't see him as a murderer – a killer, yes, but only when he's paid to do it in battle.'

Gwyn finished up his food and washed it down with

beer. 'That's not what the sheriff thinks, though he's keen for a culprit at any price. But tell me more about de Bonneville.'

The story came out readily enough from the Welshman. He told Gwyn of the gossip about the fight the two men had had in France, which was news to the Cornishman as he had left Exeter before Fitzhai had blurted out the story. However, Gruffydd took little account of this, like the coroner considering it a commonplace rough-house between rowdy soldiers. But he also told Gwyn that Hubert de Bonneville had had a squire, a Saxon called Aelfgar of Totnes. The two had met in Palestine and had travelled home through France together, in the same party as Alan Fitzhai. Gwyn tried to get a description of Aelfgar from Gruffydd, but apart from saying that he was a burly thickset fellow with fair hair – which applied to half the Saxons in England – the other was not very helpful.

'Did they leave this port together to travel to Devon?' asked Gwyn, with little hope of more information.

Surprisingly, the other man shook his head. 'No, they didn't. I tried to sign Aelfgar on for the French wars – I get a penny for every recruit,' he explained. 'But he wanted to go home to Totnes first. And, anyway, his master sent him on ahead to his own manor, some place far out beyond Dartmoor, as I remember.'

'Why didn't they travel together?'

'De Bonneville had six of his own soldiers with him. They had all travelled back from Marseille and he wanted to pay them off in Southampton. Aelfgar told me, when he was making excuses for not joining my mercenaries, that his master wanted to sell some gold loot he had acquired in Outremer. He needed the money to pay his men and wanted silver coin himself, so he was going to spend some time touring the goldsmiths and bargaining for the best price.' Gruffydd grinned and prodded Gwyn with his elbow. 'I think he wanted a week in the Southampton brothels.'

Gwyn considered this in the light of the mouldered corpse up on Heckwood Tor. 'So the squire goes off ahead of de Bonneville. And when did his master follow – any idea?'

But Gruffydd had exhausted his information. 'No, sorry, I don't know that. I saw him in the distance in the town more than two weeks after I spoke with Aelfgar, who was leaving that day. But de Bonneville could have stayed here longer than that, for all I know.'

Gwyn bought them both another pot of ale and they sat drinking companionably. Then Gwyn tried another question as a long shot. 'I suppose you haven't come across another Saxon soldier recently, a fellow with two of his fingers missing?'

The Welshman roared with laughter and slapped Gwyn on his broad back. 'Two fingers missing! I know twenty or thirty men who've run foul of either Philip's army in France or the wrong barons in England. And quite a few bowmen, most of them from Gwent, lost theirs picking the wrong side when Prince John tried his tricks last year.'

'This one's called Nebba.'

Gruffydd's mirth increased. 'Nebba! That son of a bitch! I wouldn't trust him further than I could throw a donkey!'

Gwyn's ginger eyebrows rose up his forehead in surprise. This fellow seemed to know every soldier in Christendom. 'Tell me about him, for God's sake! He's not another of this bunch that landed from Harfleur, is he?'

The mercenary shook his head. 'No, not Nebba. Crusading's not his style, though he'd sell himself to any army that paid the best. He came back from the Vexin a few months ago – he'd been fighting for Richard, but some Frenchmen caught him and deprived him of his fingers. He was lucky to lose them and not his private parts or his head.'

'So what happened to him?'

Gruffydd chuckled. 'I'd signed him up to go back to Normandy as a spearman since he could no longer pull a long-bow. While he was waiting for the ship, he ran short of money so he robbed a merchant's house, here in Southampton. The merchant caught him at it, there was a fight and Nebba stabbed him dead.'

Gwyn ran a hand through his tangled beard. 'Stabbed, eh?'

'That's the usual way of killing people in peacetime,' guffawed the Welshman. 'Anyway, he ran like hell ahead of the hue-and-cry and got to St Michael's Church and claimed sanctuary.' He stopped for a vast swallow of beer.

Gwyn looked at him expectantly. 'What happened then?'

'Oh, he broke out a couple of days later and legged it for the New Forest. The townsfolk guarding the church were pretty half-hearted. They had better things to do than a day-and-night vigil over a thief. So he turned outlaw and vanished into the woods. I lost my penny commission because he missed the boat for France. God alone knows where he is now.'

Gwyn grunted into his ale. 'I can tell you where

is. He's hiding out in a village near Dartmoor.' He pondered in silence for a moment. Could this Nebba have been mixed up in the death of de Bonneville? He had been stabbed and Nebba was a stabber – but Gruffydd was quite right that stabbings were as common as Thomas de Peyne's habit of crossing himself. Yet it was strange that the archer had turned up in two places associated with Hubert. He gave a mental shrug and took a dismissive swig of beer. 'The Crowner will be interested to hear about him, but I'm not convinced he could have had anything to do with our present problem.'

Gwyn could get nothing further from Gruffydd and, after buying the Welshman a last quart of beer and indulging in some more talk of Crusading, he decided to start for home. At least he now knew that de Bonneville had had a henchman, what his name was and that he seemed to have vanished at least a couple of weeks earlier than Bonneville's death. And Nebba's name kept cropping up.

He went back to his lodging to fetch his horse and begin the long trek back to Exeter.

The Cornishman returned to tell the story to Crowner John two days later, at the end of the afternoon, up in the gatehouse chamber. Wearily, he climbed the narrow stairway to the sounds of chanting drifting up from the little chapel of St Mary just inside the main gate.

Ralph Morin was already with the coroner and Gwyn listened to what he was saying. 'I fear for his life – he may not last long enough to be hanged,' he said. 'His whole arm is suppurating from shoulder to fingertips. I think that binding it with hay makes it

worse – I'm sure there some poison in mouldy grass
that produces pus.'

'Is he still in that foul cell?' asked John.

'He is indeed – and that gross imbecile Stigand
has not the faintest notion of how to treat a sick
man. Fitzhai is delirious with fever from that septic arm. He'll be dead in a day or two, barring a
miracle. And, of course, de Revelle and the Precentor take it for the judgement of God in proving
his guilt – though I think the sheriff would prefer to hang him, rather than lose him to suppu-
ration.'

The constable turned to leave and John called after
him that he would try to get the sick prisoner moved
to the care of the nuns, who had at least some idea
of hygiene.

'So what news have you found for me, Gwyn? Tell
me, while the little fellow is exercising his Latin.'

Thomas was sitting at the table finishing details of
that morning's hangings on his roll. Unusually, one
of the executed criminals had been a fairly rich
grain merchant, with land both outside the walls
in Southernhay and a manor at Teignmouth. He
had been caught out in an established fraud involv-
ing short weight in both buying and selling corn.
It was rumoured that several prominent burgesses
had covered up for him, for a cut of the proceeds,
but political power had kept their names out of
the scandal, the merchant himself being used as
the scapegoat. John had suspicions about Godfrey
Fitzosbern, his odious next-door neighbour in St Martin's Lane, but nothing could be proved. In any event,
the county court, spurred by howls of indignation
from the Guilds, had sent the man to the gallows,

when undoubtedly a number of eminent citizens had breathed a sigh of relief that his mouth was now finally closed. The coroner was keen to see that the value of his goods and land, forefeit to the Crown, reached the Treasury and were not spirited away by others. He therefore had Thomas making a detailed inventory of the merchant's estate and a full record was being inscribed on the rolls.

While the clerk was busy with his quill and ink, John heard Gwyn's account of his fortunate encounter with the Welshman in Southampton. 'At least we know there was a squire and that he was sent on ahead of de Bonneville to announce his master's coming,' concluded the coroner's officer. 'And this man Nebba seems to flit in and out of our sight, but how he could be involved I can't tell.'

John pondered the news, the lines running down from the corners of his mouth deepening as he concentrated. At length, he said, 'One question leads to even more problems. First, is this stabbed and cut-throated corpse really Aelfgar? And why did no one from Peter Tavy enquire about Hubert's squire?'

Squatting in his favourite place on the sill of the window-slit, the Cornishman ran his fingers through his red moustache. 'The last question is easy to answer. As far as I know, they knew nothing of Aelfgar's existence. When he left for the Crusades, he joined a few men from the Tavistock area who had taken the cross and journeyed in a group to take ship across the Channel. Hubert could have met Aelfgar anywhere between here and Acre.'

John accepted the explanation. 'But that means that they would have no means of identifying the body, even if it was in good enough a condition still to

show his features. So how the devil are we going to
know if it's this man or not?'

'He's from Totnes,' said Gwyn reasonably. 'Enquiries
there will no doubt confirm it. The problem is that,
unlike Hubert, he's beyond recognition from putrefaction by now. Even his own mother wouldn't know
him.'

'And his clothing and effects are useless, if he's been
a year or two in the Levant . . . But wait a moment –
what about that strange crucifix?'

Gwyn got up and went to the rough wooden chest in
the corner where oddments were kept. He rummaged
inside and took out the crude ornament that had
hung around the dead man's neck, together with the
empty dagger scabbard. 'But this may have come from
Palestine too,' he objected.

John took the little cross from him and looked at
it, turning it over in his powerful fingers. 'No, it's
almost pure tin. Most of the tin in the world comes
from Devon and Cornwall, so maybe he took it to
Outremer to remind him of home. Someone might
recognise it – I've not seen anything like it before.'

He snapped his fingers at the clerk. 'Up at dawn in
the morning, Thomas. You can goad that mangy mule
of yours across to Totnes, then on up to Dartmoor, to
see what you can discover about this Aelfgar.'

Thomas groaned and Gwyn, hugely amused by
his dejection, snatched the feathered quill from his
fingers and stuck it behind Thomas's ear.

'Cheer up, priest. Totnes is famed for its pretty girls.
You'll be a real hit with them – better than goosing
novice nuns, eh?'

If the clerk's crooked eye could have killed, Gwyn
of Polruan would have dropped dead on the spot.

CHAPTER FIFTEEN

*In which Thomas de Peyne plays
the spy on Dartmoor*

The following day, even though a chill easterly wind was whirling the autumn leaves from the trees, a slight thaw was noticeable in St Martin's Lane. While John was eating breakfast in solitary state in the gloomy hall, Matilda suddenly appeared and sat down at her place at the opposite end of the long table.

No words were spoken and she ignored him, but this was at least a start in the peace process after a whole week's hostilities. Mary came in and quietly set some food and a cup of hot wine in front of her mistress, winking at John over the folded white linen of Matilda's headdress.

The coroner murmured a greeting, which his wife seemed not to hear, then maintained a discreet silence, hoping to avoid any careless remark that might reopen the battle.

At the end of this strained meal, Matilda rose and stalked to the door. John, with uncharacteristic gallantry, hurried to open it for her and was rewarded with a murmur that he assumed was thanks, before she vanished to the seclusion of the solar.

'Things are looking up, Sir John,' observed Mary, cheerily, as she bustled in to clear the debris on the table.

'The mistress seems to be coming round slowly,' he whispered, always conscious of the solar window high in the wall above. The maid clattered together the two platters and mugs and brushed the remaining crusts to the floor for Brutus to chew.

'You've been a good boy the last few days, coming home every night and not spending too much time in the Bush,' she murmured. 'I reckon you'll get your bed back tonight and not have to sleep in front of the fire.'

As she went out of the door with the dishes, he reached out a hand to pat her curvaceous bottom, but she swerved to evade him and wagged a forefinger in admonishment.

He grinned, which was rare these days, then took his dagger belt and short cloak from the vestibule before setting off in the biting wind for his chamber at the castle.

The same wind, bringing an occasional flurry of sleet, had chilled Thomas de Peyne for much of the day as he travelled from Exeter to Totnes and then up to the bleaker wastes of Dartmoor.

Although Gwyn of Polruan sneered endlessly at Thomas's mule – and even the coroner had hinted at providing him with a horse – the sturdy beast had kept up a steady trot all day. Although slow compared to the great animals that the other men possessed, the animal never seemed to tire and his daily mileage was almost as good as that of the horses.

Thomas reached Totnes about three hours after dawn and soon completed the first part of his business. Although unfrocked, he still had a rapport with his brother clergy, especially if they were unaware of his unfortunate history, so he usually made one of the parish priests his first port of call.

Over a jar of weak ale – which Thomas disliked, though there was little else to drink apart from cider and water – he soon learned that Aelfgar had indeed been a native of Totnes. He had been born there and his mother and sister still worked as laundry-maids in the manor house. They were pure Saxons, the mother's grandfather having been dispossessed of his considerable estate by the Normans soon after the Domesday survey that had followed the Conquest. The priest, himself half-Saxon, said this bitterly, but the thrust of his information was that Aelfgar, a professional man-at-arms, had gone away some five years earlier and had not been heard of since. It was assumed that either he had been killed in battle or he was in some distant land, fighting as a mercenary. The priest's only description of him as a 'fair-haired man' was all but useless, but when Thomas fished in his scrip and pulled out the twisted tin crucifix, the cleric uttered a cry of surprise. 'I gave him that myself! He did me a service not long before he left. I fell from my donkey on the road to Paignton and broke my ankle. Aelfgar found me and brought me back home to safety so I gave him this cross as a token. My father is a tin-miner in Chagford and used to make these as a pastime.'

Having now established that the mummified body on Hackford Tor was that of Aelfgar, the coroner's clerk set off for Sampford Spiney, complacently satisfied with the first part of his mission. This small village was the nearest to where the corpse had lain and the coroner had ordered his clerk to inquire covertly as to whether Aelfgar had been seen there in the recent past.

Thomas took directions from the priest in Totnes and rode north to Buckfastleigh, where he claimed a meal in the abbey, and carried on north-west over the most remote part of southern Dartmoor. Following further advice from the abbey cellarer, a locally born monk, he followed an ancient trackway known as the Abbot's Way, which wound through a brown, desolate wilderness of dying bracken, heather and rock. All afternoon, the lonely little man rode up and down hillocks, through scrub-covered valleys and across bare plateaux of withered grass, keeping to an ill-defined pathway worn by shepherds and rare travellers such as himself.

Before the track reached the road across the moor from the Widecombe direction to Tavistock, he took the cellarer's advice and turned west to cross Walkhampton Common. There were no signs or markers, apart from occasional stone cairns at intersections of pathways, and navigation was almost as difficult as on the sea, even in this clear weather. Twice he was lucky enough to come across a shepherd who gave directions, vague though they were, as most inhabitants of the county spent their lifetimes without going outside the boundaries of their own manor.

The wind, relentlessly whistling across from eastern England and the northern sea beyond, cut through his threadbare cloak and the nondescript garments underneath. He had a sack wound round his chest, tied on with cord, but his hands and feet were perished by the time he skirted Ingra Tor and came to the edge of a wooded valley that looked across to the hamlet of Sampford Spiney on the other side.

It was near dusk and he had been riding since dawn, apart from his brief rests at Totnes and Buckfastleigh.

The fatigue ached through his bones and his backside was sore from sitting side-saddle on the back of the indefatigable mule.

He stopped for a moment, before setting the beast to scramble down the valley, through the little Walkham river and up the other side to the village. 'What am I doing here?' he asked himself, plaintively. A man with a good brain, who could read and write well, had been ordained as a priest and capable of high office in the Church, was now sitting in cold misery on the back of a flea-bitten mule in one of the most remote parts of England. All because of a momentary weakness of the flesh in Winchester, when the urge of his loins and the treachery of a female had ruined his life in a flash. He had no illusions about his physical failings, the crook back, the lazy eye and the bandy legs, but did God have to hand him losing cards every time? Was there nothing in him that was worthy of some commendation, at least a little comfort? Why was he always the butt of jokes, being pushed aside by Gwyn and peremptorily ordered about by John de Wolfe?

He was a good clerk – who else could write as fast or with such clarity? He was not evil, however unprepossessing he might look. He hated violence, he loved God and his Church, though not to excess. He even liked children and beasts, rare virtues in such a cruel and violent age – and yet he was treated like a leper or a beggar by most who knew him.

Sometimes he contemplated suicide, but knew he would never do it – not only because it would be a sin against God and lead to everlasting damnation, but because he was too squeamish to carry out any violent act.

All these were familiar thoughts, which came to

him every day or two. He tried to be positive and look on the credit side. At least Crowner John had been persuaded to take him on as his clerk and not let him starve in the street. Also he had the benefit of sharing a mean lodging in the cathedral close, thanks to the Archdeacon's influence.

Thomas sighed and kicked the old mule into motion, letting it pick its way down through the trees to splash through the river towards Sampford Spiney and the next stage of their investigation.

The next afternoon, a figure in the grey-white habit of a Cistercian monk walked slowly into the village of Peter Tavy. He had a long staff, recently cut from a hazel thicket, and when he begged food and a night's lodging at the manor house, he said that he was returning to Sutton, near Plymouth, from a pilgrimage to St David's in Wales.

The seneschal, the household bailiff, sent him over to one of the lean-to sheds against the tattered palisade, which housed the kitchen. He thought it odd that a monk should seek hospitality in a manor, when the huge monastery of St Mary and St Rumon was only an hour's walk down the valley at Tavistock, but soon dismissed it from his mind, thinking that perhaps Cistercians had some dispute with the Benedictines.

In the kitchen, a lame young man and two giggling girls were preparing food for the evening meal in the hall. They were amiable enough and gave the monk generous helpings of boiled vegetables, coarse bread and slices of salt ham, washed down with the inevitable watery beer.

Always curious about travellers and eager for any news of the unknown world beyond their village, the cooks plied him with questions about his journey. Blessed with a fertile imagination, he lied endlessly to satisfy their curiosity, for he had never been nearer St David's than Glastonbury.

Between their gossiping, the little man in the grey habit managed to slip in a few of his own questions and when Thomas, for of course it was he, bedded down on some clean straw in a corner of the undercroft later that evening, he was satisfied with his intelligence-seeking. He lay wrapped in the monk's thick garment, worn over his own clothes, and felt warmer than he had for two days, especially as a glowing charcoal fire burned in the centre of the undercroft. A dozen other men and some children slept or talked around him, mostly house-serfs or manor workers who had no dwellings of their own.

Thomas stared out of one of the openings in the wall at the starlit sky, brilliantly clear in the threatened first frost of the year, and rehearsed the tale he would tell Crowner John when he returned to Exeter tomorrow.

At Sampford Spiney he had sought out the local priest, a fat, indolent man whose main interest was ale and cider rather than his pastoral duties. Thomas had claimed to be a priest on his way to take up a church in a remote part of Cornwall, posted there by the Bishop of Exeter. Knowing all the personalities and the ways of the Church, it was easy for him to get away with this fabrication to a largely ignorant and certainly uninterested colleague.

He wheedled a night's lodging, which entailed having little food but an excess of drink, which loosened the tongue of his host to a satisfactory degree. Before they fell on to their hay-filled pallets in the single-roomed house attached to the wooden church, Thomas had extracted all that was known in Sampford Spiney about the dead man Aelfgar.

'He came here more than a month back,' said the priest thickly, belching out the gas from three quarts of cider. 'Came on a good big horse late in the evening, when the days were longer. Said he was making for Peter Tavy, and asked for directions. He decided he wouldn't get there in daylight, as his horse had gone lame. The hag that brews the beer keeps the nearest thing to a tavern in this place – and she has a pallet for the few travellers that may pass through, so he stayed there.'

'Why didn't anyone, especially the reeve, tell this to the Crowner when he was here after the corpse was discovered?' asked Thomas. The priest was too fuddled with drink to wonder how his visitor knew what the coroner had been told. John de Wolfe had come briefly to the village with his clerk to hold a cursory inquest, but the priest had not been around that day to recognise his present visitor as the same clerk.

'What? Get the village amerced for keeping quiet about it? Not on your life! He played dumb about everything.' He sniggered drunkenly. 'The fellow left after two nights and rode away quite alive. How were we to know that he got himself killed a few miles up the track?'

'But when your shepherds found the body, didn't they know whose it was? And what happened to his horse?'

The fat churchman had taken another great mouthful of turbid cider. 'God alone knows where his horse went – we certainly never saw it again. And as for finding the body, we knew nothing about this new crowner business, nobody ever told us. Let sleeping dogs lie, I say – and dead men, eh?'

He had cackled with laughter and swayed dangerously on his stool, the only furniture in the room apart from a rickety table.

Now, as Thomas lay on his straw in the undercroft, his mind moved on to today, when he had come from Sampford Spiney to Peter Tavy. Although there was little communication between villages, he couldn't keep using the parish-priest network, so a few miles out of the village, he tethered his mule deep in the trees, on a long rope that would allow him plenty of grazing for a day. From his saddlebag he produced the robe he had acquired a long time ago, after the funeral of a Cistercian in Winchester. Cutting a staff from the forest, he walked into Peter Tavy, hoping that no one would comment on the fresh white wood at the cut end – or his lack of a monk's tonsure. If asked about his long hair, he was ready to say that it had grown back during the three-month pilgrimage to St David's and that he had vowed not to restore it until he reached his home monastery near Plymouth. As it turned out, no one had been the slightest bit curious, wanting only to hear about the big wide world beyond their constricted horizons.

He lay watching the night sky, and recalled the information he had gleaned from the kitchen staff, the grooms and a few old men who sat around the fire in the undercroft, too arthritic to work any longer in the field strips.

It seemed certain that Aelfgar of Totnes had never arrived at Peter Tavy, even though he had set out from Sampford Spiney with the stated intention of making

221

that his next destination. It was only five miles away, little more than a hour's journey even on a plodding horse, but he had ended up as a mouldering corpse on Heckwood Tor, about half-way between the two villages. No one in the manor had ever heard of Aelfgar, which tallied with the story of the Totnes priest, who said that the man had had no link with Hubert de Bonneville when he left his own village. Having drawn a blank on the Saxon squire, the clerk had soaked up as much local gossip as possible. It seemed that the dying lord of the manor, Sir Arnulph, had been popular among the freemen and serfs alike. He had been a relatively easy-going master, firm but fair, and the village had prospered for years without fighting or famine. They did not seem so complacent about the rest of the family.

'That Hubert was a painful fellow,' confided one old man, between the fits of bronchitic coughing that racked his body every few minutes. 'He thought he was lord long before our master had his seizure, throwing his weight about and altering the way we'd done things for years back.'

Another rheumy old fellow nodded agreement. 'A cold fish he was, full of religion and morals. Should have been a priest – begging your own pardon, Brother. That's what decided him to take the Cross and go off to the Holy Land against his father's desires.'

'Good riddance, some of us said,' added the first old man, reckless in his old age. 'I never wished him dead like this, but we were glad to see him go away. Though he left a brood of brothers and cousins behind him who have prospered since Sir Arnulph suffered his apoplexy.'

Thomas gathered that Gervaise de Bonneville was

more popular than his slain brother, and the younger brother, Martyn, was looked upon as a child by the villagers, overshadowed by Gervaise. But there were three cousins, adult sons of a dead elder brother of Arnulph, who had designs on the two manors. They were manoeuvring with Winchester to be given a share of the land when Arnulph died, as the Crown now held the ultimate overlordship.

'Them cousins would like to see the other two brothers dead, as well as Hubert,' cackled the second old man. 'Wouldn't be surprised if Gervaise has a nasty accident in the forest before long.'

This started a heated argument among the grandfathers around the fire, some slandering the cousins, others defending them, but there was no more hard information for Thomas to mull over. He pulled his disguise more closely about him and composed himself for sleep.

CHAPTER SIXTEEN

In which Crowner John makes an arrest

While his clerk was wandering the cold wastes of Dartmoor, Sir John de Wolfe had been consolidating his improved relations with his wife. As the maid had predicted, the solar door had been left open for him the previous night and he regained his place in the connubial bed, even if it was on the edge furthest away from his wife.

The next evening, he returned home early from a day spent at three hangings and an inquest on a child who had drowned in a well in St Sidwell's. Matilda was sitting by the fire and gave him a subdued but civil greeting. John carefully launched into a neutral conversation, which developed into a discussion about a donation she wished him to make to her favourite church, St Olave's. John thought that her excessive show of piety and devotion to the church was more a social charade than true religious belief, but for the sake of peace he would have been willing to offer a gift to Saladin's revered mosque. By the time Mary arrived with the evening meal, they were talking together in a stilted but formally polite manner.

As things seemed to be going uncommonly well, John decided to consolidate the truce by asking Matilda's opinion on his current investigation. He recounted all that had happened in the past week or so, carefully avoiding any criticism of her brother.

'So at least now we know who the two dead men are – the eldest son of a Norman lord and his squire, both recently returned from the Holy Land. But the question is, why were they killed?'

The square face of his wife looked into the flickering fire as if to gain inspiration. 'Do you think it was by the same hand, John?' she asked, with a studied politeness the equal of his own restrained tones.

He bent forward in his monk's chair, his hands cupped around a glass of mulled wine. 'More than one hand, that's for sure. Both were assaulted by at least a pair of assassins. The wounds were similar in some ways, both stabbed in the back. But that is such a common type of murderous wound that it doesn't signify a great deal. And one had his throat cut, the other had limb wounds typical of a sword fight.'

'What does that tell you?'

'Not a lot, I'm afraid,' replied John ruefully.

Matilda tucked her heavy skirt closer around her legs as a sudden draught sighed across the floor from the east wind gusting outside. 'If the knight and his squire had been travelling together, I can see it could have been a casual robbery by outlaws,' she observed carefully. 'But the two men were ambushed weeks apart and in different places. That seems too much to be a coincidence.'

'Exactly what I think,' said John, eager to agree with her. If he had to live with her – and the alternative posed many difficulties – then he may as well try to avoid eternal daily strife.

'Who knew about them travelling westwards from

Southampton?' she asked, detective fever beginning to stir in her voluminous breast.

'Many of those returning from Palestine, I suppose,' he answered slowly. 'And that Nebba fellow, who keeps cropping up. And, of course, Alan Fitzhai.'

His wife steepled her fingers in a judicial gesture. 'This Fitzhai certainly seems the most likely candidate. He had an admitted feud with de Bonneville and you have only his word as to when he was travelling back from Plymouth, which puts him within striking distance of Widecombe.'

The coroner nodded, though he was reluctant to abandon his own illogical prejudice that Alan Fitzhai was not the man they sought. 'He could have been there for de Bonneville's killing, admittedly – but if the slaying of his squire is linked with it, he could not have been on Heckwood Tor weeks before as he was known to have been in Southampton at that time.'

Matilda was equally unwilling to concede a point against her own theory. 'He could have used an agent, some footpad he could have paid to follow the squire fellow – God knows, there's no lack of hired killers about these days. I don't know what the world's coming to with all this violence.'

Her husband grunted, torn between argument and his desire for peace. 'There's also this Saxon archer, this Nebba?' he suggested.

'Does he have an alibi for either killing?' demanded Matilda, reluctant to give up Fitzhai as her prime suspect.

John shook his head, his black locks swirling about his neck. 'The timing is too vague for that. This Welsh archer Gwyn found in Southampton, he had no real idea of when the fellow vanished. Nebba could have been involved in either of the murders. But why, in God's name, should he be?'

'He's a mercenary and an outlaw, so you say. Just the type to be hired for a killing. What if this Fitzhai paid him to follow the squire and dispatch him?'

'There must have been more than one. The squire was an experienced fighter, fresh home from the wars.'

'So? There are plenty of ruffians eager to kill for a mark or two.'

Her tone was becoming more triumphant and was beginning to weaken his hunch about Fitzhai's innocence – she could destroy every objection he put up.

'I think the answer lies at the Dartmoor end, rather than in Southampton or France,' John said doggedly.

'It might be both, husband. They were killed out west, surely, but the cause may be elsewhere. If Nebba sold de Bonneville's horse to the Widecombe reeve, can you really believe that he came upon it innocently, wandering in the forest?'

She smoothed her skirt in a preening fashion. 'If I were you, I'd find this eight-fingered bowman and put him to the Ordeal too.'

As Thomas de Peyne was away for almost three days, the affair of the slain Crusaders fell into abeyance and the coroner relapsed into his usual routine.

Gwyn reported that, contrary to pessimistic forecasts, Alan Fitzhai was surviving and that his fever was abating, in spite of the adverse ministrations of the ignorant gaol-keeper.

John had tried to get the man moved to the convent, but the sheriff had resolutely forbidden this. The coroner cynically suspected that his brother-in-law hoped that Fitzhai would die of blood-poisoning and so solve the awkward dilemma of whether to try him in the county court, then hang him, or leave him to the Justices in Eyre and then hang him.

Gwyn also reported that Eadred of Dawlish, the pig-keeper stabbed outside the Saracen tavern, had died in spite of the frantic ministrations of his young assailant to keep him alive. Another arrest and hanging seemed imminent.

In the late afternoon of the third day, the coroner and his officer were in the gatehouse chamber when a weary Thomas limped up the stairs, having left his even wearier mule in the castle stables.

John was sitting at his trestle, silently and labori-ously mouthing the Latin exercises given to him that morning by his tutor at the cathedral. Gwyn was idly sharpening the blade of his dagger on the soft red stone of the window-sill, but stopped to make a ribald comment about the bedraggled clerk who appeared in the doorway. However, with actions belying his words, he rose to get the little man a hunk of bread and cheese from their wall-shelf and pushed him onto a stool while he poured him a mug of cider, knowing his dislike of beer.

'The wanderer returns!' shouted the coroner, sur-prised at how glad he was to see the fellow home safe and sound after three days' solitary travelling in a lonely area that seemed overburdened with slain corpses.

They listened attentively to his story, without interrup-tions or even Gwyn's usual quips, and John de Wolfe, covertly rolling up his reading homework away from Thomas's inquisitive eyes, sat back for a moment's thought.

'So now we know that both de Bonneville and his squire were killed within twelve miles of each other, both *en route* for Peter Tavy, which neither reached alive.'

Gwyn, ready to split hairs, pointed out that although the bodies were found within that distance, they may not have been murdered there.

'No one is going to carry corpses far, man,' snapped John, in irritation at his train of thought being disturbed. 'But why were they killed so far apart in time? From Thomas's information, this Aelfgar left Sampford Spiney a few weeks before Hubert was slain.'

Gwyn scratched at the fleas in his red hair. 'I was told in Southampton that de Bonneville stayed behind to sell his loot and pay off his men, sending his squire ahead to announce his coming to the family.'

'Like John the Baptist and the Lord Christ,' added Thomas devoutly, crossing himself with a lump of cheese. He ventured another observation, echoing Matilda's views of a few nights earlier. 'It seems too much of a coincidence that both master and servant were killed in the same area, in much the same fashion but weeks apart. Yet I saw hardly a soul on those evil moors. There's nothing there except foxes, sheep and crows.'

'If they were ambushed, the killers must have known when they were coming,' observed the coroner, contemplatively. He turned to his clerk. 'How long did this Aelfgar spend in Sampford Spiney?'

'Two nights, the priest said. His horse went lame and he rested it for a day before going on.'

'And the village is only a few miles from Peter Tavy?'

'You could walk between them in under two hours,' replied Thomas. 'That's why I dressed as a Cistercian, in case someone in Peter Tavy knew I'd already been snooping in Sampford.'

John thought this through. 'This Aelfgar made no secret of being Hubert's squire?'

'No, I expect everyone in Sampford knew it.'

'So some thatcher or pedlar could have carried the fact to Peter Tavy the next day?'

'No reason why not.'

John looked across at Gwyn and, almost in unison, they both grunted under their breath.

The sheriff was openly contemptuous of John's suspicions and would hear nothing in favour of questioning the de Bonnevilles. 'Are you mad, brother-in-law?' he fumed, as they sat each side of the table in his chamber in the castle keep. 'The Bishop is a great friend of the family. He has already chided both of us – especially you – for not finding a culprit for Hubert's death. And now we have had God's signal from the Ordeal that this odious man Fitzhai is the villain!' He banged the table hard with his fist. 'Can you imagine my going to the Bishop's palace and telling Henry Marshall that we suspect someone in the household of his sick old friend? You must have taken leave of your senses, John.'

The coroner could see that the sheriff was adamant and would not be swayed an inch by argument, so he stood up and banged the table himself. 'Very well. You have no power over my inquiries, Richard. I will ride to Peter Tavy and see what I can discover.' He marched to the stairway door.

De Revelle shouted at his back, 'The Bishop will

crucify you for this, you fool! With Hubert Walter coming here within a week or two, you'll be lucky to keep your head, let alone your coronership.'

But John had vanished down the stairs, muttering oaths against the whole de Revelle clan, male and female.

Next afternoon, the coroner and his officer arrived at the stockade of Peter Tavy after a hard ride from Exeter, stopping only to feed their horses and themselves.

John had had no need for his clerk and left him at home to recover from his three-day mule ride. A greater problem had been Matilda: his recent return to favour was likely to be sabotaged by another night away from home so soon after their rapprochement. He carefully broached the subject at supper-time, emphasising the importance of clearing up this double murder to satisfy the concerns of dear Bishop Marshall who, to the obsessively religious Matilda, was only slightly less revered than the Pope or God Himself. He carefully omitted any reference to her brother's antagonism to his plans and prayed that the man would not turn up at the house to see her before he left for Peter Tavy in the early morning.

Rather to his surprise, she took the news of his absence with good grace. Still rather distant, her attitude of formal politeness rather than warmth, she murmured with a sniff or two into her kerchief, that she supposed that he had to do what duty demanded.

Next day, John dismounted at the foot of the stairway leading into Peter Tavy's hall and looked around him. The place seemed quiet, much less active than on their last visit. Smoke still rose from the kitchen eaves, but hardly anyone was about, just a few figures in the distance. No one came to take their horses and Gwyn had to shout into the undercroft arches to find a snivelling youth to take the bridles.

'What's going on?' he demanded of the boy.

'The master's passed on, sir. Lord Arnulph died this morning.' Armed with this news, Sir John climbed the steps to the door of the hall and found silent groups of people within, talking quietly among themselves. There were several clergymen, one in an abbot's regalia, who he assumed to be from the rich abbey of St Mary and St Rumon in Tavistock. He recognised another as Prior Wulfstan, the fat monk who had entertained him when he had stayed at the abbey on his first visit. He went over to him now and made the platitudes appropriate for a recent bereavement. It seemed that Arnulf de Bonneville had declined steadily over the past few days and eventually had had another massive stroke that had carried him off within hours.

'And what of the sons?' asked the coroner, guardedly.

'Gervaise has already assumed the lordship, as was to be expected. He had been running the two manors in all but name for months.'

'He will have to get the King's confirmation to succeed his father,' observed John. 'Especially as these are Crown lands since Prince John lost his six counties!'

'A mere formality,' said Wulfstan, with a benign smile. 'As our primate is visiting the West very soon, he can confirm him. The King is hardly likely to come back to this country, and I can't see Gervaise trailing all over France trying to catch Richard without a battleaxe in his hand.'

John looked around at the subdued knots of people. 'Where is Gervaise? I don't see him.'

'Praying at the side of his father's body, with his brother Martyn and their cousins – who still have ambitions to said part of the estate.'

'I need to see him urgently. This death has complicated my plans.'

Wulfstan's overfed face creased into a sad smile. 'Death has a way of upsetting plans, especially those of the deceased.'

The coroner had no time for facile comments and looked around the hall again. The curtain to the bedchamber swung aside and the solid figure of Baldwyn of Beer came out. He wore a dark red linen tabard reaching to his knees, laced each side at the waist, with a boar's head embroidered on the front. A black woollen tunic and black hose with cross-gartering above heavy shoes gave him a dark, powerful appearance. He was buckling on his sword belt as he came.

John went across to him and put a hand on his shoulder. The coroner was slightly taller than the man from Beer, but not so heavily built. 'I need a few words with you, Baldwyn – and with your master.'

Baldwyn frowned, a worried and abstracted look on his face. 'It's a difficult time, Crowner, especially for Sir Gervaise. He has to arrange with the abbot and Prior Wulfstan to get his father's body down to Tavistock to lie at the altar until the burial.'

John eased him by the shoulder towards the doorway. 'We can't speak in here with all these people about. Come outside. This concerns the death of your master's brother – and his squire.'

'Squire? What squire?' Baldwyn cast him a puzzled look.

At the door, they stood on the platform above the stairs, where Gwyn of Polruan waited. John squinted at the man in the red tabard. 'Doesn't any news reach you from your neighbouring village, Sampford Spiney? They're in trouble with me, amerced for concealing a dead body for weeks on end. Not just any dead body, another murdered body.'

Baldwyn looked blankly at the coroner. 'I know nothing of this. You said one was squire to Hubert?'

'Yes, a man called Aelfgar. Had you not seen Hubert's fighting companion?'

Baldwyn shook his big head, his spade-shaped beard rubbing across his chest. 'He left here for Outremer with two men-at-arms but he had no squire.' He looked anxiously over his shoulder into the hall. 'Sir John, I have much work to do, with the death of our lord. My master needs my services.'

'And I need your master!' snapped John. 'I have no wish to interrupt your mourning, but the passing was hardly unexpected. The keeping of the King's peace has to go on, death or no death. So, please, will you fetch Sir Gervaise to me? I have to speak to him urgently.'

With a barely concealed scowl, Baldwyn turned and went back into the gloom of the hall, leaving the stone landing to John and his officer. Gwyn, whose eyes were as sharp as his brain, edged up to the coroner and said in a low voice, 'Did you notice his dagger?'

John stared at the Cornishman and shook his head. What was he on about now?

'It doesn't fit the scabbard, it's too long. And it looks Levantine.'

235

'So? Plenty of soldiers have Eastern weapons. I've got one myself. So did the dead Hubert.'

Gwyn nodded. 'But that Aelfgar didn't. He had an empty scabbard. A long one. I've got it in my saddlebag there.'

The coroner folded his arms, his black cloak flying in the persistent cold wind. 'You can't hang a man on the length of his dagger.'

'No, but maybe the sheriff could!' retorted the red-haired giant. 'And it's worth looking at, I reckon.'

John sighed. One problem at a time was enough for him today.

'All right, go and get the sheath from your horse – and stay down there,' he commanded, as he saw Baldwyn and Gervaise approaching the door.

Again he made the appropriate commiserations over the death of the new lord's father, then launched straight into the strange coincidence of both Hubert and his squire being murdered *en route* to Peter Tavy.

Gervaise was shaken by the news. 'His squire also? I never knew he had one.'

'No Norman of good birth would be campaigning in the Holy Land without one,' observed John drily.

'Well, we knew nothing of him. What was his name?'

'Aelfgar, a Saxon,' said John shortly.

Gervaise turned to the impassive man from Beer. 'Did you know anything of this, Baldwyn?'

He shook his head. 'We've heard nothing more of Sir Hubert since that messenger from Palestine came last year. Never knew of any squire, certainly.'

John had been squinting covertly at the sheath on the squire's belt, which sat half-way around his waist on the right side. An ornamental knife-hilt sat high

above the sheath, with more than an inch of bare
blade exposed. On the edge of the dark brown hide,
a small white scar of recently torn leather shone like
a little star. 'Will you come down to the undercroft?'
asked the coroner, with deceptive mildness.

Puzzled, the two men followed him to where the
visitors' horses were tethered to a wooden rail. Gwyn
was standing alongside his mare, holding something
wrapped in a piece of sacking. As the other three gathered around, he flipped away the hessian and showed
them some clothing and an empty dagger sheath. They
still smelt of corruption from body-fluids soaked from
the Dartmoor corpse, but this was not what intrigued
the coroner. He saw another small rip in the top edge
of the scabbard, not white, but old and dirty.

'What's all this about?' asked Gervaise irritably. 'I
have much to attend to on this very unhappy day,
Sir John.'

'It may turn out to be unhappier than you think,'
retorted the coroner gruffly. 'Would you ask your
squire to hand me his dagger for a moment?'

The two local men looked uneasily at each other
and made no movement.

'Come on, if you please,' John barked. 'Your knife,
Baldwyn!'

Slowly, the black-bearded man withdrew his dagger
and handed it, hilt first, to John, who took it and,
with the other hand, raised the sheath from Gwyn's
sacking, sliding the blade smoothly into the leather.
The hilt-guard sat perfectly against the top edge of
the sheath. The coroner held it out towards Gervaise
and his squire.

'It seems to fit this much better than it does your
sheath.'

237

De Bonneville, flexing his new superiority as lord of the manor, began to turn away.

'I've no time for charades, Crowner. Why are you playing such games?'

'This sheath came from the man slain not five miles from here. The man you've never heard of.'

Baldwyn blustered, 'So my dagger doesn't fit my scabbard so well. Little wonder. I bought it from a man who had returned from the East after I broke my own blade.'

John was ready for this explanation. 'Indeed? Then look more closely.' He drew out the dagger again and pointed with a finger at the torn top edge of the sheath, in line with the edge of the blade. On the blade itself, two inches below the hilt, was a deep nick in the metal, where it had been damaged by being struck against something hard. A small tang of steel hooked out from it and when he slid the blade in and out of the scabbard, it was patently obvious that this was the cause of the torn leather.

'Now show me your scabbard, sir,' he demanded of Baldwyn.

With three pairs of eyes boring into him, the squire had little option but to slide the now-empty sheath around his belt to the front. John slid the dagger back in and, drawing it up and down, showed that the new tear in the leather was identical with that in the other sheath and caused by the same nick in the blade.

'What have you to say to that?' John demanded, with a dangerous softness.

Gervaise de Bonneville jumped in defensively. 'This is nonsense! Every man in England has a knife. Thousands of them have come back with the Crusading armies . . . and many knives are damaged. You are building a false story out of trivial coincidences.'

John ignored his intervention, continuing to stare at Baldwyn. 'I asked you, what do you have to say?'

Hard black eyes bored back at him from an obstinate face. 'As my master says, it is ridiculous. I have had that dagger for at least two years.'

He took it back into his hand and studied it closely.

John was unperturbed. 'I doubt if you can produce witnesses to prove that?' His voice rose in an accusing crescendo. 'I say it is the weapon of Hubert's man, Aelfgar!'

By now, a few people had stopped at a discreet distance to wonder what was going on.

Baldwyn, his face above the jet beard becoming reddened in anger, shouted back, 'I tell you the knife is mine! How can it belong to this dead man? I told you, I've never heard of Aelfgar of Totnes!'

There was a dead silence. Then John spoke, with a sinister restraint after his previous roar. 'Totnes? Who said anything about Totnes?'

Baldwyn stood, his head lowered, looking from one to the other like a baited bull between two dogs.

Gervaise opened his mouth to speak, but before he could attempt to defend his squire the dark man gave a snarl and pushed the coroner in the chest.

Caught unawares, John staggered back and Baldwyn ran towards the stables. Gwyn leaped after him and before he had gone five paces, jumped on his back and brought him crashing to the ground. Gervaise stood transfixed, but John had regained his balance and rushed to help Gwyn secure the runaway.

As he got to the heap of flailing bodies, Gwyn gave a roar and grabbed his own upper arm, where blood was flowing through his fingers. 'The bastard's stabbed me!' he yelled, and ducked as the same blade that they had just been examining, flashed past his ear.

Not for nothing had the two from Exeter been fighting-partners for a dozen years. Trapped because his legs were intertwined with the fugitive's, Gwyn made sure that he dodged the knife, confident that his master would speedily settle the affair. He was right. With a metallic rattle, John drew out his sword and, using the flat of the blade, crashed it down on the black hair of the knife-wielder. Baldwyn had no protection on his head and, though the sword was not a full-size battle weapon, its thirty inches of steel was heavy enough to stun him.

Gwyn clambered up and brushed the dirt from his front.

'Are you badly cut?' asked John.

His officer looked into the rip in the sleeve of his woollen jacket. He dipped a finger in and examined the blood that came out. 'No, nothing but a prick. My fault. I didn't expect him to knife me, the swine.' He aimed a kick at the prostrate body, which was beginning to groan and show signs of revival.

'Tie him, we're going back to Exeter with him.'

While Gwyn lashed the wrists of the groaning Baldwyn, using the belt of the dead man as an appropriate form of bondage, the coroner went back to the new lord of Peter Tavy, who stood white-faced and almost paralysed at the turn of events.

'I think your squire killed your brother and his henchman, this Aelfgar – or if he didn't kill them himself, he was present when it happened.'

De Bonneville pulled himself together and regained

his haughty poise. 'Well, I do not. And this business of the dagger is rubbish. You come here, on our day of grief, disrupt the mourning, interrupt the preparations for the funeral of one of the most respected lords in the West Country and then you make accusations against my squire, who is a friend as well as a servant.'

Gervaise was made of sterner stuff than John had thought and rapidly recovered his composure to turn defence into attack. 'My brother must have been killed by some damned outlaws on his way home. And you'll regret hinting otherwise, Coroner. I have influential friends, from the Bishop to the sheriff, and from our abbot here to others in Winchester. Release my squire at once. Perhaps I will then take a more lenient view of your over-enthusiasm.'

John bared his teeth in a sarcastic leer. 'A good try, young man. But explain to me how your Baldwyn has a dagger belonging to a murdered man and how he knew he was from Totnes, when he claimed never to have heard of him?'

'I cannot speak for what Baldwyn knows or doesn't know – or what he may or may not have done. But I cannot believe he is an evil man.'

However, banking on the influence of his powerful friends in high places, Gervaise made no further objection to the coroner continuing with his legal processes. 'You are making an error, sir, but if you have to seek better counsel over this in Exeter, I cannot stand in your way.'

Amid increasing confusion and excitement, the near hysterical Martyn now rushed out from his father's death-bed. While his brother attempted to explain and to reassure him, the groggy Baldwyn was hauled on to a horse, tied to the saddle horns and led away, roped to Gwyn's mare, for the first lap of the long journey, via a night's stop at Sampford Spiney.

CHAPTER SEVENTEEN

In which Crowner John attends a trial

The next afternoon, Gwyn lodged Baldwyn safely in the castle gaol, under the tender care of Stigand. He was lodged in a cell next to Alan Fitzhai, where he could hear the groans and curses of the mercenary, who though apparently now out of danger of death, was in constant pain and misery from his septic scalded arm.

The squire from Peter Tavy maintained a sullen, smouldering silence, as if he was bottling up his anger for a vengeful explosion once he was released – his master had promised that the full force of nepotism and undue influence would be mobilised for him, if this mad coroner persisted in trying to hang a murder charge on him.

The same mad coroner reached home and, to keep Matilda safely in her new state of tolerable temper, told her the whole story of the last two days' events.

Matilda listened to his tale in silence. Then she asked, 'You've arrested this squire. Now what are you going to do with him? And what of Gervaise de Bonneville? With his family connections, it's surely very dangerous even to suggest that he was aware of what his squire might have done?' He was strangely pleased that she took such a perceptive interest in his activities – he had been afraid that she would fly into an indignant tantrum at his audacity in tampering with the affairs of a notable county family.

'This Baldwyn has accused himself, with his stolen dagger, the slip over Totnes – and, most of all, his attempt to run.'

'But what about Gervaise? He had no dagger and he didn't attempt to escape. You've no reason to suspect him.'

John imitated his brother-in-law's nose-tapping routine. 'Motive, Matilda, motive! Baldwyn had no reason to kill either of the two men except on the orders of his master who, with his elder brother dead, now inherits the whole of the de Bonneville estate.'

Matilda shook her head slowly. 'You be careful, John. I know that house, they have powerful friends. They can make things difficult for you.'

Before he could show any appreciation for her rare concern, those difficulties began in earnest. There was a loud knocking on the street door, and before a flurried Mary could reach it from the yard, there was the sound of feet in the vestibule. The inner door to the hall was thrown open and Richard de Revelle burst in, closely followed by Precentor Thomas de Boterellis and Portreeve Henry Rifford. 'Matilda, forgive us, but we must speak urgently to this husband of yours!' The sheriff's normally urbane voice was tense with rage and apprehension.

'The Bishop is extremely distressed!' brayed de Boterellis and, not to be outdone, the portreeve huffed and puffed about the outrage felt among the town's burgesses.

John got up from his chair and stood between the visitors and the fire, as if protecting his hearth from the intrusion. 'Couldn't this wait until the morning, sirs?' he grated. 'I am taking my ease in my own home, not holding a public meeting.'

The sheriff crossed the flagstones ahead of the other men and wagged a long finger under John's nose. 'You've gone too far this time, de Wolfe! Starting a sword fight outside a death chamber and dragging an innocent squire away in bonds. Even worse, you pull the lord of a manor from his dead father's side before the body is even cold to insinuate that he has knowledge of this killing!'

The other two twittered in the background, the words 'scandal', 'Bishop', 'outrageous', 'city fathers', 'insane' and 'poor Arnulph' figuring frequently.

The lean, dark figure before the hearth listened for a moment or two, then flung up his arms above his shoulders. 'Be quiet, all of you, damn your eyes!'

The sudden eruption of this gaunt figure, who looked like some Old Testament prophet putting a curse on the Amalachites, instantly silenced the trio. 'I presume you burst into my house to complain about my arresting Baldwyn of Beer? Well, I see it my duty to take on the tasks that the sheriff of this county should be performing in apprehending criminals. This man tried to flee when accused and wounded my own officer in the attempt. His actions betray his guilt and he must be tried for his crime.'

'He is squire to the new lord de Bonneville, for God's sake!' retorted the Precentor. 'The Bishop is livid with anger that you should so upset his friends at the time of their grief.'

John snorted in derision. 'The King and his ministers and judges have sworn to dispense law and justice without fear or favour, principles set down by the two

Henrys . . . and the Saxon kings before them, for that matter. Are you telling me that there is a different law for the Bishop's friends?'

There was a pause, as no one wanted to commit himself by answering that question directly, but the Sheriff blustered his way through it. 'All right, Crowner, you shall have your trial. It shall be tomorrow, to make this poor man's incarceration as short as possible. Gervaise de Bonneville and his brother rode on your heels to bring us this outrageous news and to complain to the Bishop, who by good fortune is staying in his palace this next week to receive Walter the justiciar. So Henry Marshall will personally attend the court, together with all men of good will who wish to see redress for this shocking thing that you have done.'

He turned and marched out, forgetting even to wish his sister goodnight.

At the third hour after noon the next day, the court hall in the inner bailey of Rougemont Castle was filled to overflowing. Though the sheriff's weekly court was always busy, either with litigants, witnesses or curious onlookers seeking entertainment, the word had somehow got round that a major confrontation was likely at the trial of Baldwyn of Beer.

The arrival of Bishop Henry Marshall and a bevy of his minions was a bonus for the audience, as no one could remember such senior clerics attending this secular court before. It must be an unusual matter that brought out the Bishop on this damp, cold afternoon.

The proceedings were brief and predictable. Sir Richard de Revelle courteously greeted the Bishop, who wore a long crimson cassock and a skull-cap, and settled him in a large chair at the side of the dais behind which assembled the Precentor, Treasurer, John de Alecon, a few canons and some lesser clergy.

On the other side, Gervaise and Martyn de Bonneville sat on smaller seats, looking strained and annoyed.

The sheriff flopped into his own chair, set squarely in the middle of the platform, with Ralph Morin, several bailiffs, sergeants and a few men-at-arms scattered behind him.

De Revelle cut an impressive figure, in his bright blue tunic with a short green cloak thrown back over one shoulder, fastened on the other with an ornate gold brooch. His black breeches were cross-gartered above stylish shoes with long, pointed toes. Above his hard, tight-lipped mouth, his narrow moustache had been freshly clipped.

John de Wolfe, entitled – indeed, obliged – to be present at every non-ecclesiastical court, stood grimly at the back of the dais, as Thomas de Peyne lurked in the shadows with his pen and parchment.

Gwyn, a wide rag bound with unnecessary prominence around the slight wound on his upper arm, stood on the edge of the crowd near the stage.

The drama began when Baldwyn of Beer marched in from the keep, behind a single helmeted sergeant. Significantly, he had no chains and was not dragged in by a pair of guards, the usual mode of entry for criminals. He stood in front of the sheriff's judicial seat and folded his arms, looking both defiant and confident.

The court clerk, an older, grey-haired man with the air of a schoolmaster, walked out to the open space in front of the dais to read out the charge from a parchment, itself couched in ambiguous terms. 'Baldwyn of Beer, squire to Sir Gervaise de Bonneville of the honour of Peter Tavy, you have been accused of being involved in the death of one Aelfgar of Totnes. Do you confess to your guilt?'

Baldwyn stared at the clerk. 'Of course not. I am not guilty. In fact, I had never heard of the man.'

'What is the evidence?' asked the sheriff, in an affectedly bored voice.

Gwyn stepped forward and, in a stentorian voice, related the facts about the dagger missing from the corpse, the knife in Baldwyn's sheath that did not fit and the identical tear in each scabbard from the damaged blade.

Gervaise stood up and interrupted. 'What nonsense this is!' he said, in a tremulous but aggressive voice. 'Every man in the land has a dagger. Half of them do not fit their sheaths and the other half have a damaged blade. This is but a fairy-tale!'

John pushed through to the front of the platform. 'This Baldwyn also named the dead man as being from Totnes – yet that name had passed no one's lips. How could he know that of a man about whose very existence he denied any knowledge?'

Baldwyn looked up, his gaze passing from his master to the Bishop, then back to the sheriff. 'It must have been said by someone, or how else could I have heard it? I tell you, I know nothing of this man. Why should I? I live in Peter Tavy and rarely leave it, except to accompany my lord Gervaise. Someone dropped the name in my hearing.'

There was a buzz of discussion among the crowd until the Sheriff's sergeant, prompted by Ralph Morin, banged the stock of his spear on the dais and yelled for quiet.

Gwyn, unperturbed by the denials, finished off his tale. 'When this Baldwyn was confronted by the evidence, he attempted flight. He assaulted the King's coroner by pushing him over, then stabbed me in the arm with the dagger he carried.' He raised his arm and pointed to the thick bandage, which he had rewound that morning so that the bloodstains were visible on the outside.

'That is the evidence in this case,' John bellowed, above the renewed murmurings in the hall. 'Innocent men do not flee, nor stab their accusers as they attempt to escape.'

The sheriff looked disdainfully at the coroner. 'Are you joining anyone else in your accusations?'

John shook his head. 'Not at present – not until we have further evidence,' he added.

Richard de Revelle rose from his chair and went over to the Bishop, who had sat immobile through the proceedings. His austere face, narrow and long-jawed, revealed no emotion as he listened to the sheriff. Then he spoke a few words in a low voice.

The sheriff beckoned to the two brothers from Peter Tavy and all four conferred, with the Precentor and the Treasurer trying to get within earshot. Then the group resumed their seats. When Richard de Revelle was back lolling in his large chair, he addressed the court. 'We already have a culprit in custody, one Alan Fitzhai, whom the ritual of the Ordeal has already proven guilty of the killing of Hubert de Bonneville. He will be convicted and hanged in due course, when certain procedural difficulties' – he shot a poisonous glance at the coroner – 'have been settled. As the deceased in this case seems to have proved to be the squire of Hubert, then it seems logical to assume that the same miscreant killed them both. Thus Fitzhai must be a double murderer, in which case no other culprit need be sought.'

He stared down at Baldwyn of Beer. 'Even if that explanation was not available, the evidence of this knife scabbard, and the triviality of whether or not the word Totnes was mentioned, is unacceptable for a conviction. As to the charge of assault, it seems only natural that a man so falsely accused should take the only course open to him and try to escape. If he was then assaulted himself by the coroner's officer, who can blame him for defending himself?'

After this breathtaking distortion of the evidence, the sheriff turned to smirk at his brother-in-law. 'It is therefore the verdict of this court that no crime has been committed by the defendant and he is therefore discharged. I would also remind certain persons that, by the established legal principle of *autrefois aquit*, he can never again be arraigned on this same charge.' He stood to indicate that the proceedings were over, then went over to the Bishop to fuss over his departure from the dais. Gervaise and Martyn jumped down and slapped their squire on the back in congratulation and joined the jostling throng that was making its way out into the rain and mud of the inner bailey.

As John, Gwyn and Thomas were trailing out, they saw the trio from Peter Tavy making their way to the castle keep, where de Revelle was entertaining them to a meal before they went to an inn for the night, it being too late to set out on the long ride back to their manor. 'Some justice!' muttered Gwyn. 'Depends on who you've got for friends.'

John's lips had been clamped as tight as a rat-trap. He had not been surprised by the farce that he had just witnessed, but the way in which all the evidence had been disregarded almost instantly, with no pretence at considering even the possibility that Baldwyn was guilty, had been even more brazen than he had expected. But with the tenacity of a bull-baiting dog, he refused to contemplate defeat. 'It's not over yet, Gwyn. There must be a way of settling this.'

John failed to understand his wife's attitude to the events surrounding the de Bonneville case. From her virulent antagonism of a week ago, she had subsided into being a reasonable, if distant, house-partner. The intemperate descent of the sheriff and his cronies upon their home the previous evening had upset her far less than John had feared. He thought that she, too, might have turned on him and joined forces with her brother. But Matilda said nothing about it, neither castigating him nor supporting him. After the fiasco of Baldwyn's trial, he expected that she would wade into him as a trouble-making fool, and went home after the trial in some trepidation. To his surprise and gratification, she merely asked him, in measured tones, what the real truth of the matter might be.

As he explained to her the evidence against the squire Baldwyn, he gained the impression that she was torn between family loyalty to her brother and her loyalty to the King's coroner, her wedded husband, to whom her personal status was inevitably linked. If he fell, she fell, so he assumed that Matilda was carefully exploring the relative merits of each side in the dispute, perhaps with a view to joining the potential winner. He had been treading carefully since she had allowed him back into her bedchamber, afraid of another rupture in their relationship. Yet sharing her bed meant just that: a comfortable pallet and a good sleep, no marital privileges.

Feeling that he was treading on eggshells, John excused himself from the house after their evening meal, on the grounds that he must talk to Thomas de Peyne about next day's hangings.

Matilda made no comment and left him to go up to the solar for Lucille to arrange her hair for some function at St Olave's in the morning.

As soon as she was safely upstairs, John threw a heavy cloak over his shoulders and made his way down to Idle Lane and the Bush tavern.

It was half-way through the evening so he went straight up the wooden stairs to Nesta's bedroom, having given a discreet wink to old Edwin as he entered. He knew the aged potman would tell the voluptuous innkeeper that he had arrived and was content to flop on to her bed and stare at the dark ceiling until she had a chance to come upstairs. However, due to his discreet entrance, he missed the fact that among the crowd in the main room were not only Gervaise and Martyn de Bonneville with Baldwyn of Beer, but Gwyn of Polruan, still feeding himself extravagantly at a penny a day while his wife was away in Cornwall.

The three from Peter Tavy were staying the night, having taken advice from Ralph Morin that the Bush was the best inn in Exeter. There was no way in which they could cross Dartmoor in the dark and their journey had to wait until daylight.

They were sitting at a table behind the wattle screens where John de Wolfe often rested. Gervaise and his squire were eating and drinking with an enthusiasm that hardly suited their recent bereavement, though the youthful Martyn looked pale and ill-at-ease, picking at his food listlessly. As the potman approached, the younger brother got up and walked away towards the steps to the upper floor, obviously seeking his bed.

Edwin, his whitened blind eye swivelling uselessly as he stomped between the tables, was collecting empty pots. He was far more astute than most patrons gave him credit for and was virtually Nesta's full-time intelligence officer, sensing trouble-making drunks long before they started fights or smashed the scanty tavern furniture.

As he passed by the table of de Bonneville and his squire, he slowed to collect some jars and to wipe up spilled ale on an adjacent table. His eyesight might not have been good, but his hearing more than compensated for it and he lingered to hear what was said, until Gervaise looked up at him suspiciously and he had to move on. At the back of the room, Edwin dropped his empties into the buckets of murky water and began to fill other jars from the barrels of ale and cider that stood on wedges on a low rack. Nesta bustled up, giving orders right and left to her cook and the two serving girls, who had to provide food and blankets for the brisk trade of overnight guests that was building up. 'Sir John's upstairs, mistress, went straight up, he did.'

She nodded, pleased at the news, but busy for the moment. Edwin hesitated, turning off the spigot on the nearest barrel while he spoke in a low voice. 'Those gentlemen behind the screen . . . something going on there.'

'What do you mean, old man?'

He scratched his head with a bony finger. 'They closed their mouths when they thought I was listening,' he grunted. 'They're the people the Crowner was mixed up with in the Shire Court today. Something odd about them – they've got secrets, I reckon.'

The auburn-haired woman thought for a moment, her eyes straying across the large, crowded room. Then one of the maids called to her and Nesta had to go. 'Keep your ears open, Edwin. Tell Gwyn if anything comes of it.' She hurried away about her business.

CHAPTER EIGHTEEN

In which Crowner John surprises the sheriff

It was approaching midnight when the coroner called out to the guards of Rougemont to open the wicket gate and let him in. Even in his excitement at the turn of events, he had had the wit to call at his house on the way from the Bush to the castle, to tell Matilda that he had urgent business that night and not to expect him home until the early hours. He forbore to mention that this business had begun at Nesta's tavern, but his wife saw from his agitated manner that this was something other than spending the night in some hussy's bed, so she sleepily nodded in acceptance.

Inside the castle's inner bailey, John used the full moonlight to hurry across to the keep and again demand entry from two bored sentries sitting at the bottom of the steps. 'There'll be four others coming behind me in a few minutes,' he warned them, as he went up the outer stairs to the first-floor entrance.

Inside, he strode up the two flights of curved narrow steps, built into the thickness of the wall, and came out in the antechamber next to his brother-in-law's private quarters. On a truckle bed, the sheriff's chamberlain was snoring like a bull seal and when John kicked him he leaped up and stood trembling in his undershirt, still half asleep and hazily thinking that the castle had been attacked. The single tallow dip guttering on a table made John's gaunt figure seem like an apparition from hell, until he recognised it as the coroner.

'I have to see your master – now!' said John, in a tone that instantly cleared the sleep from the servant's eyes.

'It's not, well, not convenient,' stammered the man, a middle-aged flunkey who looked after de Revelle's wardrobe, meals and entertainment.

'To hell with convenience!' snarled John, and walked past the timorous custodian to the door of the sheriff's bedchamber. He gave a peremptory knock but, without waiting for an answer, thrust open the heavy door and walked into a room dimly lit by a couple of candles flickering on a bedside chest.

There was an immediate roar of protest and a muffled scream from the large palliasse on the floor. A bearded figure, naked to the waist, shot up to a sitting position and John could see, too, the head and bare shoulders of a woman. Her profession was declared by her red-painted lips – she certainly bore no resemblance to Lady Eleanor de Revelle, who spent most of her time at their manor in Tiverton: she abhorred her husband's official residence in Exeter Castle.

'Get out, damn you!' yelled the sheriff. The coroner was unmoved by his brother-in-law's indignation.

'I need to see you now. In your antechamber in two minutes.' John went out and slammed the door, to find the servant lighting a horn lantern and several candles. With remarkable speed, the sheriff appeared, wrapped in a coarse blanket. He was bursting with indignation at being disturbed, but John ruthlessly overran his protests. 'Never mind all that huffing,' he grated. 'If you are truly the first law officer in this county, then

I demand in the name of the King that you redress the injustice you did today in your court.'

De Revelle's protests stopped in mid-flow, incredulity at the other's impertinence momentarily depriving him of speech.

John's voice was booming again. 'I have four witnesses arriving downstairs, who will testify to a confession made by Baldwyn of Beer to the murder of Aelfgar.'

The sheriff's almost manic anger cooled a few degrees, but he was still in a towering rage. 'The matter is closed, damn you! The man has been acquitted. He cannot be charged or tried again.'

John savoured the moment. 'But my witnesses also say that he confesses to being involved in the killing of Hubert de Bonneville. He was not charged with that crime today.' Revel's emotional temperature dropped even more sharply. 'Witnesses? What witnesses?'

The coroner jerked a thumb in the direction of the stairway. 'You'll soon see when they come up here.'

The sheriff rallied to fight a strong rearguard action. 'You must be either drunk or witless! You come here in the middle of the night to disturb me . . .' He gave a quick furtive glance towards the bedroom, where the whore would be waiting apprehensively. 'This will cost you your job, John. You come with some maniac story of witnesses. Do you really expect me to take you seriously?'

The coroner was unmoved by his bluster. 'I have four persons who will separately and together testify – to the King, if needs be – that they heard this miscreant confirm that Hubert's squire was slain more than a month and a half ago. And, further, that Baldwyn helped to kill Hubert near Widecombe about three weeks ago.'

His anger-reddened face now pale, de Revelle drooped under his dun-coloured blanket. 'Do you expect me to believe this?' he whispered hoarsely.

The coroner shrugged. 'If you do not, then I'll take my testimony elsewhere. The chief justiciar visits Exeter in a week or so – a man I know and respect from fighting under him in the Holy Land.' The sheriff's confidence began to return. 'He will side with the Bishop, a patron of the de Bonnevilles,' he said.

'Patron of the dead Arnulph, you mean, whose true heir has been killed by his brother's squire. Will Bishop Marshall condone that in the face of solid evidence?' The sheriff could find no words before John went on, 'I'll go to Winchester and London with my witnesses, if I have to – even follow the King in Normandy and the Vexin. I'll not let this rest, be assured of that!'

The sheriff, conscious of the undignified figure he cut in his blanket, pulled himself erect. 'All this fantasy depends on these damned confessions you claim to have. I'd not put it past you to fabricate all of this.'

'I was given a job to do in the King's name and, by God, I'll do it, in spite of all the bishops and sheriffs in Christendom!'

However high-sounding the words, their sincerity was like a blast of icy wind around de Revelle's ears. 'Who are these people you claim to produce?' he growled.

'They include my own officer, the inn-keeper of the Bush and her servant Edwin.'

Instantly revitalised, the sheriff gave a howl of derision. 'What! Your own creature, that hairy Cornishman! A crippled potman, and your own poxy mistress, you adulterous knave! Who do you think will listen to one word from that lying crew?'

John would have dearly loved to knock his brother-in-law to the floor, but he restrained himself to deliver his *coup de grâce*.

'And your own good friend Henry Rifford, one of our respected portreeves. I'm sure you'll accept his testimony as truthful, however reluctant he may be to give it.'

'You're lying!' hissed de Revelle.

'All four should be downstairs by now. You can question them yourself, though I suggest you first put on some clothes,' advised the coroner sweetly.

By the time the distraught sheriff had dressed, arranged with his chamberlain to smuggle the painted lady out down the back stairs and interviewed the four witnesses, the night was far advanced. De Revelle did all he could to convince himself that this was a nightmare or that his cursed brother-in-law was playing some devious trick or malignant conspiracy against him. If John's evidence had merely been that of the three allegedly biased witnesses, he would have defied him and refused to give them any credibility – or even bother to listen to them. But the fact that his own crony Henry Rifford reluctantly corroborated the story made it impossible for him to dismiss the affair as a plot against his own authority.

The four witnesses had trooped into the dimly lit chamber where the sheriff, now hastily dressed in a dull brown tunic, sat behind his table to listen to them.

He still felt disoriented, having been pulled from his bed and his woman to be sledgehammered by a story that made a nonsense of the perverse judgement he had perpetrated in his shire court that morning.

Henry Rifford, the waxy-faced merchant who was one of the two leading citizens of Exeter, was given a chair before the sheriff. The others stood ranged behind him, while the coroner hovered in the background, like a chantry-master with a troop of choristers.

The upshot of their evidence was that Edwin, the old tavern servant, had caught the words 'Widecombe' and 'Southampton' as he passed back and forth near the table where the pair from Peter Tavy were drinking. The other brother, Martyn, was away in his bed in a fit of fatigue and melancholy, leaving Gervaise and Baldwyn with their heads together over their ale.

Following Nesta's instructions, Edwin had made it his business to eavesdrop on the other side of the wattle screen. What had grabbed his attention at once was Gervaise's low voice saying, 'You damned fool, Baldwyn! Whatever happens, Martyn must never know. He's got no backbone in him, he's too weak. The boy would go to pieces if he knew what had been done.'

At this point, Edwin had urgently looked about him and had seen Nesta leaning over Gwyn, who sat on a bench nearby, teasing him about the good times he could have now that his wife was away. The old potman had urgently beckoned them over and, as they had come near his side of the screen, had put a warning finger to his lips. They slid on to the bench left empty a few moments earlier when a group of noisy butchers had tipsily left.

'Listen to this!' Edwin whispered, jerking his thumb at the screen. The other bent their heads near the wattles and three pairs of ears strained to hear Gervaise telling his squire that, as long as he kept his nerve, no one need ever know what had happened on the moor seven weeks ago.

The quick-witted Nesta realised immediately that they needed a more heavyweight and reputable witness than themselves, and her eyes roved urgently around the big room until they fell on a party of leather merchants, celebrating a good contract with the Bretons. Prominent among them was Henry Rifford, whose great prosperity depended on the leather trade of which he was the undisputed leader in Exeter.

She hurried over and hissed into his ear, 'Come at once – it's a matter of life and death!' At the same time she had pulled him by the arm and Rifford, though middle-aged and portly, was mystified but flattered to be so suddenly desired by a pretty woman. Like every man in Exeter, he knew the red-headed innkeeper and occasionally had lustful thoughts about her. The intensity in her voice now compelled him to go with her to the table next to the wattle partition.

With a finger to her lips, she indicated that he should listen to the voices on the other side. Now, in front of the sheriff and rather reluctantly, but pleased at being the centre of attention, the portreeve related what he had heard.

'De Bonneville was telling this Baldwyn that he had been a fool to take that dagger from the body and that he should have buried it in the peat, as he had Aelfgar's sword.'

'Wait!' snapped the sheriff, still desperate to find

some way to discredit all this. 'How do you know it was de Bonneville speaking?'

Henry Rifford looked impatient at having his moment of drama interrupted. 'Of course I knew, Richard. I saw them at that table earlier, when the younger brother was with them. And afterwards I made it my business to pass near them to go out of the back door, to piss in the yard, so that I could confirm who they were.'

The rest of his tale, confirmed almost verbatim by the other less acceptable witnesses, was that Gervaise, his tongue loosened by the evening's drink, was impressing on Baldwyn the need for constant vigilance. The squire, who seemed somewhat resentful of his master's exhortations, replied in mainly monosyllables, but at one point, Rifford heard him say, 'Sir Gervaise, remember that it was I who helped dispose of your brother. I'm hardly likely to put myself in jeopardy for something that happened when you were half a county away.'

The eavesdropping had ended when the two men on the other side of the screen had got up and walked out, either to drink at another inn or perhaps to seek female company, easily found on the streets leading down to the riverside gates.

When the tale was told, Richard de Revelle sat silent for a moment. 'Henry, are you absolutely sure of this? You realise what it will mean if proved true?'

The bland-featured merchant looked offended. 'I am not in the habit of imagining things, Richard. I wish I had never been dragged into this but it can't be undone now. I am a devout man, and though the Bishop will be mortified, he owes it to the memory of old de Bonneville to see that justice is done.'

The sheriff looked across at John de Wolfe, still

in the background. If looks could kill, the coroner would have been felled on the spot, but de Revelle was trapped by the testimony of the portreeve. He was forced to make the best of it and sought to limit the damage. 'If this is true, which I am still not admitting without further proof, it only shows that Gervaise de Bonneville is trying to protect his squire. Nothing you have said implicates him in these deeds.'

John's face showed his almost scornful scepticism, but the sheriff was warming to his theme.

'Gervaise told his man to be careful what he said – he told him he was a fool to steal the dagger. Good counsel, albeit to a murdering rogue – but a nobleman feels a strong sense of duty and protectiveness to his squire, however misplaced.'

John grimaced at his brother-in-law. 'And what of Baldwyn's confession to having helped slay Hubert de Bonneville, eh? For what reason and at whose behest?'

De Revelle appealed to his erstwhile ally, Henry Rifford. 'You heard the rogue say that Gervaise was half a county away, so that absolves him of any implication in the death of his brother. So we have not a shred of evidence to link de Bonneville with either death. He was merely trying to shield his man from his own wicked folly.'

His explanation was met with stony silence from the faces ranged in front of him. He gave up for the moment and appealed to John about more immediate problems. 'What do you suggest is done about this? It is long past midnight. Should it not be left until morning?'

The coroner looked across at his own officer. 'Do you know where they are now, Gwyn?'

The Cornishman said that the men had not returned to the Bush by the time he had left to come to the castle.

Nesta, looking decorous under a swathe of heavy shawl over her head and shoulders, said, 'They paid in advance for a bed each in my inn and the younger brother is asleep there now. I'm sure the other two will return to bed when they've finished drinking and whoring.'

John caught the sheriff's eye as she spoke the last few words and de Revelle dropped his gaze, wondering if his brother-in-law would use his own indiscretion against him. But John kept to the issue in hand. 'It would be easier to deal with this in daylight. There's nowhere they can go until the city gates open at dawn.'

'And I don't want broken furniture and blood all over my tavern, if there's to be a fight,' put in the ever-practical Nesta.

'So we arrest them at first light?' confirmed the coroner.

De Revelle was still attempting a feeble protest. 'We take them in for questioning to see what they say to these unlikely allegations,' he countered.

'For God's sake, Richard! Do you think they'll roll over and admit it?' roared John. 'They'll lie through their teeth to save their necks. It will be the evidence of my four witnesses – and the business of the Justices in Eyre to deal with their guilt. This is one trial that I'm sure you'll be happy to leave to the King's judges, Sheriff!'

As they left, John noticed his brother-in-law give urgent instructions to his chamberlain, who hurried away through an inner door, following the route that the lady of the town had taken to vanish discreetly from the scene.

Outside, they walked back through the moonlit night to the gatehouse and the city streets. John had arranged with the reluctant sheriff to meet at the Bush an hour before dawn, with a sergeant and four men to seize the Peter Tavy trio in their beds. 'You had better keep out of the way, Nesta. Hopefully there'll be no trouble, if we catch them in their undershirts, but I don't want you involved – or you, Edwin. We need you kept safe as witnesses.'

With that back-handed concern for their safety, the two from the inn made their way back to Idle Lane, with Gwyn as bodyguard, while John strolled home to spend a few hours lying alongside Matilda, playing the faithful husband. None had seen a furtive figure slipping through the streets well ahead of them, also bound for the Bush.

CHAPTER NINETEEN

In which Crowner John uses his sword

Sir John's attempt at warming the matrimonial bed was shortlived. The cathedral bell had rung for the second hour by the time he was under the blanket and he had hardly dozed off when he felt himself shaken by the arm. It was Mary, wrapped in a shawl, trying to get him up without waking his wife.

She bent to hiss in his ear. 'Gwyn is outside! You must come, he says it's urgent.'

Unfortunately, it was Matilda who sat up first and saw the woman silhouetted in the moonlight streaming through the open door. 'Mary! What are doing with my husband? John, are you up to your tricks again?'

'No, mistress, really. It's Gwyn of Polruan, wanting the master. He says you must come to raise the hue-and-cry. Some felons have made a run for it.'

The coroner, struggling out of his dreams, gave a yell of despair. 'What? They've gone? By Christ, that can't be!'

He leaped from the low bed and scrabbled for his breeches and tunic in the silvery light. Mary disappeared down the outside steps, leaving her master to give a hasty account to his wife of the unmasking of the Peter Tavy villain.

He tumbled down the stairs from the solar, yelling to

Mary for his boots, helmet and sword. Within minutes, he was striding alongside Gwyn down the high street, dressed for trouble in a basin-shaped iron helmet, whose dents bore witness to service in many a campaign. Under this he wore his aventail, a chain-link balaclava, to protect his neck, tucked into a thick leather cuirass over his chest with mailed plates on the shoulders. A massive broadsword clanked at his waist and he had pulled on thick gauntlets, the backs covered in chain-mail.

Gwyn, wearing no protection apart from his ragged hide jacket, explained the situation as they hurried along. 'I went back to the Bush with Nesta and old Edwin. We had a dish of stew to warm us up, then Nesta went to her bed and I climbed up to the dormitory, just to make sure the birds hadn't flown . . . but they had!'

'All of them?'

'Martyn was still there. There were seven or eight people staying the night. I tiptoed among them and found the young brother sleeping like a baby – but two pallets were empty and there was no sign of the other brother or that Baldwyn.'

'They must have been warned. How else could this have happened?' snarled the coroner. 'It must be de Revelle. He's trying to save his reputation over that farce of a trial yesterday by letting them go. They'll end up in France if we don't bottle them up in the city.'

'You think that Gervaise is party to these killings, then?'

The coroner snorted as they hurried along. 'I'll be damned surprised if he's not. What reason would the squire have for being involved in the deaths? He has nothing to gain.'

Gwyn pondered on how they had been tipped off.

'Someone could easily have come into the inn. There were still a few drunks snoring on the floor downstairs and Nesta usually leaves the door open all night.'

They turned into Idle Lane where the tavern stood on a plot of wasteland, starkly visible in the light of the full moon. Edwin was standing in the doorway, a long spear in one hand and an axe in the other.

'They'll not pass me, Captain,' he said bravely, though with his eyesight he could hardly tell friend from foe.

John tapped his shoulder appreciatively. 'Go up to the castle quickly. Tell the sergeant to get the sheriff and the constable out of bed and bring half a dozen men down here. Say the coroner orders it. The hue-and-cry must be raised at once to find these people.'

Edwin, rejuvenated by the prospect of battle, stumped off as fast as he could, leaving Gwyn and the coroner to decide on the next move.

'It'll be a long while before the castle people get here. But it won't be light until seven, so those two can't get out of the gates until then.'

Gwyn grunted. 'What about their horses? They can never hope to slide out of the town on horseback?'

John looked back at the junction of the narrow streets, where Idle Lane and Butcher's Row joined. 'The stables for the inn are over there. Make sure their animals are still inside. Knock up the stable-boys and tell them not to let any horses out until we tell them.'

As Gwyn hurried one way, John walked cautiously the other, down towards Rack Lane. Apart from a few nocturnal cats, many scurrying rats and the odd whimpering dog, the streets were silent. The moon's bright orb hung in a clear, frosty sky and gave a good light, but there were plenty of shadows to hide two desperate men who had nothing to lose but their lives.

He stopped where the two streets met, unsure of which way to go. De Bonneville and Baldwyn could be anywhere in the city by now – they could have left the inn at least an hour ago.

The city walls should be an impregnable barrier, unless they could bribe a gate-keeper to open up for them – or, thought John cynically, if someone in authority gave orders for them to be let out.

He heard Gwyn coming back from the stable and stepped into the centre of the slushy road so that he could be seen and not attacked by mistake.

'Their horses are still there, so they will have to escape on foot. Where could they go, not to be over-taken at first light by mounted men?'

John pushed back his helmet a little, as the long nasal guard rubbed his prominent nose. He considered what he would do in the desperate circumstances of the two fugitives.

'The river!' he said suddenly.

They were in the south-west quadrant of Exeter, where the Watergate gave access to the quayside and to the ships that came up the Exe from the sea. John pointed down Stripcote Hill towards the inside of the town wall.

'We may as well go down that way, until the sergeant and his men arrive. The sheriff will be in no hurry to help us, though Ralph Morin might.'

As they strode down the steep slope, Gwyn asked if they should raise a hue-and-cry among the townsfolk. The law required that when a crime was discovered or a body found, the four nearest households should be roused and should chase any suspects or fugitives.

But John thought it pointless to start pounding on doors at four in the morning for sleep-fuddled citizens resentfully to stumble around the streets in the dark.

They reached the wall at a point near the West Gate, then came in a few yards to the twin towers of the gate, where they were challenged by an alert watchman.

'Someone's awake, at least,' growled Gwyn, whose opinion of peace-softened civilians was usually unrepeatable. The gateman reported that he had seen no one around for several hours and certainly would not open up his gate at any price. It was a hanging offence to risk the security of the city, even in times like this when there was no war or insurrection.

'Is there any place where two men might get across the wall?' asked John, looking up at the fifteen foot fortifications, built of the usual soft red stone. Sometimes, lack of maintenance and neglect allowed parts of city walls to crumble away.

The watchman shook his head. 'No, not a stone missing. The good city finances encouraged the portreeves to repair it last year. Sound as a bell, it is.'

They moved off eastwards, still listening for any sounds of the soldiers coming.

All was silent and they walked to the Watergate with no further sign of any human activity.

The Watergate was in the corner of the city walls, leading straight out on to the wharves. The gate was shut but they found the watchman sound asleep. After giving him a rousing telling-off, the coroner and his henchman started back into the town, taking an unsavoury lane that led towards the Shambles and eventually the cathedral Close.

Suddenly, Gwyn gripped John's arm. They listened and strained their eyes to the left, down an alley. There had been a metallic tinkle, unlikely to be rat or cat. Their own shoes were leather and the soft slime of mud and manure deadened any footfalls.

Gwyn melted into the shadows on one side of the alley and John vanished back around the corner of the lane. The opposite wall of the alley was bright in the moonlight.

They waited, frozen into statues in the blackness.

There was another slight rattle of metal on stone.

Slowly, a figure slid round the corner of the next building down the alley, and silently crossed over into the shadow opposite, the same shadow that hid Gwyn but five yards distant. Then another man, slighter in build, emerged and stood half in shadow but with part of his body still in moonlight. This part included an arm holding a naked sword.

Oblivious of the pair concealed only a few feet away, the fugitives' whispers came clear through the still, frosty air. 'Watch that bloody mace, Baldwyn. It clatters at every movement.'

'I've no sword, damn it to hell. That's still at Peter Tavy.'

'You'll never see that again. Nor yet Peter Tavy, I'm afraid.' The one in deep shadow moved again and the chain of his weapon made the same small sound, even though he tried to keep it rigid.

'Which way now? I don't know this pestilent town.'

'Turn right, then left. The Watergate will be ahead of us. If we jump the gateman silently, we can slit his throat and get out on to the riverside. There must be a boat there, to float us downstream far enough to land and make across country.'

Becoming bolder, Gervaise stepped into full moon-light and trod silently along the alley towards the junction with the lane.

Baldwyn, just visible to John, kept pace with his master in the shadows under the eaves. He was walking directly towards the immobile Gwyn and inevitably must see him within the next few seconds.

John's strategic instincts told him that he must give Gwyn the maximum advantage of surprise, so he stepped round the corner and stood in full moonlight, blocking the end of the alley. Simultaneously, he drew his sword with a flourish from its scabbard, the steel grating ominously against the bronze lip of the sheath.

The two escapers were as if struck by lightning. The sudden appearance of their persecutor from nowhere, to stand before them in the ethereal light of a full moon, seemed almost supernatural.

'Christ!' screamed Gervaise in terror. He threw away his sword, which hit the nearest wall with a clang. Then he turned tail and ran back round the corner of the alley.

'Get him, Gwyn!' roared John, throwing himself for-ward to chase the fleeing man. But Baldwyn was made of sterner stuff and stepped out to swing a murderous blow at the coroner with his chain mace. If it had connected, the heavy iron ball covered in spikes would have pulped John's head, even with the protection of the helmet. But Gwyn, his presence in the shadows unsuspected by Baldwyn, leaped forward with a yell and hacked down with his heavy sword on to the hardwood handle of the mace. The short chain that carried the ball swung up and wrapped itself around the sword-blade, preventing Gwyn from making another stroke.

The coroner, who had felt the wind of the mace-head

within an inch of his ear, staggered sideways, and before he could recover, the squire from Peter Tavy had snatched up his master's discarded sword and had jumped back to face them both.

Gwyn's sword had slid free of the mace-chain, but Baldwyn stood blocking the alley, his mace touching one wall and his sword-point the other. 'Come then, I'll have the pair of you!' he snarled, crouching slightly and swinging the mace-chain menacingly.

'Get after the other one – I'll settle this fellow!' barked Gwyn. In answer Baldwyn, who for all his evil deeds was no coward, took a great swing at both his attackers, the ball whistling across the whole width of the alley, preventing either opponent from getting close to him.

As the studded metal knob began another traverse, Gwyn jumped forward and jabbed his long sword behind it, trying to get Baldwyn's shoulder as he turned with the swing of the mace. But the man used Gervaise's discarded sword to parry left-handed, the two blades clashing like a pair of cymbals.

John dodged the mace on its return trip across the lane and, using his massive sword with two hands, slashed down at the squire's arm. Baldwyn pulled back and the blade bit into the oak stem, knocking the mace out of his hand. The black sphere spun away out of control and struck Gwyn full in the chest. His stiff-leather jerkin blunted the impact of the conical spikes, but the weight and force of the five-pound ball made him fall backwards, dropping his sword as he staggered.

With a delirious whoop of triumph, Baldwyn followed him down, his sword poised for a thrust through the neck. But not for nothing had his adversaries fought together on dozens of battlefields. In a flash

John was between them and another two-handed side stroke pushed Baldwyn's sword high in the air.

The coroner's blade skidded down the length of Baldwyn's and stopped with an arm-wrenching thud against the cross-hilt. Even before Gwyn could pick up his own weapon, John de Wolfe had begun Baldwyn's defeat. Though the younger man managed to get in one downstroke on John's shoulder, its strength was easily absorbed by the overlapping metal plates. Before the squire could lift his blade again, John had swung horizontally and hacked into the back of his hand. Baldwyn screamed as bones crunched and blood spurted. With a last desperate swing at the coroner's neck, he left himself open for a straight lunge and the point of John's sword went into his chest, through a lung and protruded an inch from his back.

Gwyn, now with his retrieved sword pointing at Baldwyn's neck, said, 'He's done for. I'll see him finished, if you want to find the other.'

As Baldwyn, his lifeblood rapidly filling the inside of his chest, slowly and silently subsided to the ground, the coroner hauled out his sword from between the dying man's ribs. He kicked the fallen weapon well clear of Baldwyn's grasp, in case of any final tricks, and sheathed his own bloody blade. 'See if he has anything to say as a dying confession – I'll try to find this other bastard. There's still no sign of the sheriff and his merry men.' Leaving Gwyn to witness the last moments of Baldwyn of Beer's life on earth, the coroner loped away up the alley where Gervaise de Bonneville had vanished.

Disturbed by the commotion, a few fearful faces peered from the window-openings of some of the mean huts in this least salubrious part of town, but no one ventured out to offer help. John could hardly blame them: this might have been just another fight between footpads.

The lanes were still deserted and there was no sign of Gervaise, who had a lead of four or five minutes, which was how long it had taken to deal with Baldwyn.

John soon came out on Bell Hill, one of the main cross streets that led to the South Gate, but this was also empty, though now a few windows showed flickering lights as the earliest risers began to crawl out of their beds for the new day. For want of any better direction, the coroner walked up to the major street junction of the city, where the roads to all four main gates crossed at St George's Church.

Here, at last, he saw half a dozen men-at-arms walking briskly down the road, with the castle constable and a sergeant hurrying behind. He hailed them and told the constable that one fugitive was dead or dying but that the other was still loose in the town. 'He came up this way, so he's not in the lower town,' concluded the coroner.

'No one crossed the High Street in the last five minutes, for we've just come down that way, Sir John,' added the sergeant.

Ralph Morin, another experienced campaigner, looked up and down the main roads, swinging his naked sword hopefully in his hand. 'I reckon he'll most likely be near the cathedral,' he said, waving an arm beyond the church of St Petroc, which stood on the opposite corner.

The mention of the cathedral caused Ralph, John and the sergeant to look at each other knowingly.

The constable sighed. 'I'll bet the swine has claimed sanctuary,' he said, reluctantly slamming his sword back into its scabbard.

CHAPTER TWENTY

In which Crowner John goes to the cathedral

No one had had much sleep, and no one had had any breakfast, so the customary snack in the coroner's chamber above the guardroom of the Rougemont gatehouse was more substantial than usual. The coroner had given Gwyn two silver pennies and his officer had come back at about the ninth hour laden with bread, pork, cheese and smoked fish. Thomas had been sent out to replenish the gallon crock of beer and had also brought some cider, which he much preferred.

Towards the end of their hearty meal, Ralph Morin came up to the bare room and accepted a jar of ale and some bread and cheese.

'I've put men at every door of the cathedral, but I don't think de Bonneville has the stomach to escape again – there's nowhere for him to go.'

'He gave us the slip well enough this morning,' said the coroner, 'although he owes that to his squire, who kept us busy long enough for us to lose him in the back lanes.'

The constable took a draught of his beer. 'The cathedral Close gates are supposed to be locked every night, but people are in and out at all hours. The canons like to go out for drink and to visit their women, and the place is infested with beggars. It's impossible for them to keep the place secure.'

'What about the cathedral itself? Is that always open?'

The clerk, considering himself the authority on matters episcopal, ventured a comment. 'The main west door is hardly ever used. It's barred most of the time. But there are smaller ones at each side of the west end. They are often left open between services – and, of course, there's a door into the chapter house and another leading to the cloisters. At the base of the North Tower, there's a small door alongside the canons' bread-house.'

The coroner sat hunched on his stool, finishing off a smoked herring. 'It doesn't matter a damn how de Bonneville got in. He's there now and we're stuck with him for up to forty days.'

'Where is he holed up?' Gwyn's curiosity got the better of his usual silence.

'Sitting at the foot of an altar in the North Tower,' replied the constable.

'Has he said anything yet?' asked John.

'Nothing apart from endlessly claiming sanctuary and hanging on tightly to the altar-cloth if anyone goes near him. A couple of canons and their vicars are circling about him, but the big men are going down there in about an hour – the Bishop himself, so they say.'

Gwyn lumbered off his window-sill to pour more drink. 'Does he get fed in sanctuary?'

They all looked at Thomas, the oracle on this ancient procedure. 'It's the responsibility of the village or the Hundred – or, in this case, the town burgesses – to keep him alive for up to forty days. That's why so many escape from sanctuary as the local people don't want the expense of feeding and guarding them.' He crossed himself spasmodically as he spoke.

The constable made a noise expressing disgust. 'And the task of guarding him falls on us – and that means half a dozen doors to watch. Why the hell didn't he choose a small church instead? There's plenty of them in Exeter, God knows, all with only one door.'

Crowner John gave one of his rare barking laughs. 'Maybe we can tempt him to move to St Olave's. My dear wife would love that, it being her favourite praying place. And, talking of the de Revelles, how is our beloved sheriff taking this?'

Morin grinned, his plain face lighting up at the thought of his superior's discomfiture. 'He's keeping his head down as much as possible. When I told him that the villain was in the cathedral, he scuttled off to see the Bishop, who for a wonder is actually staying in his palace here for a few days.' He shifted his bottom on the edge of John's table and hauled his sword scabbard into a more comfortable position. 'What's the next move?' he asked. 'There's a crowd around the cathedral already. News gets about quickly in this town.'

'No chance of his escaping again?' queried John.

'The place is sealed up tight as a drum. A mouse couldn't get out.'

The coroner got up from his bench behind the parchment-littered trestle and walked restlessly across to look down through one of the wall slits. The town looked as it usually did in early morning: all the action was out of sight in the cathedral Close. 'I'd better get down there, I suppose, to make sure those damned churchmen don't have some scheme up the sleeves of their cassocks.'

As Gwyn and Thomas cleared up the remnants of their breakfast, the constable had a sudden thought. 'This Baldwyn, whose corpse lies bleeding in my cart shed down below. Will there have to be an inquest upon him?'

John stared at him in puzzlement. 'Of course. He certainly came to his death unnaturally.'

'But you slew him yourself! Can a coroner stick a sword between someone's ribs and then investigate the death?'

John hadn't had time to consider this problem. 'What choice is there? I'm the only coroner in the county.'

The constable still felt the situation was difficult. 'But how can you be a witness in your own court? For that's what an inquest is, even if it's often held in the open air.'

As they walked down the winding steps, one behind the other, the coroner considered this problem. 'I've no answer to that, Ralph – and I doubt if it has happened anywhere else yet. Maybe I'll have to turn to Dorset or Somerset, to ask one of them to officiate – though, as far as I know, they've no jurisdiction in Devon.'

Morin laughed at John's obvious dilemma. 'That'll teach you to go hunting felons with your own sword. Leave it to the professionals, like me and the sheriff!'

John was scornful, though in good humour with the constable, whom he much admired. 'Leave it to you lot? Where were you and your merry men last night, when those two were trying to mash my head with a mace? If the coroner of this county

wants something done, he had better do it himself!'

The banter went on for while as they walked away
from the castle. Both men knew that the real object of
their derision was Richard de Revelle, whose devious-
ness made the keeping of law and order by his military
servants a stock joke in the county. The constable
was uncomfortable with this, as the men-at-arms were
mainly under his command, yet the unpredictable
behaviour of the sheriff reflected badly on his own
performance. They strode on down High Street, the
citizens greeting them with affability, respect, suspicion or downright hostility, depending on their
current relationship with law and authority.

When they reached St Martin's Lane, they turned
in towards the cathedral Close. John looked up at his
house as they passed, but made no effort to go in.
He hoped that Matilda's new-found compliance was
standing the strain of the night's events.

When they entered the Close, they found that the
idle section of the population had discovered a new
source of entertainment. Groups of people, mostly
women and old men, stood around the doors at the
west end of the huge building. Even the children
and imbeciles who usually roved among the graves,
playing ball and touch-tag, had gravitated to gape
at the cathedral entrance. There, men-at-arms were
stationed at each door and the older sergeant was
parading restlessly between them, anxious to disprove
their reputation for letting fugitives escape. Morin
went off to talk to him, while John, his officer and
clerk in tow, pushed through the sightseers. Leaving
their swords with one of the soldiers, they went in
through one of the side entrances that flanked the

big main doors of the Cathedral of St Mary and St Peter.

Inside, the poor November light left the huge building dim and shadowy. None of the side windows were glazed and birds flew in to perch on the corbels of the wooden ceiling, high above John's head. The body of the building, with its wide nave and flanking aisles, was an empty, bare vista of flagstoned floor. The many services each day were for the benefit of the clergy, and the public, who could stand in this open space, were merely passive spectators. Only at the many small altars scattered about the inner walls was there contact between priest and supplicants, where masses were said at frequent intervals.

Many religious relics were scattered around the building, most in side-chapels and on altars, where people came to pray and plead for favours to cure body, mind and purse. One of the lesser clergy acted as a guide to the splinters of the Cross, hairs of Christ, St Mary Magdalen's finger and part of the manger from Bethlehem.

But today no one had eyes for these holy artefacts as John marched the trio up the centre of the nave until they reached the quire-screen. This stood level with the sixth pair of massive columns that supported the building, separating the nave from the aisles. The quire was an ornately carved wooden cage, running back past the two huge towers towards the High Altar and the apse of the curved east end.

A few canons and lower-caste priests scurried about, disturbed by the unwanted secular activity that had descended on them this day.

'Where is this damned fellow hiding?' growled the

coroner, as they came up against the high wooden screen that separated the quire from the nave.

Gwyn saw to his left a pair of cassocked priests with their heads together, one pointing up the north aisle. 'Something going on over there, by the look of it,' he said. Bishop Warelwast's building was not truly cruciform in shape, in that the two massive towers on each side did not open as transepts to form a central crossing. Instead, the inner walls went right down to ground level, but there were small arched openings to give internal access into the base of each tower.

John walked around the corner of the quire to look up the narrow space leading to the east end, which passed the doorway to the North Tower. Here, several clergy were peering with mixed curiosity and timidity through the doorway.

'He must be in there, as Morin said. Let's have a look at the murdering bastard!' John was in no mood for delicacy or forgiveness after the events of the night.

They moved up alongside the columns of the nave to the opening that led into the bottom of the tower, a high, square chamber with a small door to the outside in the nearest left-hand corner. The gaggle of priests moved aside for them, Thomas de Peyne at once reverting to his former life by genuflecting and crossing himself. He repeated this as soon as he saw two altars against the right-hand wall of the chamber.

In front of the further one, almost in the north-east corner, a man sat on the floor, one hand firmly gripping the white cloth draped over the simple altar, dedicated to the Holy Cross, a relic of which was housed in a small brass-bound box on a shelf above it.

'There he is, our runaway hero!' shouted Gwyn, his red hair bristling, unconcerned about disturbing the sanctity of the place.

'Be quiet, you barbarian! You're in the House of God!' hissed the outraged Thomas, standing alongside the three priests, who glared disapprovingly at the noisy, roughtly dressed Cornish giant.

Gervaise de Bonneville, dishevelled, his cheeks and chin stubbled below his fair moustache, looked up in terror at the officer's bellow. He convulsively seized the altar-cloth even more firmly and crouched nearer the square table, which carried a gilded crucifix flanked by two candlesticks. He stared fearfully at the archway, unable to see clearly who was standing there in the gloom.

'Who's there? I claim sanctuary, whoever you are.'

His voice was tremulous with fear, as if he could already feel the coarse rope around his neck.

'It's the King's coroner, John de Wolfe, whom you well know by now. We met last half-way through the night, sir. If you'd not been so craven a coward, you'd have seen me spit your man Baldwyn on the end of my sword.'

The man from Peter Tavy rose slowly to his feet as the other came fully into the chamber. He kept one hand firmly on the altar of the Holy Cross.

'Baldwyn? Baldwyn is wounded?'

'Wounded? Baldwyn is dead – with my sword through his chest. But at least he stood his ground to fight, sacrificing himself to let you escape. You ran like a frightened rabbit and left him to die.'

De Bonneville's head sank to his chest and he subsided to the floor in front of the altar. They could only just hear his voice from across the wide room.

'Baldwyn – oh, God, have mercy on him!'

'And on you, Gervaise de Bonneville,' boomed the coroner, 'for you're a cold-blooded killer, a murderer of your own brother, for which you'll rot in hell.'

The fugitive held his head in his hands as he leaned against the base of the altar, mumbling something inaudible.

The coroner called to him again. 'De Bonneville, will you come out of this place and surrender yourself to me or to the constable?'

Without looking up, the man at the altar screamed, 'No, never! Leave me in peace. I am in sanctuary, I claim the protection of this holy place.'

Before John could reply, he felt a tap on his shoulder and turned to see Morin behind him in the doorway. 'I was about to tell him a few truths about sanctuary,' said the coroner.

The constable backed away a little into the arch, to look over his shoulder down the nave. 'You'll have to wait on this lot before you do that, John. Here's a procession of priests. I saw them assembling outside the cloisters. A full delegation of God's henchmen – and our dear sheriff with them.'

The coroner put his head out of the doorway to see an impressive group approaching with a stately, measured tread. First came a canon's vicar bearing a high processional cross, then the Archdeacon, John de Alecon, with a black cloak thrown over his chasuble and alb. He walked solemnly in front of Bishop Henry Marshall, who was in full regalia of embroidered cope over his other vestments. He carried his crosier – the gilded shepherd's crook – and his lofty brow bore the mitre as if he was attending some major ceremony at the high altar.

He was closely followed by the Precentor, Thomas de Boterellis, who walked with Richard de Revelle. The sheriff was in his best finery, wearing a dark red silk tunic to his knees, covered by a long cloak of green linen. A matching green capuchin was around his head, the tail falling elegantly to his left shoulder. John thought he looked more like a baron at court in Winchester than the law keeper of a far-western county, but perhaps his outfit reflected new political aspirations.

The vanguard was brought up by the cathedral Treasurer, John of Exeter, and a posse of prebendaries and assistant clergy. The coroner assumed that the personal friendship between the Bishop and the late Arnulph de Bonneville had led to this unprecedentedly grand delegation – and perhaps, also, it was an attempt to cover the sheriff's embarrassment at having protected Gervaise and his squire at the court the previous day. Normally, a sanctuary-seeker would be lucky if a mere canon or vicar came to check that the secular authorities had not violated the ancient right of temporary shelter for fugitives. It was unheard of for a bishop in full regalia to intervene – but, then, it was not every day that the lord of a manor sought sanctuary for conspiring to murder his own elder brother.

The coroner, his men and the castle constable stood aside, Thomas de Peyne jerking like a marionette as he attempted to cross himself repeatedly and bow low at the same time. The canon's vicar dipped the cross to get under the arch and led the episcopal convoy into the transeptal chamber. Here they contemplated the miserable figure crouched at the altar of the Holy Cross.

There was a heavy chair against the opposite wall

and two junior clergy hastily dragged it across, placing it behind the Bishop. His throne was up in the chancel near the High Altar, but it would have taken ten men to shift it. Henry Marshall sat on this lesser seat and arranged his voluminous cope carefully around his legs.

The rest of the entourage formed a semi-circle behind him and John's group came in to stand in the background. When the Bishop was settled, there was an expectant silence. His long chin turned towards the apprehensive figure crouched in the far corner. 'Gervaise de Bonneville, come here,' commanded the high-pitched voice of the prelate.

The figure slowly got to its feet, showing himself to the onlookers as a blond young man of average build. He was dressed in a crumpled dark green surcoat that reached to his knees over a lighter green tunic and trousers. The lower part of his legs, gartered above stout shoes, was splattered with mud from his flight last night through the filthy lanes. He stood, but made no move to go forward, keeping a firm grip on the edge of the altar.

'I said come here – and kneel at my feet,' snapped the Bishop.

De Bonneville's mouth opened and closed a few times indecisively. Then he said, 'I claim sanctuary, your grace, so I am afraid to leave this holy altar.'

Henry Marshall showed his impatience. 'You stupid boy, you have no need to cling to that table as if it were a raft in the ocean. The whole cathedral – indeed the whole Close – is included in our ancient mercy of sanctuary. You can go out and stroll in it just as safely, so come away from there!'

Only partially reassured, Gervaise let go of the

altar-cloth and slowly walked across the few yards of flagstone towards the Bishop's chair. He sank to his knees and bowed his head.

The prelate restrained himself from holding out his hand for his ring to be kissed – he had a politician's wariness of siding with losers.

'It saddens me to see you in this state,' he said sonorously. 'I was a friend of your father for most of my life. To hear within such a short time of his death, then the death of his eldest son and now your mortal predicament is almost too much for me to bear.'

John thought that in spite of his words the Bishop seemed to be bearing up quite well.

Then the Archdeacon took up the interview. 'De Bonneville, you say you seek sanctuary, so do you confess your sins?'

Gervaise shook his head vehemently. 'Of course not, Father. I am innocent. I am the victim of circumstance and conspiracy. My squire, Baldwyn of Beer, may have been a villain, though I can hardly believe it. But it is a foul conspiracy to claim that I am involved. You already have a culprit proven by the Ordeal, this Alan Fitzhai.'

His voice almost cracked with emotion. Then there was a long silence. The Bishop chewed his lip. Should he continue his previous ardent championship of de Bonneville with the risk of it all falling about his ears? Or should he throw him to the wolves and wash his hands of the whole affair?

He decided to try a middle path, leaving his options open until the matter became clearer.

'I am not concerned with the secular authorities – but whatever the eventual truth, I will defend to the death the inviolacy of sanctuary.' He looked hard at the sheriff, the custodian of secular power in Exeter. Everyone present still had the spectre of Thomas Becket's murder hanging over them and bishops were always happy to rub the noses of royal servants in the memory of that epic breach of sanctuary only twenty-four years before.

He turned back to glare at de Bonneville. 'As far as the Church is concerned, you have the set period of sanctuary allotted to you, without fear of violation. I will ensure that this is held sacrosanct. Whatever else you may arrange within that period is between you and the law officers.'

Gervaise, still on his knees, nodded vigorously.

Henry Marshall turned again to the coroner and the constable, who had moved to stand alongside de Revelle. 'No one may dare take him from this place against his will. He must be given food and water – but that is the responsibility of the city, not of the cathedral.'

The sheriff nodded. 'I will inform the portreeves, your grace. They have that duty. In fact, they have also the duty to guard the fugitive against escape. These are burdens for the city. But in this case I will detail a sergeant and men-at-arms from the garrison. The constable will see to that.'

It seems that Richard is trying to run with both the hare and the hounds, thought John.

The mitre turned slightly to face Ralph Morin. 'On the subject of such guards, I would remind you that the cathedral Close is not part of the city of Exeter. It is subject only to the rule of canon law and the King's officers and the burgesses have no jurisdiction within these precincts.'

The constable stared stonily at the Bishop. It was

obvious that he was going to be made the scapegoat in this, to avoid Henry levelling his criticisms directly at de Revelle.

'Well, what have you to say? Your men are trampling all over my Close, in places where they have no right to be.' He made it sound as if the soldiers' boots were ruining exquisite lawns and gardens rather than a quaguire of grave-pits and rubbish.

For a moment, Gervaise's face lightened with a flicker of hope; he wondered if the Bishop was trying to get the guards called off. This might give him a chance to escape.

But John entered the fray. His deep voice boomed from the back, 'It is true, Bishop, that the ground of the cathedral Close is outwith the responsibility of the town but I would remind you that the roads and paths through it remain the property of the borough. Men-at-arms are fully entitled to stand upon these roads, even if they should not venture on to the soil between them.'

Marshall swung round to identify the speaker and his face darkened when he saw that it was the coroner. But John was secure in his facts and they could not be denied.

'Very well, it may be so,' the prelate conceded. 'But I am still concerned that some heavy-footed, sword-happy man-at-arms might be tempted to violate the sanctuary I bestow upon this unfortunate soul.'

He decided to take the plunge and leaned forward to lay a hand on de Bonneville's head muttering an almost inaudible blessing as he did so. Then, having decided that he had become far enough involved in this messy business, he rose from his chair and turned away from Gervaise without another word, leaving the man on his knees.

He moved at a dignified, slow pace towards the doorway, preceded by his cross-bearer and followed by most of his entourage.

Only de Revelle and the Archdeacon stayed behind with the constable, and the coroner and his men.

In spite of the Bishop's assurances, the fugitive got to his feet and backed away again into his corner, pushing himself into the gap between the altar and the angle of the wall.

The sheriff advanced on his brother-in-law, his face twisted with rage. 'See what troubles you've unleashed now, John!' he snarled. 'Why couldn't you leave well alone? A couple of men dead – what's that when we lose thousands each year in wars and pestilence?'

The coroner, two hands' breadths taller than the other, glowered down into his face as they stood but a few inches apart.

De Revelle, as uneasy as the Bishop over the whole affair, advanced on de Bonneville, who, well aware of the previous partiality the sheriff had shown him, looked at him with tremulous hope.

'I have to ask you this straight away, Gervaise. Will you surrender to me and face trial on these allegations?'

The heir to Peter Tavy shook his head. 'I am innocent, Sir Richard. It must have been Baldwyn, acting without my knowledge.'

The sheriff looked even more unhappy that before. 'Such matter will be explored at the trial. If you have false accusers, this will become apparent when you face your judges.'

'How can I defend myself against false witnesses?' asked Gervaise wildly.

De Revelle tugged at his pointed beard in agitation. He wanted himself out of this place and this situation as soon as possible. 'I have said, the court will discover the truth,' he claimed with pious vagueness.

'Will it be your county court or the burgess court? Or will it be before the royal justices?' persisted de Bonneville, with panic in his eyes.

This was a thorny problem and de Revelle was not going to commit himself with so many onlookers present. 'That will have to be decided,' he said stiffly. 'The matter in hand is whether you will give yourself up to me now.'

Gervaise looked from one face to another. He saw frank hostility in Gwyn of Polruan and the coroner, distaste from the constable and evasive duplicity in the sheriff.

He backed away, hands out in front of him, as if fending off attack. Stumbling back to the altar, he shook his head vigorously. 'No! I'll not surrender to you! You'll chain me – imprison me – torture me, then hang me, whatever I say.' His voice rose to a shriek of fear that reverberated around the bare stone chamber.

De Revelle turned on his elegant heel and caught John by the arm. His face was white, but the coroner couldn't decide whether it was from anger or anxiety. 'Come out of earshot, through into the nave,' he hissed, pulling John by the elbow.

They passed back through the arch and stood around the corner against the high, cold stone.

'You are poised on a knife-edge, brother-in-law,' snarled the sheriff. 'The man Baldwyn was evil and treacherous – I admit I was wrong about him – but Gervaise de Bonneville! If it turns out, as I hope and expect, that he was merely an innocent trying to be faithful to his own retainer, then you are in deep trouble, Master Coroner!'

John's long, saturnine face showed no trace of anxiety and he failed to tremble at the sheriff's threats. 'What are you going to do about it, dear Richard?' he answered. 'Perhaps you can ask your good friend Prince John to bring his influence to bear on Hubert Walter – or even our royal king himself, eh?'

The sheriff's pallor was flushed with the a mottled ruddiness of true rage. 'You've always got some cheap answer to divert truly serious advice, sir! Watch your back on dark nights in lonely streets, John. I'll not want to see my sister a widow before her time.'

The coroner grinned, infuriating the sheriff even more. 'I think last night showed that I can more than hold my own in lonely alleys at dead of night! I can still shove a broadsword through a murderous heart – and I'd have saved you a hanging if the other knave hadn't thrown down his weapon and run off like a jack-rabbit!'

Frustrated beyond endurance, de Revelle swung back into the archway and called, in a voice quivering with spite, 'You have had your chance, de Bonneville! Now settle the matter with the coroner here.'

He vanished, abdicating any further responsibility to his brother-in-law.

CHAPTER TWENTY-ONE

In which Crowner John takes confession

Crowner John dragged the chair used by the Bishop nearer to the altar of the Holy Cross and sat down to parley with the fugitive. He had been up virtually all night and was feeling the strain of dodging chain-maces and indulging in sword fights.

'So you'll not give yourself up to me or the sheriff?' he began conversationally.

The man from Peter Tavy pressed back into his niche and shook his head again. 'Never! I might as well hang myself now from that window.' He gestured dramatically at the centre bar of a small opening above them.

'Save us a lot of trouble and expense if you did,' grunted Gwyn. 'I'll willingly supply you with a rope.'

John leaned forward to the man in the corner. 'You'd better understand well the situation regarding sanctuary. You've managed to evade arrest by getting in here. The fact that you ran away and sought refuge will be damning evidence against you when the matter comes to trial – which, I assure you, will be before the King's judges, not the sheriff's court.'

De Bonneville seemed to recover some of his for-mer defiance now that the sheriff and the episcopal contingent had left. 'Don't try to tell me that flight means guilt, Crowner! The level of justice in this land means that many an innocent man takes to his heels to escape false accusation.'

John wasn't disposed to argue with him. 'That's as maybe, the court will decide that. In any event, you managed to reach sanctuary.' He fixed the younger man with a steely eye, not concerned to hide his contempt for a killer and a coward. 'Sanctuary gives you forty days' respite in here, understand?' Gervaise crouched transfixed, like a rat mesmerised by a snake. 'At the end of that time, your food and water ceases, the place is sealed up and you either come out or you die in here.' He stabbed a finger towards de Bonneville. 'Anyone helping you after those forty days are up is himself liable for summary execution, so don't expect any aid.'

Gwyn couldn't resist adding a brick to the burden. 'And if you come out after the forty days, anyone is entitled to slay you on the spot – preferably by beheading.'

'Apart from the formality of a short inquest on the spot,' added the coroner, anxious to maintain his stake in the process. 'And my legal obligation to take the severed head to the castle gaol.'

John de Alecon, who as Archdeacon had a little more compassion than the two fighting men, threw a lifeline to the cringing Gervaise. 'But there is an alternative, as the Crowner will no doubt tell you.'

John settled back in the chair, his black-clad arms folded across his chest. With some reluctance, he spelled out the way in which Gervaise could evade justice, if he so wished. 'You can abjure the realm of England, leaving these shores never to return during the reign of King Richard. You will forfeit all your property, even down to the clothing you now wear.'

The Archdeacon chipped in again. 'Of course, your inheritance of Peter Tavy will be lost to you. If you had already been confirmed in it by the King, then the honour would have been forfeit to the Crown.' His lean, ascetic face was as earnest as that of a schoolmaster instilling lessons into his pupils. 'As it is, you cannot in natural justice benefit materially from the fruits of murder, so it was not yours in the first place.'

De Alecon has a good grip on secular as well as canon law, John thought.

'But as you are not so confirmed, then I presume that Martyn will become the new lord of Peter Tavy, as long as he can keep his cousins at arm's length. But that is no concern of ours.'

Gervaise had listened to all this with mixed emotions. The catalogue of his lost possessions, even down to his undershirt, was offset by the prospect of not swinging from a gibbet. Of course, he knew of the principle of abjuration of the realm but, like most folk, had never before needed to go into the details.

'I will abjure!' he exclaimed eagerly. 'What do I have to do?'

John set out the procedure for this cumbersome sequel to sanctuary. 'First, you must confess your guilt to me before a jury, in a form which I will tell you.'

'But I am innocent!'

'Then you cannot abjure. You can surrender now or you can step out of the door and be killed – or you can rot in here after the forty days expire. The choice is yours.'

Gervaise began to shake with a mixture of fear and

fatigue. 'There is no choice, it seems,' he muttered in anguish.

John went on relentlessly, 'You will cast off your own clothing, which will be confiscated and sold. You will be given an ungirdled garment of crude sackcloth and you will be given rough-hewn wood from which you must construct a cross with your own hands.'

Here John de Alecon added, 'De Bonneville, the cross must be held before you in your hands every inch of the way when you leave here to show people that you are a felon and a sinner, who has been granted mercy by the Holy Church.'

John picked up his official version, which he was obliged to relate to every would-be abjurer. 'You will tell passers-by what you are on your journey, the direction and length of which will be decided by me.'

He paused for a moment. 'Do you still wish to abjure or will you surrender?'

De Bonneville had no doubts: the alternative was execution, with or without a trial.

'I will abjure – as soon as it can be arranged.'

The ritual was to take place the next day, as soon as a jury could be summoned, a sackcloth robe sewn and two pieces of rough wood found in the refuse lying around the cathedral Close for Gervaise to lash together to make a crude cross.

Later that day, after he had examined an alleged rape and another non-fatal assault, John walked wearily down to the the Bush in the twilight, before going home to Matilda and his dinner. It was too early for the inn to be busy, so Nesta sat with him behind the same wattle screen that had concealed the eavesdroppers from the Peter Tavy conspirators. 'Looks as if the fellow will escape retribution, after all.' John glowered as he sat with one hand on the comforting plumpness of the innkeeper's thigh.

The auburn-haired woman seemed relieved. 'Then I'm glad there'll be no need for us to appear as witnesses before the court. Especially as people would snigger at the coroner's mistress being so deeply involved. And it would do your relations with your wife no good at all, Sir Crowner!' As usual, she saw the sensible and practical side.

Old Edwin came across with refills for their mugs. He looked ten years younger after the stimulation of his part in the previous night's excitement. 'You settled that fellow properly, Captain,' he wheezed gleefully. 'I'd a' come out myself with the firewood axe to help you, if I'd known it was going on so near.' He stumped away, chortling to himself, as Nesta leaned closer to John, both enjoying the warmth of the log fire before them.

'This abjuration – where does he have to go?' she asked.

'Depends where I choose to send him. I've heard that some coroners – for there were a few in some counties even before September – are perverse enough to make them walk the length of the country.'

'And what are you going to do?' she persisted.

'I've not made my mind up yet. But the further they have to travel, the greater the chance that they get killed on the way.'

'I thought you'd be happy to see his throat slit,' she said.

John blew a long sigh through his beard. 'I hate to see him escape the noose, but the law is the law.

Few abjurers arrive at their destination – many throw away their cross around the first bend in the road and vanish into the forest to become an outlaw. And many others are set upon by the families of their victims in revenge.'

'Are they allowed to do that?' she asked, sipping his ale.

'Not if the abjurer sticks to the road as he is instructed. But who's to say what happens once they are out of sight? In the Palatine of Durham, I'm told the Bishop sends an escort to see the man safe out of his territory – but I can't imagine our dear sheriff going to that trouble or expense.'

They sat in comfortable silence for a moment.

'Can I come to see what happens at this abjuration affair tomorrow?' she asked.

He gave one of his rare grins. 'Why not? The rest of the town will be there, I'll bet.'

At noon the next day, the cathedral bell boomed out its message to the town as a large crowd gathered in the Close. It was Wednesday, so there was no rival attraction at the gallows and several hundred of Exeter's five thousand population were clustered around the West Front of the great building to see the entertainment.

Nesta was there and John had been surprised to receive Matilda's announcement at their early meal that she intended to watch the proceedings too. He could not decide whether she wanted to be there from sheer curiosity or to see her own husband the centre of civic attention.

Though the de Bonnevilles were not well known in the city, coming from the distant lands at the other end of Dartmoor, the fact that a Norman gentleman was in such disgrace was an unusual attraction to pull in the crowds. It was a secular ceremony, even though the concept of sanctuary had religious origins, so the clergy were keeping a fairly low profile. The Bishop had decided to keep away but the Archdeacon and the Precentor stood in one of the doorways of the West End to keep a watch on the formalities.

The sheriff was also notable by his absence, the sergeant and a few men-at-arms the only token of the forces of law and order, apart from the coroner. John, with the abjurer, was the focal point of the ritual.

As the bell tolled midday, the Coroner led a drab figure out of the north tower and down the nave towards the cathedral doors. The great central oaken door was never opened except on high festivals or for the rare visitation of the Archbishop or the King, so one of the lesser flanking doors was used to allow them out into the daylight.

Gwyn of Polruan followed closely behind the fugitive, his face suggesting that he hoped de Bonneville would make a run for it as soon as they got outside the weaponless zone of the cathedral so that he could cut him in half with his sword. However, as Gervaise was shortly to be released alone on to the high road, there was little point in him escaping anywhere and Gwyn had to be content with a threatening attitude and an occasional prod in the back. Thomas de Peyne trailed along behind, carrying his bag of writing instruments.

Gervaise's clothing had already been listed for sale, as the abjurer now wore a shapeless tube of hessian, the ragged hem of which came to his ankles. He was barefoot and his long curly hair had vanished – Gwyn had arbitrarily decreed that it be cut off – leaving an irregular stubble over his scalp, which looked worse than if it had been fully shaved. As far as John knew, there was nothing in the rules on abjuration that insisted on shearing the hair, but he was in no mood to deny Gwyn his last chance at humiliating the man.

As they lined up outside the door, there was a chorus of jeers from the crowd and a few rotten vegetables were thrown. As they were as likely to hit the officials as the villain, the sergeant roared at the culprits and smacked a few heads with his mailed hand; he was dressed up to show off for this occasion, in chain-mail hauberk to his knees and a round helmet with the usual nose-guard.

The shouts and catcalls died down and the coroner began the ceremony. Gwyn had dragooned a dozen men to be a jury and they stood in a double semi-circle behind John, to witness Gervaise's confession. The two cathedral priests also joined the group.

'On your knees before the King's coroner,' yelled Gwyn.

The wretched de Bonneville sank to the ground. His humiliation was all the greater for the contrast with his former station in life – good clothes, horses, money and aristocratic elevation above his fellow men.

'You will now confess your crimes to me,' grated John. 'Unless it is full and genuine, your confession will be invalid.'

At this point the Precentor upstaged the Archdeacon by throwing in a further warning of eternal damnation. 'And the mercy of the Church and perhaps your eventual absolution also depend on your contrition and truthfulness. Otherwise the fires of hell await you.'

Haltingly and reluctantly, de Bonneville came out with the story.

It had begun many months earlier when a soldier fresh from Outremer had brought the news to Peter Tavy that Hubert hoped to be home before long. 'We had thought Hubert dead, either in Palestine or on the arduous journey,' murmured his brother. 'Many of those who took the Cross never returned home, so my expectations of being heir to my father's honour had been accepted by all.' His voice rose in almost petulant defiance. 'I ran the manors, did all the business when my father was struck with the palsy, it was to have been mine by right. I had earned it through three years of Hubert's absence.'

Gervaise, who had long resented his brother's seniority and superior attitude, had seen his hopes of becoming his father's heir diminish to almost nothing. The only vestige that remained was that Hubert would not survive the homeward journey, as more Crusaders fell prey to disease and other dangers of travel than to the weapons of the Mohammedans. He admitted now that he had often talked to Baldwyn, his squire and confidant, about this possibility. Somehow it developed into an open hope that some fatal accident might befall his elder brother, though there seemed little that they could do to foster the likelihood of this happening.

Then, by sheer chance, Baldwyn had been in Sampford Spiney some eight weeks ago, visiting a woman he knew there, when he heard that a man staying at the tavern was on his way home from the Holy Land. Anxious to know whether this traveller might have more recent news of Hubert de Bonneville, Baldwyn sought him out and was amazed to discover that this Aelfgar was actually his servant-cum-squire. He was on his way to Peter Tavy to announce that his master was in Southampton and would be home in about two weeks.

'Baldwyn kept his identity secret from the man, then rode home and told me of what he had discovered,' announced Gervaise, in a flat, hopeless voice.

After a few hours of agonising discussion, they had decided that Aelfgar could never be allowed to deliver his news to their manor. Although Sir Arnulph was incapable of understanding, Martyn, the cousins and all the manor inhabitants would know of Hubert's imminent return and any plan to usurp him would be frustrated.

By now, Gervaise was purging himself of his misdeeds in an orgy of penitence. Still on his knees in the mud, with the jury and a sizeable part of the townsfolk of Exeter hanging on his every word, he carried on his confession, in a voice that varied from a dull monotone to cracked emotion. 'We decided to kill Aelfgar and somehow prevent Hubert from coming home, which was far more difficult.'

Baldwyn knew that the Saxon was coming from Sampford Spiney the next day, after his horse had recovered from lameness. 'I provided my squire with money and he soon found a rough outlaw begging on the rim of the forest above Tavistock who, for a couple of marks, was willing to help him dispatch the Saxon.' There was an outraged murmur from the front rank of the crowd.

'Baldwyn and the ruffian lay in wait for Aelfgar

on the road out of Sampford Spiney. The two easily unhorsed him, stabbed him and Baldwyn cut his throat. They threw his body over his horse and took it to that nearby tor, where they hid it in a cleft.'

His voice rose suddenly in plaintive justification. 'I had no part in it, I was miles away at our other manor. Baldwyn was keen to do this thing. Without me as lord of Peter Tavy, he would never have advancement under Hubert, who disliked him and would have put in his own man as seneschal.'

Crowner John bristled at this. 'You miserable hog, don't try to excuse yourself! It was you who gave the money for your man to hire another killer. All you can plead is cowardice, not innocence.'

Gervaise's head dropped in shame, but he still attempted to excuse himself. 'This was merely getting rid of some paltry bodyguard, something to delay the news of my brother's return until we thought of another plan. We had no intention to kill Hubert. I thought perhaps I could arrange for him to be kidnapped and dumped in Ireland or Brittany, where some accident might still befall him.'

John gave him a push with the flat of his boot that sent him tumbling into the ordure on the ground. 'You're as big a liar as you are a villain! You meant Hubert's death from the outset. No other way would grant you your father's heritage. But then what happened?'

Gervaise used his crude cross to push himself up to a squatting position. He looked so abject in his misery that Nesta almost felt sorry for him, until she reminded herself of his mortal sin of fratricide.

'That fool Baldwyn couldn't resist stealing the man's dagger. Then they took the Saxon's horse into the

305

wilds of the moor, stripped it of its harness and let it run wild to get rid of it,' he mumbled.

'What happened to this outlaw and his Judas pieces of silver – or is that some other figment of your evil mind?' snapped the coroner.

De Bonneville shook his head violently. 'He was real enough – until Baldwyn killed him!'

John raised his arms in despair. Framed in his black cloak, he looked like a huge bat hovering over the culprit.

'Mother of God, another corpse! Where will we find this one?'

Gervaise was anxious to shift the blame from himself. 'It shows what manner of evil rogue Baldwyn was!' he said, in a complete reversal of his former concern for his squire. 'I knew nothing of it, but he told me later that he felt it wise to get rid of any witnesses.'

'Where and when?' demanded the coroner grimly.

The aspiring lord of Peter Tavy shrugged. 'He never told me other than that he had caught the man unawares and run him through with his sword in some remote spot. He did say that there was no fear of the body being found, as he threw it down the shaft of an old tin mine.'

Gwyn of Polruan was outraged at this endless story of treacherous killings. 'And I'll gamble that your fine squire took back his blood money from the corpse's purse before he dropped it down the hole, the swine!'

'So how did you later find your brother, wretch?' demanded John, who was getting angrier as the story unfolded.

The jurymen and those in the crowd who could hear what was being said, or had the proceedings relayed to them by those in front, were also growing restive. Hisses and jeers were frequent, in spite of the men-at-arms' efforts to keep order. John felt that if he had thrown Gervaise to the mob, they would have torn him limb from limb or hanged him from the nearest tree.

De Bonneville, who now cowered on his knees close to the protection of the coroner, explained what had happened.

'It was not I who killed my brother!' he pleaded. 'I never laid eyes on him. It was Baldwyn who went to Southampton just before the time that Aelfgar had claimed that Hubert would leave that port. He was the one who slew him, on the promise that I would give him advancement and wealth when I achieved my inheritance.'

John was disgusted with him. Violence was commonplace, but Gervaise's cold-blooded plan to assassinate his own's brother was outrageous. 'You might as well have held the knife yourself, you evil worm!' shouted John.

Gwyn came up to whisper something in his ear. The coroner turned back to look down scathingly at the craven figure in sackcloth. 'The wounds on the body of your brother strongly suggested that he had two attackers . . . and you claim you were not there?'

Gervaise shook his head at the earth beneath his face. 'Baldwyn again hired some outlaw to help him. First he went to Southampton and found such a fellow. The hired man had to seek out Hubert, as Baldwyn was well known to my brother. It was no problem tracing him, but then Baldwyn and his man waited until he left Southampton and covertly followed him.'

There was a sudden commotion at the back of the

crowd. 'Here's someone who can vouch for that – the felon himself!'

Gervaise's tale was interrupted by a shout from beyond the circle of onlookers. They parted to allow a man-at-arms push a way through for the constable of Rougemont.

Behind him came another soldier, shoving a be-draggled figure with chains on his wrists and ankles – a man with two fingers missing from his right hand.

After the hubbub had died down, Ralph Morin joined the inner group and stood alongside the cor-oner, his hands on his hips.

Nebba, for certainly it was he, was forced down alongside Gervaise to kneel in the mud, completing de Bonneville's ignominy: the Norman aristocrat now had to share the same filthy ground as a base outlaw.

'We found this creature by sheer chance, Crowner,' related Morin conversationally. 'Early this morning, he robbed a merchant of his purse just outside the North Gate and made a run for it. Unfortunately for him the trader's own son saw him, raised the hue-and-cry among the other stall-holders and overtook him before he reached the woods beyond St David's.'

The coroner reached down and grabbed the hair of the outlaw, jerking his head back so that he could look more closely at his defiant face. 'You keep turn-ing up in this matter, Nebba!' he said. 'Widecombe, Southampton . . . but I suspect that this will be your final appearance.'

Morin gave the former archer a kick in the ribs. 'He was recognised as an outlaw by those who seized him this morning – some were for lopping off his wolf's head on the spot and collecting the bounty money. But then he spun some tale about bargaining for his life with some information about Gervaise de Bonneville here so, from curiosity, I listened to his tale.'

The Saxon bowman, ever an optimist, cried out in his own defence, 'This is hallowed ground, I claim sanctuary, just as I hear Sir Gervaise has done!'

Morin gave him another blow with his boot. 'Sanctuary, be damned! My soldiers brought you here and my soldiers will take you out again. Now, tell the Crowner the same tale you spun to me, to see if he believes you.'

Nebba seemed fatalistically calm, compared to the nobleman alongside him in the dirt. He knew that he would hang soon, but a violent death was almost the inevitable end for a mercenary and an outlaw. The only doubt about it was when – rather than if – it would happen. His time had run out and that was that. Everyone has to die sometime.

The castle constable prodded him again with his toe. 'You told me that you were the ruffian that Baldwyn of Beer hired in Southampton, eh?'

Nebba nodded, his matted hair bobbing over his dirty forehead. 'He seemed to have an eye for a man who would do any task for a few marks. Found me in an inn, bought me some ale and offered me a job.'

'I knew nothing of this!' whimpered Gervaise. 'I was many leagues away in my own manor.'

John and Morin ignored him. 'What then? Did Baldwyn say, "Kill me a man for two marks"?' asked John sarcastically.

'I knew nothing of that to start with, I just had to wander around Southampton and find this Sir Hubert. The Welsh agent, Gruffydd, eventually pointed me in the right direction.'

Gwyn grunted in surprise. 'He never told me that when I was talking to him!'

Nebba continued his story resignedly. 'Baldwyn said we needed to follow him without being seen. He said nothing of slitting his gizzard at that stage, but I soon got the drift of his intentions.' He grinned at a sudden recollection, in spite of the certain knowledge that within days he would be hanging by the neck. 'I had to run for it even then, as I'd relieved a fat merchant of his purse to get some drinking money – the damned fool resisted, so I had to stick him between the ribs to get away. But I arranged to meet up with Baldwyn again next day in the forest near Lyndhurst.'

The rest of the unhappy tale was plain. The two assassins had tracked de Bonneville across Hampshire and Dorset. When their best opportunity came, on a bare moorside above Widecombe at dusk, they attacked Hubert together but, a seasoned fighter after his Crusading, he fought them off and raced down towards the village. 'He nearly got away from us, blast him, but his horse put a foot in a rabbit hole and threw him off. We caught him up near Dunstone and continued the fight on foot.'

'Two of you against one – a brave performance!' John was cynical this morning.

'He put up a good fight, I'll say that,' admitted Nebba, with some admiration. 'Though I was never much good with a sword, I was brought up to use a long-bow.'

'But you managed to stab him in the back, while that squire cut him in the arm from the front,' snarled Gwyn, unable to conatin himself any longer.

Nebba's silence was as good as an admission of guilt.

'What about the mare, the one with the black-ringed eye?' demanded the coroner.

Nebba sighed, as if realising that he could only be hanged once, so it made little odds what he confessed to now.

'We dragged the body into some bushes near the hamlet of Dunstone and set his horse loose to wander away.'

'If you left Hubert's body in a thicket in Dunstone, how did it come to be found in a stream in Widecombe?' John asked. Even as he spoke the words, he realised that his earlier suspicions about the Dunstone reeve were probably true and that the village had foisted the corpse on their neighbours to avoid trouble.

Gwyn of Polruan picked up on another matter. 'If you turned that grey mare loose, how did it come to be sold to Ralph the reeve?'

Nebba shuffled his feet, his ankle chains clanking. 'I didn't trust that Baldwyn. One night he told me about the killing of that other fellow, that Aelfgar. Though he didn't say outright, after a gallon of ale he made hints that he'd silenced the man for safety's sake.'

'So?' grunted the Cornishman.

'I didn't turn my back to him for fear of getting it stabbed. I got him to pay me what he owed me, then slipped off back into the woods. I gave him time to clear off, then came back to find the mare.'

'And sold it to the village reeve,' finished John. 'Well, I'll see you at the hanging tree.'

He jerked his head at Ralph Morin, who gestured to his men-at-arms to take Nebba back to the castle. Undoubtedly the next time he emerged it would would be for a one-way trip to the gallows. The gap in the crowd fused together after he had clanked mournfully away and attention was once more focused on the sorry figure of the abjurer, still kneeling in the mud.

Gervaise seemed to have run out of confessions and John began his own part of the ritual. 'You are a killer and a liar, and have enough felony on you to be hanged a dozen times over. But I have to accept your confession, as it seems to fit the sorry facts. Now you will take the oath of abjuration.'

He turned to the motley collection of townsfolk behind him. 'You, the jury, will witness everything that is said here.'

The Archdeacon came forward with a copy of the Gospels from the cathedral and the kneeling penitent put his right hand on the cover. John de Alecon took care to keep the valuable book well away from the mire.

Gwyn bellowed for silence and John then spoke the words of the oath, making Gervaise repeat them after every line.

'This hear thou, Sir John de Wolfe, that I, Gervaise de Bonneville of Peter Tavy in the county of Devon, am an instigator and conspirator in the murder of Aelfgar of Totnes and my own brother, Hubert de Bonneville. And because I have done such evils in this land, I do swear on this Holy Book, that I will leave and abjure the realm of England and never return without the express permission of our lord Richard, King of England or his heirs.'

Gervaise stumbled over the words many times and his voice dropped to become inaudible now and then, but the coroner remorselessly made him repeat any faulty passages.

'I shall hasten by the direct road towards the port which you have allotted me and I will not leave the

King's highway under pain of arrest or execution. I
will not stay at one place more than one night and
I will diligently seek for a passage across the sea as
soon as I arrive. I will tarry there only one flood and
ebb, if I can have such passage. If I cannot secure
such passage, I will go every day into the sea up to
my knees, as a token of my desire to cross. And if I
cannot secure such passage within forty days, I will
put myself again within a church ... and if I fail in
all this, then let peril be my lot.'

Satisfied with this, John then told the felon to rise
and lifted the right hand that clutched the rough
cross high into the air. It was merely two sticks, one
as tall as Gervaise, the other a two-foot cross-bar,
which the abjurer had been made to bind together
with some rough twine. Then he was given a pair of
crude wooden-soled shoes and the time to send him
on his way had finally come.

The crowd were still growling at him and a stone,
thrown with unerring aim by an urchin, hit him
on the side of the head, causing blood to trickle
down between the ragged clumps of shorn hair. John
grasped him by the shoulders and turned him to face
away from the cathedral.

'You will walk from here bare-headed to Plymouth
to seek a ship to France or Brittany. You have been
given sufficient of the contents of your purse to pay for
a passage and to keep you alive for a number of days.
You have two days and two nights to get to Plymouth
on foot, which should be ample. Remember, you must
abide strictly by the terms of your oath. If you fail, by
staying more than one night in any place or by straying
an inch off the highway, people are entitled to treat
you as the wolf and behead you. And if you ever set

foot in England again, you will be outlawed and your wolf's head forfeit to any man who can lift a sword.' The coroner gave him a token push. 'Now go!'

The Archdeacon and the Precentor chanted, 'May God have mercy on your soul,' and made the sign of the cross in the air, feverishly mimicked by Thomas de Peyne, who had been writing energetically on his roll draped over a large stone left by the masons.

To the jeers and abuse of the crowd, Gervaise jerked forward and began to walk towards the exit of the Cathedral Close, which led to the West Gate, the river and the road to Plymouth.

The sergeant and his men beat a path for him through the hostile crowd and a man-at-arms walked alongside the abjurer to make sure that at least he got out of the city in one piece.

The coroner stood watching, with Gwyn and the Archdeacon at his side. 'There he goes! It seems unjust that he kills two or three men and walks away, while a child who steals a jug is hanged.' John was bitter and philosophical at the same time.

'What about that man who was made to suffer the Ordeal?' enquired John de Alecon. 'It seems that he was unjustly accused.'

The Precentor naturally took an opposite view. 'It proves the efficacy of the ritual. As he survived the scalding, it proved his innocence.'

'He damned near died,' John snapped. 'Only his strong constitution saved him. Let's hope the ministrations of the holy sisters will make him fit again.'

Thomas de Boterellis had no answer to this and kept a sulky silence when the Archdeacon expressed the hope that Alan Fitzhai would find it in his heart to forgive the sheriff for his actions.

The crowd dispersed and, though a few youths and idiots had followed de Bonneville to the gate, the mass hatred seemed to have faded as readily as it had come.

Yet John was still uneasy about the abjurer, as he disappeared into the distance. 'I keep thinking about the Palatine of Durham and the way they shepherd their exiles,' he said to Gwyn.

The Cornishman was unimpressed. 'Good riddance, I say. If someone wants to take a swing at him with a battleaxe or broadsword, then good luck to them.'

His bloodthirsty sentiments were interrupted by Matilda who had left a conversation with another woman spectator and was approaching John. Gwyn melted away, there being mutual dislike between them. John noticed that Nesta, too, had diplomatically vanished.

'You seem to have done something right for a change, husband,' said Matilda. In spite of her two-edged words, the tone was not critical, and John sensed that she was pleased with him for once.

'I hated seeing that evil young man get away so easily, but sanctuary and abjuration have long been our custom,' he said.

His wife failed to think that Gervaise had suffered too lightly. 'He's lost everything, hasn't he? Pride, position, possessions and inheritance.'

All these losses would be worse than death to Matilda, thought her husband. 'Abjurers have a strange way of coming back, lady,' he forecast gloomily. 'Even if – God forbid – King Richard were to die, it's not clear whether the exile only lasts for his reign. And many an abjurer has slipped back quietly into the country after all the fuss has died down.'

315

'That's no concern of yours, John. You did your duty well and that's all that can be asked of you.'

As they walked slowly towards St Martin's Lane, he still had a nagging concern about his responsibility to the ragged abjurer, now plodding to Plymouth to find a shipmaster willing to take him to France.

At least John was content that his contempt for the man had not allowed him to be vindictive in his choice of port. Yet the anger of the crowd, short-lived though it seemed, made him wonder if de Bonneville would see Plymouth alive.

He found that, during his reverie, they had arrived outside their house and his wife was speaking to him. 'Are you going to eat now or this evening? Mary can make something if you're hungry.'

Matilda's concern for his well-being was a novelty and John was surprised at how he welcomed it. Not because he had discovered any new-found affection for her, but as a relief from the usual sparring and fighting. However, he had other things on his mind. He came to a sudden decision. 'No, but I'll come in to change my cloak and get my riding boots.'

As he pulled on his travelling outfit and hung his baldric across his shoulder to carry his sword, Matilda wanted to know where he was going. 'To follow our abjurer – I want to see that he at least gets well away from the city alive.'

Leaving her on the doorstep, shaking her head in a resigned lack of understanding of the man who shared her life and her bed, the coroner hurried across to the stables and helped the farrier to saddle up Bran, his huge stallion.

He trotted away towards the West Gate, more than

an hour after Gervaise had trudged off in a welter of abuse.

Eager to put as much distance between himself and Exeter as possible, still fresh and not yet footsore, de Bonneville had covered quite a distance in that hour. He was already well into the trees towards Alphington when John, now walking his horse quietly, saw him in the distance.

The Plymouth road was moist after a shower during the night, but not too deeply rutted in mud. It was deserted apart from the bedraggled figure in brown sackcloth, who held the cross before his chest like some talisman to ward off evil, even though, as far as the coroner was concerned, he was the epitome of evil himself. John kept pace with him at a considerable distance, so that Gervaise remained unaware of his presence. Now that he was out of sight, as he thought, of the law officers who had ruined his life, the man from Peter Tavy was turning over in his mind all the options. Should he throw away his cross and step into the trees to become an outlaw? There seemed little point in doing that here, so the next option was to walk on until he came near Tavistock and his manor. But what could he do there? By that time, the news of his disgrace would have reached his home.

He had seen no sign of Martyn, who must have forsaken him in loathing. He had not even come to see him in sanctuary and had been conspicuously absent at the abjuration ceremony that morning. Martyn had worshipped Gervaise and would never forgive him for what he had done. Return to Peter Tavy seemed pointless, as his only real ally, Baldwyn, was dead. The cousins were waiting like carrion crows to pick up what they could of the inheritance and this affair could be nothing but a delight to them. Now they had only the weak, malleable Martyn to deal with, the brother who should have taken holy orders, rather than the sword.

As he marched along with his crude cross, the clogs were starting to chafe his heels and toes and Gervaise realised that the fifty miles to Plymouth were not going to be the easy march he had first imagined, but he resigned himself to taking ship from there to France. He had distant relatives in Normandy, and as long as they had no news of his disgrace, he could start to rebuild his life – anything was better than dangling by the neck on the end of a rope.

He trudged on for another hour, past the village of Kennford, where several children and some dogs came to jeer and bark at him. A few carters' wagons passed him in the other direction, the drivers ignoring him.

He was still oblivious of John, a quarter of a mile behind him, Bran's hoofs muffled in the soft slime.

On a long curve of track, where the forest came right to the edge of the road, he was suddenly aware of a noise in the tall trees on his right, but he could see nothing. Feeling naked without a sword or even a cudgel, he was wary of attack, but the crackling stopped and he carried on, though the hairs on his neck had risen in tense apprehension.

John was thinking of giving up his impromptu escort duty and returning home – he began to wonder why he had wasted his time in the first place. The curve in the track had taken the abjurer out of sight but when he came round the bend the situation had dramatically changed.

The cross was lying in the road and two men,

dressed in rough clothes little better than rags, were attacking the man in the long sackcloth robe. One ruffian was using a piece of branch as a crude club and the other was pulling at the abjurer's arm, trying to drag him off the road into the trees. The unarmed Gervaise was putting up a vigorous fight for his life, punching and kicking as he yelled at the top of his voice, but the outlaw with the branch was putting in repeated blows at de Bonneville's shoulder and arm, slowly driving him off the road as his accomplice hauled him from the other side.

John spurred his great horse into a gallop and shot down the road, rapidly closing the gap between him and the struggling trio. The heavy thump of the warhorse's hoofs and his own bellowing froze the tableau ahead. All three men stopped fighting and looked open-mouthed at the apparition bearing down on them.

With a yell of fear, the two ruffians let go of Gervaise, who fell to the ground. They ran for their lives into the trees and by the time that John's stallion pounded up to the stricken abjurer they had vanished as if they had never existed.

John stared for a long moment into the tree-line where the men had disappeared, then slid from his horse and hoisted Gervaise to his feet. The man was bruised and bleeding down the right side of his face and had deep scratches on his neck and arm. 'Are you badly hurt?' asked John, immediately feeling the incongruity of concern for the health of a man whom he would gladly have hanged a couple of hours earlier.

De Bonneville staggered to his feet, gingerly touched his injuries with his good hand and examined the blood on his fingers. He winced as he moved his neck and right arm, but said he was free of any serious damage.

John walked a few yards and picked up the cross, which he gave back to Gervaise. 'Then walk on, as you are bidden by your oath.'

The man groaned, but turned and began to limp again down the centre of the track. One blow of the cudgel had caught him on the thigh and his heels were now rubbed raw by the clogs.

John put a foot in a stirrup and hoisted himself on to Bran's back. He walked slowly behind de Bonneville and, after a few hundred yards, said, 'Chudleigh is the next village. You can stop there this night and recover. I'll give you an extra day and a night travelling time to Plymouth, in the circumstances.'

They carried on for a few more minutes until the coroner spoke again. 'I'll see you safe to that village. After that, you're on your own, for better or worse.'

Later, John never understood why he was so reluctant to tell Gervaise that when he had looked into the trees back there, he had seen Martyn de Bonneville waiting, a naked sword in his hand.